"A parable of black feminist self-reliance, couched in poetic language and the structural conventions of classic SF."

—*Village Voice*

OUTSTANDING ACCLAIM FOR
NALO HOPKINSON

THE NEW MOON'S ARMS

**Sunburst Award for Canadian
Literature of the Fantastic
Locus Recommended Reading List**

"A significant figure and a singular talent...A most impressive work, *The New Moon's Arms* has everything a reader could want: a compelling storyline with mysteries at its heart; a firm rooting in myth and history; keen social sense; and, most importantly, a focal character it is impossible not to fall in love with. It is a novel that sweeps the reader into its world: vivid and richly nuanced, utterly realistic yet still somehow touched with magic. Hopkinson's writing is lush and note-perfect...The dialogue crackles, and Calamity's narrative voice is direct and winning...one is left with a sense of wonder."

—*Toronto Star*

"*The New Moon's Arms* is a dance of lost-and-found. Hopkinson knows not to get too sentimental, thanks in large part to her heroine's unsinkable sense of humor. It let me hear the mermaids singing."

—*Washington Post Book World*

"Considerable talent for character, voice, and lushly sensual writing...her most convincing and complex character to date."

—*Locus*

"Hopkinson has had a remarkable impact on popular fiction...[Her] work continues to question the very genres she adopts, transforming them from within through her fierce intelligence and her commitment to a radical vision that refuses easy consumption...With sly humor and great tenderness, [she] draws out the hope residing in age and change."

—*Toronto Globe and Mail*

"Shows new depths of wisdom, humor, and insight...Like life, Hopkinson's novel doesn't resolve every mystery. But Hopkinson has answered the essential questions in *The New Moon's Arms*, and she's wise enough to know we need nothing more."

—*Seattle Times*

THE SALT ROADS

Nebula Award Final Ballot
Shortlisted for the Hurston-Wright Legacy Award

"A book of wonder, courage, and magic...an electrifying bravura performance by one of our most important writers."

—Junot Díaz, author of *The Brief Wondrous Life of Oscar Wao*

"Sexy, disturbing, touching, wildly comic. A tour de force from one of our most striking new voices in fiction."
—*Kirkus Reviews* (starred review)

"Succeeds impressively as a powerful and passionate meditation on myth and survival."   —*Locus*

"A brilliant and multilayered tale."
—*Black Issues Book Review*

"Whirling with witchcraft and sensuality, the latest novel by Hopkinson is a globe-spanning, time-traveling spiritual odyssey...The novel has a genuine vitality and generosity. Epic and frenetic, it traces the physical and spiritual ties that bind its characters to each other and to the earth."
—*Publishers Weekly*

"Rollicking, sensual...Required reading...[from] one of science fiction's most inventive and brilliant writers."
—*New York Post*

SKIN FOLK

Winner of the
World Fantasy Award for Best Collection
New York Times Best Book of the Year

"Vibrant...stunning...Hopkinson puts her lyrical gifts to good use."   —*New York Times Book Review*

"Hopkinson's prose is vivid and immediate."

—*Washington Post Book World*

"An important new writer." —*Dallas Morning News*

"A marvelous display of Nalo Hopkinson's talents, skills, and insights into the human conditions of life...everything is possible in her imagination." —*Science Fiction Chronicle*

"Hopkinson has already captured readers with her unique combination of Caribbean folklore, sensual characters, and rhythmic prose. These stories further illustrate her broad range of subjects." —*Booklist*

"An ideal place for the new reader to discover her fertile imagination, profound empathy and extraordinary voice."

—*Toronto Globe and Mail*

MIDNIGHT ROBBER

Final Ballot for the Nebula Award
Finalist for the Hugo Award
***New York Times* Notable Book of the Year**

"Deeply satisfying...succeeds on a grand scale...best of all is the language...Hopkinson's narrative voice has a way of getting under the skin." —*New York Times Book Review*

"Caribbean patois adorns this novel with graceful rhythms...
Beneath it lie complex, clearly evoked characters, haunting
descriptions of exotic planets, and a stirring story...[This book]
ought to elevate Hopkinson to star status."   —*Seattle Times*

"Spicy and distinctive, set forth in a thoroughly captivating
Caribbean dialect."   —*Kirkus Reviews*

"Hopkinson's rich and complex Carib English is...quite beautiful...believable, lushly detailed worlds...extremely well-
drawn...Hopkinson owns one of the more important and
original voices in SF."   —*Publishers Weekly* (starred review)

"Highly recommended."

—*Library Journal (starred review)*

"Employs Caribbean folk elements to tell a story that is by
turns fantastic, allegorical, and contemporary."

—*Washington Post*

BROWN GIRL
IN THE RING

BROWN GIRL IN THE RING

NALO HOPKINSON

GRAND CENTRAL
PUBLISHING

NEW YORK   BOSTON

Grateful acknowledgment is given to reprint from the following: The lullabye "Rocking My Baby," excerpted from *And I Remember Many Things: Folklore of the Caribbean*, compiled and edited by Christine Barrow, published by Ian Randle Publishers, Ltd., Kingston, Jamaica, 1992. An excerpt from the play *Ti-Jean and His Brothers* by Derek Walcott.

Grand Central Publishing
Hachette Book Group
1290 Avenue of the Americas
New York, NY 10104

www.HachetteBookGroup.com

Printed in the United States of America

LSC-C

First edition: July 1998
Reissued: November 2012

20 19 18 17 16 15

Grand Central Publishing is a division of Hachette Book Group, Inc.

The Grand Central Publishing name and logo is a trademark of Hachette Book Group, Inc.

The Hachette Speakers Bureau provides a wide range of authors for speaking events. To find out more, go to www.hachettespeakersbureau.com or call (866) 376-6591.

The publisher is not responsible for websites (or their content) that are not owned by the publisher.

The Library of Congress Cataloging-in-Publication Data:

Hopkinson, Nalo.
    Brown girl in the ring / Nalo Hopkinson.
        p. cm.
    ISBN 978-0-446-67433-1
    I. Title
PR9199.3.H592776 1998
813'.54—dc21   97-39151
                                                            CIP

Dedicated to my father, Slade Hopkinson. Daddy, thanks for passing on the tools of the trade to me.

PROLOGUE

Give the Devil a child for dinner,
One, two, three little children!

—Derek Walcott, *Ti-Jean and His Brothers*

As soon as he entered the room, Baines blurted out, "We want you to find us a viable human heart, fast."

"Bloodfire!" Rudy cursed, surprised. "Is what you a-say?" He stared at the scared-looking man from the Angel of Mercy transplant hospital up by the Burn. Douglas Baines had obviously never ventured into Rudy's neighbourhood before. The pudgy man had shown up in a cheap, off-the-rack bulletproof that dragged along the floor, his barrel chest straining at its buttons. He looked foolish, and he looked like he knew it.

Rudy watched Baines give Melba the bulletproof. Underneath it he was wearing a poorly made jacket and a cheap white shirt. Rudy picked at a nonexistent bit of fluff on the sleeve of his own tailor-fitted wool suit. His ostentatious lack of protection against attack carried its own message. He was guarded in other ways. "Sit down, man." With his chin, Rudy indicated the hard plastic chair on the other side of his desk. His own chair was a plush upholstered leather, the colour of mahogany.

Baines sat, fiddling nervously with the case of his palm-book. "We need a heart," he repeated. "For, ah, an experiment. We're hoping that your people can help us locate one."

Something didn't sound quite right to Rudy. "And how come oonuh nah use a swine heart? Ain't is that you have all them pig farms for?"

"Yes, well, of course the Porcine Organ Harvest Program has revolutionized human transplant technology. . . ."

Eh-heh. He talking all official. The way he using all them ten-dollar words, this one go be big. Rudy leaned his elbows on his desk and steepled his fingers, making the gold ring on his thumb flash. "I hearing you."

"Well, ah, I'm afraid that porcine material just won't do in this case. Ethics, you know?"

As he heard that spluttered word "ethics," Rudy was suddenly sure that he knew what this was all about. The man was spouting someone else's party line. Rudy smiled triumphantly at Baines. "Is Uttley, ain't? Oonuh need a heart transplant for she, and she nah let you put no trenton in she body?"

"Trenton?"

"Pig."

Baines looked troubled, then gave a resigned shrug and said, "Fuck, I hate this. I just want to do my job, you know?"

Rudy gazed calmly at the man. As he expected, his silence seemed to fluster Baines even more. Baines babbled, "This is all on the q.t., you understand?"

"Mmm."

"Well, yeah, it's Premier Uttley all right. She's demanded a human donor. Says the porcine organ farms are immoral. You know the line: human organ transplant should be about people helping people, not about preying on helpless creatures, yadda, yadda, yadda. Says she's confident that if she's meant to have a new heart, it'll come from the human population. Fat chance, when almost no one in the world runs human volunteer donor programs any more. But her position is pulling in the voter support. Polls are tipping in her favour since she started up this 'God's creatures' thing. She might actually get voted back in next year." Baines pursed his lips, shook his head. "And it looks like she's not leaving a lot to chance, either." More softly he said, "Somebody's quietly going to a lot of trouble to have the hospitals procure a human heart for her. It might bring Angel of Mercy good business if we're the ones to pull it off. It could put us back on the map."

Rudy put on his bored face. "And what that have to do with we? Posse ain't business with politics. Is we a-rule things here now." It was true. Government had abandoned the city core of Metropolitan Toronto, and that was fine with Rudy.

• • • •

Imagine a cartwheel half-mired in muddy water, its hub just clearing the surface. The spokes are the satellite cities that form Metropolitan Toronto: Etobicoke and York to the west; North York in the north; Scarborough and East York to the east. The Toronto city core is the hub. The mud itself is vast Lake Ontario, which cuts Toronto off at its southern border. In fact,

3

when water-rich Toronto was founded, it was nicknamed Muddy York, evoking the condition of its unpaved streets in springtime. Now imagine the hub of that wheel as being rusted through and through. When Toronto's economic base collapsed, investors, commerce, and government withdrew into the suburb cities, leaving the rotten core to decay. Those who stayed were the ones who couldn't or wouldn't leave. The street people. The poor people. The ones who didn't see the writing on the wall, or who were too stubborn to give up their homes. Or who saw the decline of authority as an opportunity. As the police force left, it sparked large-scale chaos in the city core: the Riots. The satellite cities quickly raised roadblocks at their borders to keep Toronto out. The only unguarded exit from the city core was now over water, by boat or prop plane from the Toronto Island mini-airport to the American side of Niagara Falls. In the twelve years since the Riots, repeated efforts to reclaim and rebuild the core were failing: fear of vandalism and violence was keeping 'burb people out. Rudy ruled with his posse now, and he couldn't have cared less about Premier Uttley's reelection platform.

• • • •

"We'll pay for the assistance." Baines named a figure.

Rudy was immediately interested, but he didn't reply for a moment. He pretended to be considering. Let the hospital's procurement officer sweat it out a little more.

Baines stammered, "I, um, I mean, it's not like it's illegal or anything. No laws about human organ donation on the books any more, right? No need, when you can just phone up the farm and order a liver, size three, tailored to fit."

"Mmm."

"This is a tough city, right? You people see a lot of terminal injuries?"

Seen, Rudy agreed wordlessly. *Half the time, is we cause them.* That amused him. Baines was just coming directly to the source.

"We're only asking that you call us when that happens," Baines continued. "We'll do the rest. Head wounds are the best. Don't want too much trauma to the chest cavity. If any one of them has a heart that's compatible for the Premier, we'll pay you a bonus."

No. That nah go work, just having them come and pick it up easy so. Nah go push the price high enough. Rudy took his time thinking it through, figuring out all the angles.

Baines tensely tapped ash from his cigarette into the ashtray on Rudy's desk.

"Melba," Rudy said softly to the haggard, blank-eyed woman who had been dusting around the office, "wipe out the ashtray."

Moving slowly, eyes irising in and out of focus, Melba took the ashtray from under Baines's hands, wiped it clean with her dustcloth, and stood holding it, staring into its empty bowl.

"Thank you," Baines said, smiling nervously at her. She didn't respond.

"Put it back on the table now," Rudy instructed her. She obeyed. She was getting too thin. He'd have to tell the boys to remind her to eat more often.

"Keep on dusting, Melba."

Melba walked woodenly over to a marble coffee table she'd already cleaned three times and resumed meticulously wiping her dustcloth over and over its surface in slow circles. Baines gulped. Rudy smiled at that. The man couldn't even begin to suspect what he was dealing with. All right. He knew how this was going to go. He said to Baines, "Once my boys find the body, oonuh have to reach fast, right? Before the person heart stop beating?"

"Well, yes, but—"

"And what if is in one of them streets that full up of garbage, or oonuh get swarmed by a kid gang? Any delay and you go lose your donor."

"Oh. You might be right." Baines frowned at him worriedly. "This is too important to take a chance."

"Well, Mister B., I think today is oonuh lucky day. We have just the fella to set the donor up right for you, keep the heart beating till you reach."

"You do? Who? It needs someone with the right training to put the body on ice."

"Let we just say, a ex–medical professional. A nurse." Rudy was pleased that he'd thought of this. Tony was going to be useful to him after all. "The man know him business," he said unctuously. "Him was a good worker. Just him misfortune that him couldn't resist the temptation of buff, you know? His employers do right to let he go. He does do one-one little job for we now, helping out, you know? While he try to kick the habit."

"Well, maybe . . . yeah, I guess he could do it. We could supply him with a call button that would bring an ambulance on the double. Yeah, that'd work. He could certainly test the blood type." Baines continued to mutter to himself, ticking items off on his fingers. "And we could give him the fortified Ringer's Lactate, laser pen to seal off any bleeders, portable CP bypass machine . . ."

"Good. I glad you agree. For me think say we could help oonuh."

"Excellent. Let me—"

"But all like how we taking such a risk, me want you to increase that bonus figure, *seen*? Say, another ten percent?"

Baines sighed. "Done."

So easy! Briefly Rudy wondered if he should have held out for more. Well, that's how dealing went. Some days you wouldn't win as much as others.

"Okay," Baines said, looking as though he had a bad taste in his mouth, "don't forget, we only want the flatliners that are in pretty good condition. Healthy, well, before they died, that is; not too much deep tissue trauma. And tell your man we're particularly interested in anyone who's very small framed and has blood type AB positive."

"Somebody small? Oonuh could use a child? Like a youth, say?"

"Teen or preteen? Well, yes, we could, come to that. None of the street kids, though. Most of them have had buff-addicted mothers."

Pity. No one would have noticed a few more of the rats going missing.

Baines opened up his palmbook and tapped at the keys. "I'm requisitioning the equipment you people will need." He scribbled on a business card, swiped the card through the slot in his palmbook, then gave it to Rudy. "Tell your man to bring this when he comes over to the hospital to pick up the equipment. Today, mind. Before four." Then he stood, shook Rudy's hand as though he were palping rotting carrion. "We'll be in touch."

He picked up his bulletproof from the chair where Melba had draped it. The view off the observation deck caught his eye, and he went over to the window. "God, we're a long way up, aren't we?"

"Hmm."

"You know, I never visited this place back before the Riots. Funny how you can live all your life in a city and never visit its main attractions, eh?"

Rudy didn't answer. Man needed to leave his office now, let him get on with his business.

Baines blushed, pulled up the hood of the bulletproof, adjusted its clear Shattertite beak so that it jutted out to protect his face. It was the trademark uniform of the Angel of Mercy Hospital. On the street, they were called the Vultures. The price for established medical care was so high that only the desperately ill would call for help. If you saw a Vulture making a house call, it meant that someone was near death.

Rudy escorted Baines to the door, watched Jay go with him to the elevator. He nodded in satisfaction. He wasn't going to pussyfoot around until they found a compatible donor. He would make sure that Tony got the heart they needed as fast as possible. He turned to the thin, wiry man standing guard outside his office door. "Crack, where Tony? Go and find he. I have a job for he to do for me."

CHAPTER ONE

What can you do, Punchinello, little fellow?
What can you do, Punchinello, little boy?

—Ring game

Ti-Jeanne could see with more than sight. Sometimes she saw how people were going to die. When she closed her eyes, the childhood songs her grandmother had sung to her replayed in her mind, and dancing to their music were images: this one's body jerking in a spray of gunfire and blood, that one writhing as cramps turned her bowels to liquid. Never the peaceful deaths. Ti-Jeanne hated the visions.

Rocking along in the back of a pedicab, she held Baby, cradling her child's tiny head in one hand to cushion it from the jolting. Undeterred by the shaking of the pedicab, Baby was trying to find his mouth with his thumb. Ti-Jeanne took his hand away long enough to ease the little blue mitten onto his fist. "Sherbourne Street," she told the pedicab runner, "corner of Carlton."

"No prob, lady," he panted. "Wouldn't catch me going into the Burn, anyhow."

The pedicab was at Sherbourne and Carlton in a few minutes. Ti-Jeanne got down, pulled her baby and her package into her arms, and paid the runner. She'd have to walk, carrying Baby the rest of the way to the balm-yard her grandmother had set up on the old Riverdale Farm.

The runner moved off quickly, not even looking around for more customers. *Coward,* Ti-Jeanne thought to herself. It was safe enough in this part of the Burn. The three pastors of the Korean, United, and Catholic churches that flanked the corner had joined forces, taken over most of the buildings from here westward to Ontario Street. They ministered to street people with a firm hand, defending their flock and their turf with baseball bats when necessary.

Ti-Jeanne shivered in the chilly October air and hoisted Baby higher onto her hip. The package in her other hand consisted of four worm-eaten books tied together with string. Her grandmother would be pleased with the trade she had made for the eczema ointment. When she'd shown up to deliver the medicine, she'd found Mr. Reed, self-appointed town librarian, balanced on a stepladder just inside the doors of the old Parkdale Library. He'd been pinning slips of newsprint to the bulletin board. "Hey, Ti-Jeanne; whatcha think of my display?" He'd hopped down and moved the ladder so that she could inspect his project. At the top of the bulletin board was a hand-lettered sign that read TORONTO: THE MAKING OF A DOUGHNUT HOLE.

He'd cut headlines from newspapers that were twelve, thirteen years old and pinned them up in chronological order.

"How you mean, 'doughnut hole'?" Ti-Jeanne had asked.

"That's what they call it when an inner city collapses and

people run to the suburbs," he'd answered. "Just a little bit of history. You like it?"

Ti-Jeanne had read the headlines:

TEMAGAMI INDIANS TAKE ONTARIO TO COURT: AMNESTY INTERNATIONAL FUNDS TEME-AUGAMI ANISHNABAI LAND CLAIM

FEDERAL GOVT. CUTS TRANSFER PAYMENTS TO PROVINCE BY 30%, CITES INTERNATIONAL TRADE EMBARGO OF TEMAGAMI PINE

JOBLESS RATE JUMPS 10%: TEMAGAMI LAWSUIT IS FUELLING ONTARIO RECESSION, SAYS LABOUR MINISTER

CRIME AT ALL-TIME HIGH BUT BUDGET CUTS FORCE ONTARIO PROVINCIAL POLICE TO DOWNSIZE

TORONTO POLICE THREATEN MASS WALKOUT: JOB TOO DAN-GEROUS, NOT ENOUGH BACKUP, SAYS UNION

JOBS LEAVE TORONTO: 7 LARGEST EMPLOYERS RELOCATE, SAY TORONTO'S NOT SAFE

TORONTO CITY HALL MOVES TO SUBURBS: SAFER FOR OUR EMPLOYEES, SAYS MAYOR

HUNDREDS KILLED IN RAPID TRANSIT CAVE-IN: TORONTO TRANSIT COMMISSION BLAMES FEDERAL CUTBACKS TO ITS MAINTENANCE BUDGET

CAVE-IN PROTEST SPARKS RIOT: THOUSANDS RIOT: THOUSANDS INJURED, DEAD

RIOT COPS LAY DOWN ARMS, ARMY CALLED IN: TORONTO IS "WAR ZONE," SAYS HEAD OF POLICE UNION

The next two headlines in Mr. Reed's display were written in smeared, blurry letters on lavender paper.

"The major Toronto papers jumped ship soon after the army came in," Mr. Reed had told her.

The headlines had been taken from the *New-Town Rag*. Ti-Jeanne knew the newspaper; a mimeographed 'zine that someone named Malini Lewis churned out by hand whenever she could find paper and ink:

TEMAGAMI NATIVES WIN LAWSUIT: TRADE EMBARGO LIFTED, TOO LATE FOR TORONTO?

ARMY OCCUPATION OF TORONTO ENDS: NOW WHAT?

"It's nice," Ti-Jeanne had said uncertainly, not knowing what else to tell the man. All of that was old-time story. Who cared any more? She'd given him his medicine. In return, he'd dug through his book stacks and come up with an encyclopedia of medical symptoms, two gardening books, and the real find: *Caribbean Wild Plants and Their Uses.*

"Tell your grandmother that I can't give these outright to her," Mr. Reed had said. "It's a loan. If anyone else asks for them, I'll have to send for them."

Ti-Jeanne had just smiled at him. Mr. Reed had grinned and shaken his head. "I know, I doubt anyone will ask for them, either." When Ti-Jeanne left, he was rubbing the ointment luxuriously into his moustache, where the skin was cracked and flaking. Dermatitis: "Seborrheic eczema," Mami had called it, before cooking up a nasty-smelling paste to treat it, made from herbs grown in their garden. Mami freely mixed her nursing training with her knowledge of herbal cures.

"Ti-Jeanne, tell he to stop drinking that elderberry wine he does brew. I think is that irritating he lip. And tell he to stop smoking. Tobacco does only aggravate eczema."

Ti-Jeanne just hoped the ointment would work. Sometimes the plants Mami used had lost their potency, or perhaps were just a weak strain. Too sometime-ish for Ti-Jeanne's taste. She'd slipped some vitamin B tablets and a tube of anti-inflammatory cream into Mr. Reed's package. Mami still had lots of that kind of stuff left in her stockpiles.

Paula and Pavel had set up their awning at the corner of Carlton and Sherbourne, next to the shack from which Bruk-Foot Sam sold reconditioned bicycles. Braces of skinned, gutted squirrels were strung up under Paula and Pavel's awning. Ti-Jeanne could smell the rankness of the fresh raw meat as she walked by. It must have been the morning's kill. The couple had claimed the adjacent Allan Gardens park and its greenhouse, which they farmed. In the winter, Paula and Pavel were the Burn's source of fresh vegetables for those who lacked the resources to import them from outcity. And the overgrown park hid a surprising amount of wild game; pigeons, squirrels; wild dogs and cats for the not too particular. Paula and Pavel defended their territory fiercely. Both brawny people, they each had a large, blood-smeared butcher knife tucked into one boot: warning and advertisement. Nobody gave them much trouble any more, though. It wasn't worth the personal damages to try to steal from the well-muscled pair. Rumour had it that those who crossed Paula and Pavel ended up in the cookpot. Besides, vegetables and fresh meat were scarce, so people tried to stay on Paula and Pavel's good side. Those who lived in the Burn were still city people; most preferred to barter or buy from the couple, rather than learn how to trap for themselves.

Hugely pregnant, Paula was arguing the price of two scrawny squirrels with two gaunt young women who had their arms wrapped possessively around each other. They'd probably take the meat across the street to Lenny's cookstand, where for a price he'd throw it onto the barbecue next to the unidentifiable flesh he skewered, cooked, and sold for money or barter.

"Good evening, Ti-Jeanne," Pavel called out as she went by. He and his wife, Paula, had been lecturers at the University of Toronto before the Riots changed everything. "We got something for your grandmother; leaves from that tree—soursop, I think she calls it?"

"Yes," Ti-Jeanne replied. Mami would like that. Soursop leaf tea made a gentle sedative, and the old greenhouse was the only source of the tropical plant.

"Good," Pavel said. "Tell your grandma we'll be by with them later, eh? We'll trade her for some cough syrup for our little Sasha."

Ti-Jeanne nodded, smiled, looked away. In the eleven years since the Riots, she'd had to get used to people talking out loud about her grandmother's homemade medicines. Among Caribbean people, bush medicine used to be something private, but living in the Burn changed all the rules.

Ti-Jeanne walked past Church Row. An old woman bundled into two threadbare coats sat shivering on the steps of the Catholic church; maybe from the icy fall air, maybe a buff-trance. The heavy oaken door opened and Pastor Maisonneuve stepped out. His black shirt and dog collar gave him a formal air, despite his patched jeans.

"Hello, Pamela," he said to the old woman. "Some lunch for you today?"

She turned her head slowly, seemed to be having trouble focusing her eyes. "R-Reverend, I'm hungry."

As Ti-Jeanne walked by, she heard Pastor Maisonneuve say, "All right, dear, but you know the rules. Give me that knife first, then a bath, then you eat."

The next place Ti-Jeanne had to pass was Roopsingh's Roti Parlour: Caribbean and Canadian Food. Nervously she eyed the twitchy huddle of men hanging out in front of the roti shop. Crapaud, Jay, and Crack Monkey, hustlers all, *liming* till the next job, looking for trouble. She knew them well from her days with Tony. She had always managed to be very busy in Tony's rooming house kitchen when they came to visit. And, of course, there was Tony, liming with them. She *would* have to bump into him on her first excursion since Baby had been born. Ti-Jeanne sped up slightly. Tony looked at her. Did she hear him softly say her name? No. He and Crack had put their heads together, whispering about something. Tony didn't look too pleased at what Crack was telling him.

Tony was trying to catch her eye. She could feel the pull of his gaze. She risked another glance at him. His features were as fine as she remembered: skin smooth as hot cocoa; square jaw; full, well-defined lips; deep brown eyes. Baby's eyes looked just like that.

She should be ignoring Tony, not staring at him like this. She sidestepped a flock of gulls that were fighting loudly as they picked at a near frozen, orange bolus on the ground, probably the sour remains of last night's meal that someone had vomited onto the sidewalk. Pulse thumping, she began to edge past him and his friends, trying to seem very interested in picking her way through the garbage on the sidewalk.

As Ti-Jeanne walked past the men, Crack Monkey called out to her, "Hey, sister, is time we get to know one another better, you know!" Big joke. They all laughed, though Tony's voice sounded nervous.

"Ah say," Crack hollered, "is time I get to know you better!"

The men's mocking laughter spurred Ti-Jeanne to move faster. She hugged Baby closer to her and scowled at Crack. Tony glared at him, too, but she knew Tony wouldn't say anything to his boss's right-hand man.

Abruptly, the visions were there again. Ti-Jeanne froze, not trusting her eyes any longer to pick reality from fantasy. She was seeing:

Crack Monkey, a wasted thing, falling to the ground and gasping his last. No one around him would care enough to try to help. (Crick-crack, monkey break he back in a ham sack);

Crapaud, the old souse, in a run-down privatized hospital, finding the strength to scratch fitfully once more at his bedsores before his final, rattly exhalation. His sphincters would make a wet, bubbly noise as they released their load into his diaper. Cause of death? Metabolic acidosis. Cirrhosis of the liver. Rum. (Down by the river, down by the sea, Johnny break a bottle and blame it on me);

Jay, killed by love; running to the aid of his sweetheart, a transvestite hooker who would be attacked when her john realised she was actually a man and pulled a knife. Jay's death would come from a belly wound. Ti-Jeanne was sure that no one in the posse suspected that Jay was anything but arrow-straight. (Riddle me ree, riddle me ree, guess me this riddle; or perhaps not).

Ti-Jeanne couldn't see her own death, or Baby's. She couldn't see Tony's death, not anyone close to her. And she didn't see blind Crazy Betty until the woman was right in front of her, sightless eyes turned toward Baby, who was snuggled in Ti-Jeanne's arms, happily gumming the mitten on one tiny fist.

"That is my child! He's mine!" shouted the bag lady. Her wrinkled arms reached to pluck Baby away. "What you doin' with my baby? You can't make a child pretty so! You did never want he! Give he to me!"

The old fear of madness made Ti-Jeanne go cold. She jerked Baby out of Crazy Betty's reach. Alarmed, the child began to wail. Madwoman in front of her. Hard-eyed men just behind. But at least the men had *something* behind their eyes, some spark of humanity. Ti-Jeanne chose. She turned and ran back the way she'd come.

"Hey, Ti-Jeanne!" Tony reached for her arm. She yanked it away, pushed between Tony and Crapaud. She dragged the door open and ran into the roti shop. The warm, fragrant air on her face was a shock. How come she was outside, and why was it warm? Ti-Jeanne looked around her, then jumped as she felt Tony's hand on her shoulder. "Ti-Jeanne, what's up? You all right?"

She didn't answer. She appeared to be in a green tropical

meadow. A narrow dirt path ran through it, disappearing in the distance as the road curved gently downward. The scent of frangipani blossoms wafted by on a gentle breeze. Baby stopped fussing.

A figure came over the rise, leaping and dancing up the path.

Man-like, man-tall, on long, wobbly legs look as if they hitch on backward. Red, red all over: red eyes, red hair, nasty, pointy red tail jooking up into the air. Face like a grinning African mask. Only is not a mask; the lips-them moving, and it have real teeth behind them lips, attached to real gums. He waving a stick, and even the stick self paint-up red, with some pink and crimson rags hanging from the one end. Is dance he dancing on them wobbly legs, flapping he knees in and out like if he drunk, jabbing he stick in the air, and now I could hear the beat he moving to, hear the words of the chant:

"Diab'-diab'! Diab'-diab'! Diab'-diab'!"

Ti-Jeanne shrank back, trying to hide Baby's face from the terrifying sight. But he chortled and stretched baby-fat hands out in the direction of the Jab-Jab. Tony had more sense. Behind her, she could hear him whisper, "God Almighty! What the hell is that?"

The Jab-Jab turned its appalling grin of living wood in their direction. It hopped right up to the three of them, split its wooden lips wide, and hissed in their faces—a hot, stiff wind.

• • • •

Which was exactly how the roti shop felt. As the tune of the Caribana hit "Raise Your Hand in the Air" crashed against her eardrums, Ti-Jeanne opened her eyes again, to find herself in Roopsingh's roti shop. As always, the roti shop was hot and noisy. The single, rickety ceiling fan only stirred the super-heated air around. The roti shop smelled of curry and frying oil and stew peas with rice. People pushed to get to the counter, yelling out their orders; raucous soca music blared from the grease-splattered ghetto blaster. In disorientation Ti-Jeanne asked Tony, "What happen? Is where we was?"

Tony frowned at her. "Huh? We were outside, you started running, I followed you inside. You shouldn't be scared by Crazy Betty, you know."

What was he talking about? Slowly, Ti-Jeanne's surroundings registered on her and she realised: Tony hadn't seen what she had! Fear was like ice in her chest. Lately the visions had been growing stronger, more vivid. This was the worst one yet.

Tony didn't seem to notice how dazed she was. He turned to the shop owner, a slight, middle-aged East Indian man, and said, "God Almighty, Roopsingh; what the hell is that crap you playing on the stereo?" He was speaking to Roopsingh with almost the same words he'd used in her vision. Showing off as always for her benefit, Tony switched into the creole his parents had spoken to him when he was a child. Tony had been raised in Toronto by Caribbean parents; his speech wavered between creole and Canadian. "You ain't have any-thing more tasteful? How many years I coming in here, and all I could hear is some so-so road march?"

Ti-Jeanne felt the gears slipping between the two worlds.

Roopsingh's face crinkled into a grin as he looked up from

stirring the huge pot of curry chicken. This game with Tony was an old one. Roopsingh's response never varied. "You don't like it, you could take you skinny black ass down the road, you hear? You could always catch a burger and fries from the cookstand Lenny have on the corner. I don't know where he gettin' his meat, oui? You might be eatin' rat burger and thing. But if you don' like my music, I sure cookstand food good enough for you."

"Nah, nah, nah, man, is all right. God, Roopsingh, you know is only joke I joking. You know I would walk any distance, listen to any old bruk-down *kaiso,* just to taste your roti!"

Ti-Jeanne couldn't spare the time for the teasing game both men always played. She had to figure out what to do about the waking dreams. Squeezing past a woman hollering for "two patty and a ginger beer," she headed for the door.

Maybe it was just the stress of learning how to cope with a newborn baby. Maybe if she ignored the second sight, it would go away. She dared not tell her grandmother. Lord knew how Mami would react. Ti-Jeanne's own mother had had a vision one day, back when the Riots were just starting. She'd told Mami about it, and they had quarrelled. Ti-Jeanne's mother had seemed to go mad in the days after that, complaining that she was hearing voices in her head. Maybe it was hereditary? Ti-Jeanne didn't want to go mad, too. Her mother had disappeared soon after the voices had started, run away into the craziness that Toronto had become. She had never come back.

It was just turning dusk; the loungers outside the roti shop had left. The temperature had dropped. A light early snow was falling. Crazy Betty must have crawled away to the abandoned car where she spent her nights. No one in the Burn could figure out how the madwoman knew where she was going. Caught up in her thoughts, Ti-Jeanne was well on her way back to the balm-yard before she realised that Tony was loping after her, leaping the garbage piled up in the gutters to catch up with her.

"Hey, Ti-Jeanne! Wait for me, nuh? Why'd you run off like that?"

She turned to glare at him, when what she really wanted to do was smile, brush away the melting snow that was twinkling in his hair. His soft brown eyes had a hurt look to them. Returning his gaze, she felt like that snow, melting.

"So what's up?" he asked. "Why haven't I seen you in so long?" He glanced shyly at the baby.

"What you want, Tony? I have to get home and feed this child."

"I only . . . the baby okay?"

"What that is to you? Baby okay, baby-mother okay, and we both going home."

"I just want to tell you . . . I want you to know . . . I mean, don't tell anyone, all right, but maybe I'll be going away soon." He hesitated, then, "Come with me?"

Startled, Ti-Jeanne said, "Come with you where? But you can't just . . . where you going, Tony?"

"Just away. Can't tell you yet."

Same old Tony, loving drama too bad. Ti-Jeanne heard her irritated voice swinging into her old harangue: "Why you can't ever just settle down and live good, eh, Tony? What happen to the work Bruk-Foot Sam say he would give you, helping he fix up bicycles?"

He sucked air through his teeth, making a "steups" sound of disgust. "And what good would that do me? Eh? Penny here, penny there, never enough to really live on, never have anything nice? Is a good way to die poor, Ti-Jeanne! Anyway. I don't have time for that now. I might have to leave."

"Leave and go where!"

He pursed his lips, frowned. "Maybe out to one of the 'burbs."

"Why, Tony?"

"Not telling you more than that. Either you come with me, or when you don't see me, I gone." He sighed, hesitated, then said quietly, "This posse shit get to be too much for me, Ti-Jeanne. Selling buff here and there is one thing, but man, them posse raggas crazy can't done, oui? Crack just told me that Rudy's asking for me."

Ti-Jeanne blurted out in dismay: "Posse? Lord, Tony; I thought you tell me you done with that stupidness!"

"Soon done now, girl. I don't know what Rudy wants me for, and I don't want to know. I'm going to get out of here while I still can."

"Man, why you can't use the sense God give you? Is what you gone and mix up with now?"

"Woman, don't give me none of that! You don't understand any of it. Once you're hooked up with the posse, it's not so easy to 'done with that stupidness,'" he mocked her. "Posse come in like Mafia nowadays. I can't make them think I turn Babylon on them. If I don't do what them tell me to, next thing you know, you go be bawling over a box with my body in it."

"Tony, don't—"

"Besides, I thought you done with me . . . you don't business any more with what I mix up in, right?"

She opened her mouth to contradict him, to say . . . what? Tell him that she did care about him? Tell him she would stand beside him against the posse, follow him no matter what trouble she'd be going into? Baby squirmed in her arms, clasping at her coat buttons with his tiny mittened hands. Mami Gros-Jeanne had shown her how to knit those mittens. Living with her grandmother, she could give her child a secure life. Ti-Jeanne shook her head at Tony, deliberately made her words harsh, repellent. "Well," she said acidly, "you lie down with dog, you get up with fleas. Is you get yourself into this, oui? You have to deal with it by yourself, too."

But Tony's face got so sad, Ti-Jeanne couldn't bear it. She softened a little. "All right, all right. You go on where you going, and when you get settle, send word and let me know. Maybe I come and visit you."

"You will?" His smile was like the springtime sun. If she didn't watch herself, Ti-Jeanne knew she would do any kind of foolishness just to see more of that smile. Trying to change the subject, she asked him, "How you going to get out of the city?" It had been years since she had seen a working car, except for the Angel of Mercy ambulances—the Vulture Vans, people called them—and Rudy's elegant, predatory Bentley. Who could afford gas, batteries, tires? Most people only travelled as

23

far as a bicycle could take them. Sometimes it was hard to believe that there was even still a world outside.

"I don't really know, love." (Ti-Jeanne's heart leapt at the sound of that last word.) "And it's better if I don't tell you too much, all right? Can't take the risk. So you really going to make me go away all alone, Ti-Jeanne?" Tony's eyes looked so lonely. But she said:

"Yes, Tony. You go be on the run. Suppose I come with you, and the posse catch the two of we? I can't put this child in danger like that. Send and tell me when you have a job and a place to live, and I go think about it."

She touched his arm, then quickly stepped back before the touch could turn into a hug. "I going home now. Go good, Tony." She blinked hard two or three times and marched away. She imagined Tony staring after her through the dark.

Tony could give sweet, sweet talk. Words so nice, they would charm the money from your pocket, the caution from your heart, the clothes from your body. Words so sweet and soothing, they sounded like love, like let me hold you the way your mama never held you, like come and be my only special one, my doux-doux darling. Words that promised heaven.

Ti-Jeanne had not told Tony that Baby was his child. She had left him and his room in the rooming house when her belly began to get big. She'd gone back to her grandmother and refused to see or speak with him. Let him think she'd been cheating on him and was ashamed. Something had made her want to keep the little person she was growing all to herself. It would be the one human being who was totally dependent on her and would never leave her.

To her surprise, Tony had barely seemed to consider the possibility that she might have been horning him with another man. He was more concerned about getting her back. He had braved her grandmother's cutting eyes and hard-set mouth to visit Ti-Jeanne at the balm-yard. He sent little notes via her grandmother, written with a dull pencil on torn, crumpled paper. Mami would thrust them sullenly at her. In the notes, Tony apologized for anything he might have done to hurt her. He told her that he was going to leave the posse, going to get a straight job. He told her all the old things that used to set her to dreaming about the cozy life they'd have together. But he'd never done any of them. She told herself she couldn't believe him any more, that she had done the right thing to go back to her grandmother to bear her child. Whenever Tony appeared at their door, Ti-Jeanne would send her grandmother to answer it, and finally he would no longer face Mami Gros-Jeanne's implacable glare.

The last time he had tried to visit had been early in the summer. Ti-Jeanne had been watching from the cottage window. Mami had been in the herb garden in front of the old Simpson farmhouse that they'd made into their home. She was safe within the magic circle of stakes that she had shoved into the ground, surrounding the farmhouse. Each stake had a deep blue Milk of Magnesia bottle jammed upside-down onto it, protection against duppies, dead people's spirits. Tied on below the Magnesia bottles, triangles of coloured cloth fluttered from the stakes.

Hunched over the basil plants in her worn black dress, Mami had been picking snails off the leaves and popping them with a crunch between thumb and forefinger. Sun on the duppy bottles made blue lights dance over her face and hands, so that she looked like a duppy herself. Mami knew which plants could kill as well as cure. She had moved on to inspect the spiky aloe plants in their clay pots and plastic margarine tubs. The sticky sap from the leaves soothed burns and healed blemishes. It was Ti-Jeanne's job to move the plants inside for the warmth every fall. Mami said that her baby would come before then, by midsummer.

Ti-Jeanne's breath had caught in her throat as she saw Tony come striding along the path to the cottage. At the same time, the baby in Ti-Jeanne's belly writhed, as if in anger. Ti-Jeanne moved one hand in soothing circles around her distended navel. She yearned for Tony so badly, but he was no good for her.

Tony had opened the garden gate. Mami looked up at the creak it made. Tony had looked at her, then hesitated, waiting for permission to enter. Mami had straightened from her weeding. Somehow, her tiny, fierce body had seemed to tower over Tony's six-foot frame. She had stared at him for long seconds and then muttered, "If you don't stop coming here, I goin' to put mal 'jo upon you, you know." *Evil eye.* Tony was terrified of the small-boned seer woman. Ti-Jeanne knew that for all his medical training and his Canadian upbringing, he'd learned the fear of Caribbean obeah at his mother's knee. His face went grey. He swallowed, stepped back, then turned and hastened away. After that, he hadn't tried again.

Baby had been born a few weeks later, and then Ti-Jeanne had had no time for thoughts of Tony. Learning to look after her sickly newborn had kept her busy.

• • • •

Tony took a deep breath for calm as Crack Monkey beckoned him into Rudy's office. The elevator ride up one hundred and thirteen floors had increased his nervousness. The door shut with a hollow thud, like a coffin lid slamming down.

Rudy was sitting in a leather executive's chair behind his huge, highly polished oak desk. With a manicured hand, he indicated that Tony should sit in the chair on the other side. Tony sat, tried out a smile on Rudy. The posse boss's thick, blocky body nearly obscured the plush padded leather of the chair. The man's neck was almost as big around as his head. Tony suspected that Rudy augmented his strength with steroids. He'd once seen him wrap one hand around a man's neck and lift him right off the ground. Crack Monkey, a whippet-thin man with cords for muscles, stationed himself in front of the door, feet apart, hands held loosely behind his back, exposing the gun at his belt.

Poor Melba was there, standing beside Rudy's desk, a dust-cloth tucked into the waistband of her thin cotton skirt. She was holding a glass jug filled with water and ice cubes, ready to refill the goblet of water that Rudy kept on his desk. She was deathly still. Condensation ran off the jug. It glistened on her hands and tracked runnels down her forearms to drip onto the grey plush carpet. Tony had the impression she'd been standing in just that position for a long time. Her fingernails were edged blue from the jug's cold. It must have been heavy. Her thin, wasted arms were trembling with the weight of it, but she didn't move, said nothing, just gazed absently ahead, looking at nothing. Rudy noticed Tony staring at her and smiled. Tony shuddered. Whatever hold Rudy had on the woman had to be more than just buff addiction. Her will, her *volition*, seemed to be gone. Tony knew that she would do whatever Rudy told her, and only that, until he gave her a new order or her body collapsed from exhaustion. She even had to be told when to relieve herself. She was only in her mid-twenties, but in the past few months her face had become lined and worn, and her hair was whitening rapidly. She wasn't the first that Rudy had used like this, either. It was one of the reasons Tony had come to feel he needed to get away from the posse's influence.

Trying to look calm, Tony turned to Rudy. "Afternoon, Mr. Sheldon," he said quietly.

"Afternoon, brother. How you keeping? Crack treating you all right?"

"Yes, sir."

"Good. Now Tony, you been with we for a few months now, right? Crack tell me you doing a good job."

"Thank you, Mr. Sheldon."

"Don't thank me yet, me brother." Rudy settled back farther into the chair, linking his hands behind his head. Every movement he made sent a thrill of fear up Tony's spine. Why had the posse boss sent for him? Rudy continued:

"Crack say you have one little problem, though. You does dip into the deliveries every so often."

Behind him, Tony heard Crack Monkey's insane little giggle. They knew! He'd thought they wouldn't miss a few pinches of buff here and there. The fine hairs on Tony's arms raised in terror. "I, I," he jabbered.

"Nah, nah, is all right, brother. Me understand." Rudy held up one hand in a calming gesture. "Life hard. Sometimes a man does get, ah, dependent on he pleasures, you understand me?"

"Mr. Sheldon, I can pay it back, I can—"

"Yes, that is exactly what you go do. Pay me back." Rudy's face was serious for a moment. Then he skinned his lips back from his teeth in an oily grin. A snake probably looked like it was smiling, too, when it opened its jaws to strike. "You go pay me back by doing this one little job for me, just the way I tell you. But don't feel no way. If you pass this test, I go know I could trust you. I go know say you is a true member of the posse. Is that you want, right?" Rudy's meaningful stare made the only correct answer obvious. Tony nodded quickly. Rudy smiled again.

"Seen. I did take you for a man with brains."

Tony could feel his heart thumping in his chest. "What do you need me to do, Mr. Sheldon?"

"Mercy Hospital need a fresh human heart for a transplant."

"What!?"

"You hear me. You going to find a donor for we. You going

to send for the ambulance to come and get it, and while you waiting, you going chill the body down and keep the heart beating. I go give you the equipment to do it. It go be easy."

"But Mr. Sheldon, how'm I going to find a donor? Why can't they use the porcine program? The odds—"

"Brother, you nah business with none of that. You just going to have to improve the odds, seen? Find somebody the right size, the same blood type, healthy, and arrange for them to be in a condition to donate their heart. You get me?"

Appalled, Tony could only stare. Rudy was asking him to commit murder.

The jug fell from Melba's hands and crashed onto the floor, spraying her with water and broken glass.

"Fuck!" Rudy shoved himself out of his chair, brushed his pants leg where some of the water had splashed him. He motioned to Crack. "Clean this up. Melba, too."

Crack hurried to his side and started picking up shards of glass. Melba just stood, staring at nothing, hands still curled to hold a jug that was no longer there. Goose bumps lifted on Tony's arms. He had no choice but to do what Rudy told him.

CHAPTER TWO

Rocking my baby, I know you are sad,
Baby, you were naughty; Baby, you were bad.
I'm sorry to whip you my darling, but true,
My Mama whipped me, so I'm bound to whip you.

—Lullabye

Lost in thoughts of Tony, Ti-Jeanne hurried home. Despite her distractedness, she automatically kept a watchful eye about her. You always had to be on the lookout for trouble in the Burn. She crossed the street a number of times to avoid drunken fights or men offering presents in return for "a little time" with her: "You look so healthy, darling, so nice." Most men only asked, though. She was Mami Gros-Jeanne's granddaughter, and nobody wanted Mami mad at them. They needed Mami when the winter coughs were racking their lungs or their women were giving birth.

A knot of street kids whirled around her, a grimy rainbow of all colours, screeching with laughter and nearly knocking her off balance. They chanted as they ran: "Nigger, nigger, come for roti, all the roti done!" As they jostled her, Ti-Jeanne could smell the dirty little bodies, feel small hands quickly patting her body, looking for anything to steal. Someone

31

tugged at the package of books. Ti-Jeanne yanked it out of the child's grasp.

"Allyou get away!" she shouted. "I ain't have nothing for you!"

Baby, fascinated by all the activity, didn't know enough to be frightened. He just stared, wide-eyed. Ti-Jeanne held on tightly to Baby and her books until the children were gone to wherever they went for the night.

Ti-Jeanne kept walking. She couldn't keep her mind off Tony. She'd lived with him for a year and a half. A year and a half of him making a few dollars from odd jobs, then using it to score a few slashes of buff, spending the night flat on his back on the mouldy futon in his one-room apartment, eyes wandering from the muscle-relaxing effect of the drug. Next day he'd be queasy and weak, unable to work for days. Ti-Jeanne had kept them fed by working in Roopsingh's restaurant, but it hadn't been enough for two people to survive on. Tony was good with his hands, talked about opening his own little bicycle repair shop like Bruk-Foot Sam, but never did anything about it. He could even have used his medical training to do what Mami had done: opened a small private practice to treat simple ailments. But it had been easier for him to start running errands for the posse. It took no thought. He just followed orders and saved all his initiative for figuring out where he was going to score the next slash.

Baby nuzzled hungrily at Ti-Jeanne's chest, rooting where he knew her breast was. Ti-Jeanne put her finger in his mouth to soothe him until they reached home.

Tony had sounded serious today. Maybe this time he'd finally break away from the posse, and she and Baby could make a home with him at last. Maybe a little apartment in one of the suburban cities outside the Metro core. Maybe North York or Scarborough, where she'd heard there were jobs and people could afford to drive cars and wear store-bought clothes. They would both find work, and Mami could come to live with them and leave Toronto people to their own hell.

"You would like that, my bolom baby? Eh, no-name baby?" Baby's eyes followed hers. He sucked fretfully at her knuckle. "Well," she continued, "you almost old enough for your nine-week naming now. Next week, me and Mami go do that, and maybe in a little while, me and you and Tony going to live together, and I go buy a baby pram to push you in, and toys for you to play with. You would like that, Bolom?"

Ti-Jeanne smiled at the child in her arms, hugged him closer to her, but he frowned and whimpered, clenching his hands into fists. She scowled at him. "Hush now."

He kept on whimpering. Ti-Jeanne sucked her teeth. She loved him, but when he got like this, it irritated her. Her mother and grandmother had raised her with the strap; it was what she knew of discipline. "Hush, I tell you. You best had learn fast to mind me when I speak, you know."

But by the time she'd tromped through the fallen leaves in the park to reach their farm, Baby was screeching with hunger. Ti-Jeanne hated the noise. She shook him a little, hoping to startle him into silence. Instead his screaming took on a desperate edge. Guilt burned at her.

"Shut up, Baby," she said. "You must learn to listen when I talk to you." She rocked Baby in her arms and made soothing noises, trying to make up for shaking him. He got a bit quieter.

Mami Gros-Jeanne was waiting at the door of their cottage, a hardened knot of a woman in her limp black dress.

"Is where the ass you been all day? You don't see the child hungry? Get inside and feed he! You just as bad as your blasted mother!"

"Yes, Mami. I goin', Mami." Ti-Jeanne scuttled inside, unbuttoning her blouse as she went so that the child could suck.

"Stupidness," Mami muttered behind Ti-Jeanne's fleeing back.

Baby was soon full; he would sleep for a few hours. Ti-Jeanne spent the rest of the evening as she so often did, braiding Mami's wiry salt-and-pepper hair while the old woman sat and chopped herbs at the "kitchen" table.

Riverdale Farm had been a city-owned recreation space, a working farm constructed to resemble one that had been on those lands in the nineteenth century. Torontonians used to be able to come and watch the "farmers" milk the cows and collect eggs from the chickens. The Simpson House wasn't a real house at all, just a facade that the Parks Department had built to resemble the original farmhouse. There was a front porch that led into a short hallway. To the left and right of the hallway were two small rooms in which the Riverdale staff had led workshops in spinning and weaving. Mami used the right-hand room with its fireplace as her parlour/dining room, the left-hand one as her examining room. Upstairs had been two offices. Those she had converted into bedrooms: one for herself and the other for Ti-Jeanne and Mi-Jeanne. Now that Mi-Jeanne was gone, Ti-Jeanne shared her bedroom with her baby son. The back of the house had consisted of male and female public washrooms, but they were no use now in a city without a sewage system. Mami's followers had built her an outhouse just outside with a cesspit and had converted the two washrooms into a cold-storage room and a ventilated kitchen where she cooked on a wood stove that someone had found for her.

"You minding me, Ti-Jeanne? For foot itch, you must pound garlic, and mix it with pot salt to put between the toes. That does kill it." Mami Gros-Jeanne was always training Ti-Jeanne in the work she did as a healer.

"Yes, Mami."

"This batch for Papa Butler. He coming Sunday for it. I done tell that man that he must wash he foot every day. He does wear one pair of stinking socks from September to June. Stupidness."

"Yes, Mami."

"What you does put on a cut to heal it?"

Damn. One of Mami's spot tests. "Ah, aloe?"

"And if we can't get aloe no more? Tell me a Canadian plant."

Shit. It was the one with the name like a tropical plant, but it was something different. What, what? Oh, yes: "Plantain leaf."

Her grandmother grunted. Ti-Jeanne had given the correct answer, but that grunt was the only acknowledgment she would get. She swallowed her resentment.

"And for headache?" Mami continued.

That one was easy. "Willow bark."

Tony had once teased Ti-Jeanne almost to tears about her grandmother: "What's that crazy old woman doing over there in Riverdale Farm, eh, Ti-Jeanne? Obeah? Nobody believes in that duppy business any more!"

"Is not obeah, Tony! Mami is a healer, a seer woman! She does do good, not wickedness!" But Ti-Jeanne herself wasn't so sure. There was the drumming that went on in the crematorium chapel, late into the night. The wails and screams that came from the worshippers. The clotted blood on the crematorium floor in the mornings, mixed with cornmeal. Obviously, other people than Mami still believed in "that duppy business."

Ti-Jeanne didn't place too much stock in Mami's bush doctor remedies. Sometimes herbs lost their potency, stored through Toronto's long, bitter winters. And they had to guess at dosages. For instance, willow bark made a good painkiller, but too much of it caused internal bleeding. Ti-Jeanne would have preferred to rely on commercial drugs. They could still get them, and Mami's nursing training had taught her how to dispense them. People brought stuff to her nearly every day, loot hoarded from drugstores during the Riots that had happened after the bankrupt city had disbanded its police force. People often had no idea what the Latin names on the packages meant; they just hoped it would be something Mami would consider to be fair payment to treat whatever ailed them. She had built up quite a stockpile of antibiotics and painkillers, so Ti-Jeanne didn't understand why Mami insisted on trying to teach her all that old-time nonsense. If Mami didn't know how to cure something, she could look it up in one of the growing piles of medical books lining the walls of the cottage.

Only half listening to the old lady's muttering, Ti-Jeanne fretted silently about Tony. Suppose the posse boss realised that he was trying to make a break for it?

• • • •

When horse dead, cow get fat.

—Traditional saying

Fretfully, Uttley shifted a little under the thin blue sheets, glancing over at the telemetry readout beside her bed as she did so. Even that slight movement sent the three green lines of the readout careening into a crazy S-curve before it settled back down into the irregular, thready rhythm of her failing heart. Catherine Uttley lay back in her hospital bed and brooded. Anything more strenuous than that exhausted her alarmingly quickly. *Cool it, girl,* she told herself. *Stick this one out, and you'll sail right into another five-year term.*

The Ontario premier had never been physically strong, but she'd always kept in the best shape that she could: healthy diet, as much exercise as her work and her body, weakened by meningitis as a child, would allow. She'd refused to accept the fact that her health would eventually fail her. But of course it had. When the doctors first confirmed that she was going into heart failure, she'd been furious, so much so that they'd hospitalized her immediately, fearing that her soaring blood pressure would bring on a full-blown heart attack. She'd been livid. Damn it, there were senators twenty years her senior still hale and hearty!

It was Constantine's visit that had put her on an even keel again. Good man. A lot of people underestimated her soft-spoken policy advisor with his smooth, nothing features and his smooth, nothing body. She'd laughed with him about it often, called him her spin doctor. Doctor Shark. He'd shown up that day while she was sulking in her hospital room. It seemed like he'd just materialised, so nondescript that it was hard to remember just when he'd entered a room. He'd sat down quietly on one of the standard hospital-issue green plastic chairs.

She'd greeted him gloomily. "Come to get me to transfer the reins?"

"Premier, you understand that this is an opportunity for you, not a setback?"

"Fuck you. I don't understand anything of the sort. Election in seven months, and I've hit rock bottom in the polls. They're going to vote for Brunner, damn his tanned, muscled hide. Or Lewis, God forbid, with her smarmy make-work programs."

"Madam Premier," Constantine had said then in his lecturing voice, "your voter pop's been down ever since the Temagami thing. Brunner's been a shoe-in for months."

"Constantine, you know I had to give the blasted Indians their blasted stewardship. I practically had orders from the feds, what with Amnesty International breathing down our necks. Their international sanctions had been starving the Canadian economy for years. We needed to be able to export Temagami pine and water again."

Her telemetry'd gone sailing off the scale. A nurse stuck her head in the door. "I'm all right," Uttley said irritably, waving her away. "I'll be good."

"Seriously, Premier," Constantine continued. "Fact of the matter is, once you get a new heart, you'll be back on your feet in two, three months. And when you go on air before the operation and announce that you won't have it unless it's a human heart—"

"What?!"

"Calm down, calm down. Here, lie back. Let me get you a glass of water."

"Constantine, sit the hell down and tell me what you've got up that greasy sleeve of yours."

Constantine took his palmbook out of his attaché case, tapped in a code, and held it out for her. "The latest polls. Support for porcine organ farms since VE made its appearance."

The disease that had jumped from pigs to humans through the an-antigenic porcine organ farms was so new that the scientists had only named it "Virus Epsilon." The acronym had stuck. Uttley glanced at the graph. "Yes?"

Constantine tapped in some more data. "Twenty-three percent of those polled are voters. Look at what happens to your chances of reelection when we sway them to your side by having you bring back voluntary human organ donation." He keyed in a new chart. Uttley felt her eyebrows rise at the result: 62 percent voter support in her favour.

"Nice," she said. "And we get them to vote for me by telling them I'm going to die because I insist on a medical procedure that no longer exists?"

"You'll make it exist again. Introduce a bill to the House. Use VE to justify the need for the bill. Make a statement to the press that you're convinced that this is the safe, moral way to go: 'People Helping People,' you're going to call it. Tell them you're so determined that you'll back your words with your life; you've demanded the medical system find you a compatible human heart, and you're imploring the public to sign the voluntary organ donor cards you're going to distribute in all the local papers. Tell them you'll refuse the operation unless it's a human heart. Voters'll eat it up."

Uttley smiled. "You son of a bitch. I'm going to dazzle them with my moral courage!"

"Exactly."

"But what happens if I don't find a human heart in time? I don't suppose any of the hospitals follow voluntary organ donor protocols any longer."

"Oh," Constantine replied mildly, "I've got some leads. Besides, if it comes down to the wire and they have to operate before finding one, just put in a pig heart. We'll make up some story to cover."

It was a brilliant plan, and it was working beautifully. Polls showed her support at 58 percent and rising. Only one problem—no donor yet. Very few people were completing the donor cards. Seemed people weren't prepared to signs parts of themselves over after all, even if they were never going to use them again. Human heart or no, her doctor was determined to operate within the next few days. "I don't care what you tell the media we put into your chest, Premier, but by next week, I'm going to have a healthy heart beating in there."

Uttley tapped at the remote in her hand to raise the head of the bed a little higher. Yes, that was better: she could breathe a little more easily now. Slowly she slid over to the side of the bed, got her palmbook from the bedside drawer. She lay back again, gasping as though she'd just run a marathon. When she could find the energy, she punched in the number. "Constantine? Found a donor yet?"

CHAPTER THREE

Bluebird, bluebird, through my window,
Oh, Mummy! I'm tired.

—Ring game

Ti-Jeanne was having the usual nightmare. This night, as every night, it startled her awake. She opened her eyes into the dark of the tiny bedroom. Nothing there. The weeping echoing in her ears was only Baby, crying for his four A.M. feed.

"Lord, keep quiet, nuh? I coming!" Ti-Jeanne stumbled over to the narrow crib, changed the fussing child, then brought him back to her bed to feed him. Sitting up against the headboard, Baby in her arms, she drowsed, lulled by his rhythmic sucking. She started to think about Tony again.

It hadn't been Ti-Jeanne's decision to leave Tony; it was Baby's. Three months into her pregnancy, the bolom inside her had begun to move. It would kick, making Ti-Jeanne think of the shoes those kicking feet would soon need. And clothes, too. And food for its growing body. Those things had to be bartered or paid for. When she was with Mami, she could at least earn her keep by preparing poultices and wrapping bandages. Grateful customers would give her goods and sometimes money. Mami said anything she got was her own, so she lived well by helping her grandmother.

When she'd gone to live with Tony, though, they survived mostly on what he could bring in by running errands for the posse. Roopsingh kept asking her if she didn't want to work in his nightclub. The back of Roopsingh's restaurant was actually a club that opened late in the evening hours and went until cockcrow. Roopsingh hand-picked the attractive waiters and waitresses who danced in the floor shows and hooked on the side. They made good money, but it wasn't for her. In any case, Tony wouldn't have let her do it. So even though she hated his involvement with the posse, hated him selling drugs, she put up with it, believing he would find honest work soon.

When she became pregnant, she had known it almost immediately. She'd worked too long for Mami not to know the signs. As she fought down the nausea every morning, she began to worry about how she'd look after the baby. Tony wouldn't be much help. He was too flighty to make a good father.

Ti-Jeanne had tried to ignore the thoughts fighting in her head; she wanted to think only of Tony. Tony's hands on her body, making her skin tingle. Tony's lips, whispering honey, following where his hands had been. She resented being forced to think about the future, about anything but Tony. Resentment battled with the urge to care for the baby growing inside her. The two feelings fought and grew, swelling as her belly swelled. Love and resentment scrabbled, punched, kicked inside her till she had thought she was carrying triplets and her belly would burst with the weight. Finally she went back to her grandmother, who had simply made a kiss-teeth noise of disgust, then brought her fresh sheets for the bed in her old room.

• • • •

Ti-Jeanne opened her eyes. Baby had drunk his fill and gone back to sleep, one tiny fist still clutching absently at her breast. She sighed; went and settled him in the crib; turned as she heard a step behind her. Mami?

The back of Ti-Jeanne's neck prickled at what she saw:

A fireball whirl in through the window glass like if the glass ain't even there. It settle down on the floor and turn into a old, old woman, body twist-up and dry like a chew-up piece a sugar cane. She flesh red and wet and oozing all over, like she ain't have no skin. Blue flames running over she body, up she arms, down the two cleft hooves she have for legs, but it look like she ain't even self feeling the fire. She ol'-lady dugs dripping blood instead of milk. She looking at me and laughing kya-kya like Mami does do when something sweet she, but I ain't want to know what could sweet a Soucouyant so. The thing movin' towards me now, klonk-klonk with it goat feet. It saying something, and I could see the pointy teeth in she mouth, and the drool running down them:

"*Move aside, sweetheart, move aside.*" *She voice licking like flame inside my head.* "*Is the baby I want. You don't want he, ain't it? So give him to me, nuh, doux-doux? I hungry. I want to suck he eyeballs from he head like chennette fruit. I want to drink the blood from out he veins, sweet like red sorrel drink. Stand aside, Ti-Jeanne.*"

Terrified as she was, Ti-Jeanne stood firm beside the crib, planting her body between Baby and the hag. She would not let it have her child! The Soucouyant tried to get around her, but Ti-Jeanne blocked its way. *Lord help me!* she thought.

Another figure ran in through the doorway on jokey back-ward legs. *Oh God, not the Jab-Jab!*

The Jab-Jab stopped behind the Soucouyant and with a bamboo-clack of a voice called out, *"Old lady! Like you don't know me?"*

The Soucouyant forgot Baby and turned to spit fire at the Jab-Jab, but the flames didn't reach him. Brandishing his stick to block her way, the Jab-Jab threw something to the ground from the other hand—rice grains? They scattered all over the floor. The Soucouyant stiffened up when she saw the rice, then dropped to her knees. Ti-Jeanne didn't understand. Why was the creature picking up the rice grains and counting them? Why wasn't she fighting back?

Now the Jab-Jab was dancing around the Soucouyant, hit-ting her with the stick, and shouting, *"Yes, you old witch, you!"* (Whap! with the stick.) *"Bloodsucker!"* (Whap!) *"Is my spell on you now: count the rice!"* (Whap!) *"I bet you don't finish before sunup! Is where you hide you skin? Eh?"* (Whap!) *"You not get-tin' back inside it tonight, I tell you!"* (Whap!) *"Baby blood not for you! You must leave little children alone!"* (Whap!)

With her back against the crib, Ti-Jeanne watched the bizarre battle. Crouched on the floor, the Soucouyant tried to scuttle away from the Jab-Jab's rain of blows and struggled to count the grains of rice, picking them up one by one with her wrinkled fingers, trying to keep them cupped in one shaking hand. But with each blow that connected with her oozing, skinless back, the grains of rice flew from her hand and she had to start all over again. The Jab-Jab danced around her, taunting, striking. The Soucouyant shrieked in terror and frustration and spat flame at the wooden creature.

It seemed as if the battle had been going on for hours. Then the Jab-Jab yelled, *"Ti-Jeanne! Draw back the curtain!"* Baffled, terrified, Ti-Jeanne edged over to the window and pulled the curtains open. The first light of the morning sun shone full on the Soucouyant. She screamed, threw her hands up to ward off the killing light, and dissolved into smoking ash. The Jab-Jab grinned at Ti-Jeanne. It said, *"Soucouyant can't stand the sun, you know."*

And vanished.

They were really gone. Sobbing, Ti-Jeanne checked on Baby, who was still sleeping soundly.

"Ti-Jeanne! What you crying for, child? What happen to Baby?" Never asleep for long, Mami came bustling officiously into the room.

"No, Mami—watch out for the rice!" Ti-Jeanne rushed to prevent her grandmother from tripping, grabbed her by the shoulders, and looked down. The floor was bare. Mami frowned at the clean linoleum, met Ti-Jeanne's eyes: "Doux-doux, why you think it have rice on the floor in front of the baby bed?"

Ti-Jeanne threw herself into Mami's arms, sobbing as she tried to explain. Mami walked her over to the single bed, sat down with her, and listened while Ti-Jeanne gulped out the story of what she'd seen. "Mami, this ain't the first time I see something like this. I going mad like Mummy, ain't it?"

At that, Mami's gentle air vanished. She pulled back and frowned at Ti-Jeanne. "This happen to you before?"

Ti-Jeanne shrank back into herself. "Two-three times now, Mami," she mumbled, looking down at the floor.

Mami grabbed her wrist and held on tight, forcing Ti-Jeanne to make eye contact with her. "Two-three time? Child, why you never tell me what was goin' on with you?"

Sullenly Ti-Jeanne replied, "What I was to tell you, Mami? I don't want to know nothing 'bout obeah, oui."

Mami shook a finger in front of Ti-Jeanne's face. "Girl child, you know better than to call it obeah. Stupidness. Is a gift from God Father. Is a good thing, not a evil thing. But child, if you don't learn how to use it, it will use you, just like it take your mother."

Frightened, Ti-Jeanne could only stare at her grandmother. She remembered that night so many years ago. She had been only nine years old, living with her mother and grandmother in a cramped, run-down apartment in Saint James' Town. The city was still being governed but was gradually collapsing economically as transfer payments from the province dwindled, taxes rose, and money, businesses, and jobs fled outward to the 'burbs. Young Ti-Jeanne didn't really understand what was going on, but she could sense people's resentment and apprehension wherever she went. She and her mother, Mi-Jeanne, used to share a bedroom. That particular night, Mi-Jeanne had woken up screaming. She'd dreamt of people trapped in some sort of box, drowning as water rushed in through its windows. She'd dreamt of angry fights in the streets, heavy blows breaking glass, of heads being blown apart like melons. Mami had tried to calm her, but Mi-Jeanne had become hysterical. The Riots had started a week later. For Ti-Jeanne, they were mixed up in her mind with memories of her mother lying helpless in her bed, besieged with images of the worst of the rioting *before* it happened. Mi-Jeanne refused her mother's help. She spat out all of Mami's potions and screamed at her to stop her prayers. And the power of the visions had driven her mad.

Mami's voice broke into Ti-Jeanne's reverie. "It look like you turn seer woman like Mi-Jeanne, doux-doux. I could help you. No time to waste. Your education start now. Tell me about your visions, nuh?"

So Ti-Jeanne began describing her visions to the old woman: the Jab-Jab, the Soucouyant, the nightmare she had had every night now for three weeks. As she spoke, Baby woke, crying for his morning feeding. Ti-Jeanne gave him the breast and continued to talk:

"And in this dream I have now, I does see a tall, tall woman in a old-fashioned dress, long all the way down to the floor. She head tie-up in a scarf, and Mami, she teeth pointy like shark teeth!"

"What her feet them look like?"

"She have one good foot and one hoof like a goat."

"Jeezam Peace, child! La Diablesse visitin' you! What she does do in your dream?"

"I does see creeping through the streets at night. She have a glow around she, like she cover up in fire, but nobody ain't seeing she. She does be hiding in alleyways and thing, just waiting, waiting. And then a street kid does come walking down the alleyway, whistling to heself, not looking around. And I could

48

see the woman getting ready to spring out at the little boy. And all I screaming and crying at the boy to turn back, to run away, he don' hear me; he just keep coming closer and closer."

"Lord have mercy," said Mami quietly. "Wait right there. I go tell you what this mean."

She stood and went into her own bedroom. Ti-Jeanne could hear her rummaging about in the old wooden press in which she kept her valuables.

As he suckled, Baby's hands found one of Ti-Jeanne's plaits and gave it a good pull. Irritably Ti-Jeanne pulled the plait away from him and was about to slap the mischievous hand when Mami came back into the room. "Lord, Ti-Jeanne; just let the child play a little, nuh? Don't be rough with he so."

Ti-Jeanne frowned up at her grandmother. Mami continued, "Ti-Jeanne, I know you did never want no baby. Sometimes you almost feel to just get rid of he, don't it?"

Shamed, Ti-Jeanne nodded.

"Don't feel no way, darling; children does catch you like that sometimes. It ain't easy, minding babies, but if you don't make the time to know you child, you and he will never live good together. I know."

"Yes, Mami; sorry, Mami; I go do better."

Ti-Jeanne wasn't really listening. She stared at the deck of brightly coloured cards in Mami's hand. She'd never seen anything like them. Mami's eyes followed her gaze. The old woman sat on the bed and fanned the cards out.

"You know Romni Jenny, who does live in the old Carlton Hotel? She people is Romany people, and she teach me how to read with the tarot cards, way back before you born. This deck is my own. Jenny paint the cards for me, after I tell she what pictures I want."

"How come I never see you using them before, Mami?"

"I used to hide it from you when I was seeing with them. I don't really know why, doux-doux. From since slavery days, we people get in the habit of hiding we business from we own children even, in case a child open he mouth and tell somebody story and get them in trouble. Secrecy was survival, oui? Is a hard habit to break. Besides, remember I try to teach about what I does do, and you run away?"

"But Mami, obeah . . ."

Mami stamped her foot. "Is not obeah! You don't understand, and you won't let me teach you, so don't go putting your bad mouth 'pon me!"

Ti-Jeanne pouted, but she held her tongue. It felt good to be unburdening her problems to Mami. If she pushed the old woman too far, she would only retreat into silence again.

The cards were like none Ti-Jeanne had ever seen. Larger than playing cards, they were pictures of men and women dancing in colourful, oversized Carnival costumes.

The words "Masque Queen" were on one card. The Masque Queen's costume was a gown of blue and silver sequins with a cloak that dragged behind. Jutting up from the dragging fabric was a city with castles and towers, also in blue and silver. The cloak formed a float that loomed high over the Masque Queen's head. She clutched a large book in one hand and a wand in the other. She seemed to be performing a graceful pavanne, despite the bulky float she was pulling behind her.

Ti-Jeanne reached out to touch the cards, then looked at Mami. Her grandmother nodded in encouragement. Ti-Jeanne turned up one card after another. The Five of Cane, five men dancing the Stick Fight; the Jab-Jab; a prancing, nearly naked man, his body completely covered with red paint, horns stuck to his head, and a snaky, rude-looking tail tied on to his body. *But thing I see was some kinda animal,* thought Ti-Jeanne, *not a man in costume.*

Mami took the cards from Ti-Jeanne and began to shuffle them with an economical ease. "These will tell me what your dream is about. Here. Cut the deck."

Ti-Jeanne cut. Mami took the pack back from her and laid the cards out on the bed between them. Baby chortled and reached toward the bright colours, but Ti-Jeanne held him out of reach. He had to be content to suck on his own thumb. The cards lay in a cross on the bed. Mami muttered over them, divining the pattern. "Cowrie King reverse, the La-Basse, Ten of Cutlass, and look; see La Diablesse there so? The Devil Woman? Somebody you know in trouble, Ti-Jeanne; somebody mixing up heself in some business he can't handle."

Tony; I did feel so, thought the younger woman. "What kind of trouble, Mami?"

"I don't know, darling, but wherever La Diablesse go, she leave death behind she."

The two women stared somberly at the image on the card, a tall, arrogant-looking mulatto woman in traditional

51

plantation dress and head-tie. Her smile was sinister, revealing sharpened fangs. Behind her ran a river, red like blood.

Mami resumed, "When the Cowrie King card come in upside-down, it mean a man in trouble, a dark man, maybe a Black man. And the trouble have to do with money. Is that Tony, ain't it?" She stared accusingly at Ti-Jeanne. "You still seein' that sweet-talking sagaboy?"

Ti-Jeanne felt her face heat up with embarrassment. Mami always seemed to know her secrets. "No, Mami, I ain't seein' he, really. I just bump into he on the street last night." No need to tell her grandmother about the conversation she had had with Tony.

"Ti-Jeanne, I want you to leave that boy alone. I don't want you to mix up with he and the posse."

Ti-Jeanne stared down at the baby asleep in her arms. He frowned in his sleep, just like Tony did. She took a deep breath for courage. "I know Tony is nothing but trouble, Mami, but he is my baby-father. He have a right to get to know the baby, ain't?" She had no idea why she was fighting for Tony like this. She hadn't even planned to tell him that Baby was his child, much less allow Tony to visit him. She wondered if Tony would want to come to know the child he'd fathered. Mami opened her mouth, probably to protest, but Ti-Jeanne interrupted her:

"Mami, you ain't want to know the rest of my dream? The little boy come running down the alleyway, and La Diablesse jump on he and fasten she teeth in he throat. I could see blood running down he neck and he screaming, screaming."

Mami looked horrified. Satisfied that her grandmother hadn't noticed the change of subject, Ti-Jeanne continued, "And is me who stop La Diablesse. I grab she, and wrestle she down to the ground, and break a bottle over she head. A blue bottle. She lie down there and turn to ashes." She'd kept telling the story only to distract Mami from talking about Tony, but now Ti-Jeanne felt herself pulled back into the dread of the dream that had been haunting her for weeks. She whispered, "You know what, Mami? I 'fraid. I ain't know what it is I seeing, but I 'fraid too bad."

Baby began to cry, twisting his tiny body and wailing in despair.

Someone was knocking at the door.

"Ti-Jeanne, go and see who that is, coming here so early in the morning. It might be Pavel; Paula baby due any day now."

But it wasn't Pavel. Tony stood in the doorway, looking back nervously over one shoulder. Ti-Jeanne put her hand on her hip and stared a challenge at him.

He licked his lips nervously. "I could come in, doux-doux? I have to talk to you and your grandmother." As he spoke, he plucked nervously at the shoulder straps of a knapsack he was wearing. Its design was odd—a broad, flattish square.

Tony hadn't braved her doorway in a long time. Ti-Jeanne felt her face get hot at her second encounter with him in two days. Not trusting herself to speak to him, she hoisted Baby into a more comfortable position on her hip and simply stood back to let him in. He closed the door quickly behind him.

"Is Tony, Mami," she shouted to the upper level of the cottage.

A loud kiss-teeth sound came from inside. "Speak of the devil," Mami said as she clumped down the stairs to confront Tony. "What trouble you bringing for we now?"

"I'm sorry to disturb you, Mistress Gros-Jeanne, but you and Ti-Jeanne are the only two people I have to turn to. I really need help." Tony looked imploringly at Ti-Jeanne. In his nervousness, he had taken the woolen tam off his head and was twisting it into a rag between his hands.

Mami's mouth set hard. "The only help you getting is to help yourself out from my front door, oui. Stupidness."

"Mami, let we hear what he have to say, nuh?"

"No! Ti-Jeanne, you have to break good with this good-for-nothing boy, or you go find yourself mix up in he story again. You see it in the cards for yourself; whatever Tony get into with he posse this time, he ain't getting out of just so." Mami hissed at Tony, "Get your worthless self out of my house now, before I put mal 'jo upon you!" She advanced on him, eyes narrowed, one hand held up above and behind her head—to slap or to conjure, Ti-Jeanne didn't know.

Tony blanched. He turned for the door. The words came bubbling out of Ti-Jeanne before she knew what she was saying. "Tony, you stay right here. This is my home, and you is a guest. Mami, stop frightening the man. You know your heart too soft to put evil eye on anybody."

For some reason, Baby chortled out loud just then.

"Child," Mami spat at Ti-Jeanne, "I used to change your diapers. Don't give me this back talk in my own house!" Mami Gros-Jeanne's bottom lip was quivering with anger.

Ti-Jeanne remembered how the back of Mami's hand used to feel when it connected with her face. *But I is a big woman now,* she thought. *She ain't beat me for years.* She gathered her courage around her and stood up to the old woman again.

"I ain't mean to be rude to you, Mami, but I want to hear what Tony have to say. Let we sit down and listen to he, nuh? Just listening can't hurt."

Mami cut her eyes at Ti-Jeanne and sucked her teeth, but she said no more. She went and sat stiff-backed in one of the wooden chairs in the front room. Ti-Jeanne felt her heart leap in triumph. Mami had given in!

Ti-Jeanne sat on the couch, pointing out another chair to Tony as she did so. "Take a seat, Tony." *Act normal, girl.* "Ah, you want some mint tea?"

Mami looked daggers at Ti-Jeanne, said nothing.

I think I enjoying this, Ti-Jeanne thought.

Tony shook his head in response to her question and refused the chair she indicated. "I don't have time for that now. I have to do this quickly. Don't want to make Crack suspicious."

Ti-Jeanne made a face, thinking of Crack Monkey with his mean, ferret-like eyes.

"All right, then, ask we what you have to ask we."

Tony closed his eyes, took a deep breath, and briefly told them the story.

"Jesus, Tony!"

"That man wants me to kill somebody for him, and I can't do it. *I tried. . . .*"

"What!" Ti-Jeanne exclaimed. "You try to do what?"

"God, Ti-Jeanne, you don't understand—I went out with Crack tonight. That was the agreement. We went on a prowl, looking for likely donors, you know, people who looked healthy, but maybe like no one would miss them? Street people, shit like that. He, he cold-cocked a couple of them so I could check their blood types. In alleyways and stuff, where no one would see us."

Outraged, Ti-Jeanne just gaped at him. She clutched Baby closer to her.

"Don't look at me so! I couldn't do it, you don't understand? The first two weren't the right blood type. The third one, it wouldn't have mattered if she was. Hepatitis eating her up. When Crack started stalking the fourth one, I told him I couldn't do any more that night, that I was feeling sick. He laughed at me. Said I'd better find the stomach to do the job, or Rudy would set him on me. I thought he was my friend. He smiled at me. No humour in that smile. Is like my soul just shrivelled up and died inside me to see that smile. I've seen Crack do some things I don't want to think about. On the street, they say that Crack would follow the Devil himself into hell to fetch him back for Rudy."

"Yes," Mami said bitterly. "Rudy have a way to get what he want, oui?"

Tony looked at her with frightened eyes. "Mistress Gros-Jeanne, I'm begging you. You could work a obeah for me? You could hide me from them people?"

Mami just sneered at him. "For why? Far as I concern, if them do for you, is nothing but good riddance to bad rubbish."

"Mami!"

"Good riddance, I say! Ti-Jeanne, what this mamapoule

man ever do for you? You don't see he is a fool?"

Baby chortled, cooing and pulling at Ti-Jeanne's hair. Probably he was enjoying all the noise and carrying on. Mami turned on Tony again. "Any idiot could have tell you this is the kind of thing that does happen when you mess up in that Rudy business! Playing big man, saying you running with posse, selling dope. You know how many patients I get because of people like you? You know how many of them draw them last breath in my hands? Is best the posse kill you, yes; one less murderer on the streets!"

"Mami!" Ti-Jeanne was almost glad for the flush of indignation she felt. It kept her from thinking too much about the enormity of what Tony had done. "Tony begging your help. Is so you talk to people? He is my guest!" Ti-Jeanne's heart was pounding, her hands sweating. She'd never crossed Mami in anything before; what had gotten into her tonight?

The old woman leaned toward Ti-Jeanne, shook a cold-chapped finger in her face. "Guest? What make you turn big woman and have any 'guest'? This is my house! If I say go, both of allyou go have to leave!"

And there it was. Out in the open. Mami expected Ti-Jeanne to dance to her tune or find somewhere else to live. A cold anger washed over Ti-Jeanne. "All right, then, Mami. We go do that. Come, Tony. Let we go talk somewhere private."

She stood up and marched toward the front door, Baby on her hip, Tony following uncertainly after her. She had one foot through the door before Mami said quietly, "Wait, Ti-Jeanne. Come back, doux-doux."

Ti-Jeanne couldn't believe her ears. From stubborn, close-mouthed Mami, that simple request was a plea. She turned back and stared at her grandmother. "What you say?"

Mami Gros-Jeanne stood in the living room, her eyes brimming with tears. "Don't go. Don't get vex and leave. Is just so your mother did leave me, in anger. I ain't see she from that day to this. Stay nuh, Ti-Jeanne?"

The loneliness in the old woman's eyes tore at Ti-Jeanne. But she wasn't going to give in so easily, not the first time that Mami had ever acknowledged that she was an adult in her own right. "If I stay, Mami, you have to talk to Tony."

Her grandmother scowled. Her lips worked in frustration. Then, "All right," she growled, almost too softly to hear.

"And you go try to help he?"

Mami glared at Tony. "That ain't for me to say. Suppose the spirits don't want to help he?"

"Don't beat around the bush, Mami. You go try?"

"Yes."

Trying to hide her smile of triumph, Ti-Jeanne took Tony's hand boldly in hers (the rough, warm feel of it, the way it completely covered her own hand, the granulated line of the scar where he'd taken a knife cut in the Riots) and came back into the parlour, her baby in her arms and his father at her side.

"I can't stay," Tony muttered uncertainly, "I have to leave tonight—"

"I ain't promising nothing, you understand," Mami interrupted him, "but maybe I could help you get out of town, past the eyes of the posse. I could try and make it so them can't see you or hear you."

"Oh God, thank you, Mistress Gros-Jeanne."

Defiantly she straightened her shoulders. "But allyou have to stop calling the thing 'obeah.' I don't work the dead, I serve the spirits and I heal the living."

"Yes, Mami."

"And I have one more condition. You have to leave Ti-Jeanne here with me."

Ti-Jeanne began to protest. Mami held out her hands pleadingly. "Just for a while, doux-doux, just until you learn about your seer gift."

"I don't want to know 'bout it, Mami!"

"Child, is not just me being selfish, trying to keep you with me. If you don't learn to use the gift, things going to go hard with you. You want to come like the crazy people it have wandering the streets? Eh? Not knowing if you have clothes on your back or what day it is, just walking, walking and seeing all kinda thing that ain't there, not knowing what real and what is vision? Is that you want, Ti-Jeanne? That is just stupidness!"

Ti-Jeanne thought of Crazy Betty and how the mad, blind woman had frightened her that afternoon. She swallowed. "Okay, Mami. I go stay for now." She took a deep breath. "But when Tony leave here tonight, I want to go with he, only as far as the highway. I want to see that he get away safe. Then I go come back."

Mami pursed her lips and scowled at Tony again. She frowned. "All right, doux-doux. I go make it so the posse people wouldn't be able to see neither you nor Tony."

CHAPTER FOUR

Moonlight tonight,
Come make we dance and sing.

—Traditional song

Mami said they had to wait until nighttime to do the ritual. Throughout that day, Mami kept Ti-Jeanne busy, one eye on her at all times. Ti-Jeanne made the cornmeal porridge and fried dumplings they had for breakfast, Mami right beside her to make sure that she sprinkled some brown sugar into the dumpling batter and that the porridge didn't burn. Like she didn't know how, after all these years. But it was good to see some of the life come back into Tony's face as he ate. God knew how he was eating, now that he was living by himself again. He smiled a thanks at Ti-Jeanne, and she felt her face get hot. She had scarcely finished eating her own meal when Mami decided she needed help bringing in the washing from the line they had strung between the house and the small barn. Mami didn't usually let her bring in the wash, claimed that she didn't know how to fold the clothes properly and always put wrinkles in them. But today Ti-Jeanne was cor-ralled into carrying the laundry basket as Mami dropped the clean, dry clothing into it. Mami was giving her a lecture on the best way to fold sleeves. Ti-Jeanne wondered what Tony was doing. Her grandmother was obviously trying to keep her from being alone with him. She needn't have worried; Ti-Jeanne was trying to avoid him, too. It made her uncomfortable to have him so near. She felt confused and unhappy, the same way she'd felt when she had left Tony's rooming house to come back to her grandmother's to have her baby. In her head, she kept going over the litany of Tony's faults: he drank too much, he was lazy, he ran drugs for Rudy. But his smile made her feel like she was flying.

Mami must have sent Tony to fetch water from the lower pond at the bottom of the hill. Ti-Jeanne could see him struggling back up the pathway with two full buckets. His strength and grace were obvious, even dressed as he was in a bulky windbreaker. He stopped for a rest and looked her way. Ti-Jeanne glanced down at her feet. Tony had been fired from the hospital for using buff; he was irresponsible. Still, she found herself wondering if his windbreaker was warm enough. Maybe she would knit him a pair of gloves for the winter. Jenny spun wool from their sheep into yarn. . . .

Mami dumped a pile of clothing into her basket with such force that she almost dropped it.

"Keep your mind on your work, Ti-Jeanne!" she scolded. "Nothing in your head but man."

"Mami, you know that ain't fair."

Mami kissed her teeth in disgust but said nothing more. Since Ti-Jeanne had successfully stood up to her grandmother this morning, she was feeling more self-assured. Something had changed between them. They were two women now, no longer an adult and a child.

Tony carried the buckets into the kitchen and came out a few minutes later with Baby in his arms. To Ti-Jeanne's surprise, he had thought to dress the child warmly against the fall air. Too warmly. Baby was probably sweaty and uncomfortable in the heavy winter bunting that Tony had put him in, but at least he wouldn't catch a chill. Tony sat on the porch steps and tried to play with Baby, chucking him under the chin and making silly noises at him. The child squirmed in his arms and whimpered for his mother.

"Mami," Ti-Jeanne said, "I should go and get Baby. He ain't take to Tony."

"Hmph. Child got some sense, then. More than some I could name. But leave he there. He have to learn that he can't always have what he want."

Two of the cows in the paddock started lowing mournfully. Their udders were full.

"Mami, I have to go and milk the cow-them."

It looked as though the old woman were going to protest, but just then there was a knocking at the front gate. A gaggle of street kids stood there. Mami hurried over to let them in. There were about five of them, carrying a sixth in a sling made of their dirty hands clasped together. It was a little girl, her leg swollen and bruised and twisted at a strange angle. Her mouth was open wide, eyes squinched shut tight as she tried not to cry from the pain. Street kids learned early not to make too much noise.

"Come. Bring her inside," Mami said, switching to the more standard English she used when she was speaking to non-Caribbean people.

The little girl whimpered, clutched at her friends. "No, no! She's a witch! She's going to eat me! Don't make me go in there!"

"Just shut up, Susie!" said the eldest of the children, a young woman of about fifteen with matted hair and torn clothing. "If you don't behave, I'll let her eat you, too. I told you not to go jumping off things." Despite her fierceness, the young woman looked worried for the little girl.

"Is all right," Mami told her. She knelt, bringing herself eye level with Susie, who cringed to have her so close.

"Susie," Mami said gently, "my name is Mistress Hunter, and you know what I like to eat?"

Susie's eyes opened wide. "B-bones?"

Mami shook her head. "Apples," she replied. "Apples, and pears, and chestnuts, and strawberries, and raspberries. But I don't eat bones. And I don't eat children. See," she said, pointing to Ti-Jeanne, "this is my granddaughter. I didn't eat her, did I? She lived with me, and grew up with me, from a little girl into a big woman. And you see she's fine?"

"Yes," mumbled Susie.

"Well, then. So that proves I don't eat children."

Susie still looked doubtful. Mami said, "Does your leg hurt, doux-doux?"

"Yes. We was playin' on the old rusty cars over by the orange building there? We was jumping down into the

63

leaves, you know, the way the wind piles the leaves up? It's real soft and everything. Only I landed on a big rock inside one of the piles."

"Made a big crack, like a old tree branch breaking," volunteered a little boy of about seven. He reached for Susie's hand.

Susie's lip began to quiver. "It hurts so bad. Is it broken? Is my leg broken?"

"I think so, darling. If you let your friends bring you inside, I can look at it, and give you something to make the pain go away."

"No," quavered the little girl, shaking her head from side to side, eyes wide. She put her hand to her mouth, started chewing on a knuckle. "You're gonna eat me."

"I tell you what, Susie. Your friends can watch me the whole time I'm examining you. They'll make sure I don't hurt you."

"Can Clem hold my hand?"

"Until you're ready to let go, sweetheart." Mami smiled at Susie. The little girl looked at her, then looked at the young woman who'd brought her.

"'S okay, Susie," she said. We'll watch out for you."

"Well, okay, then."

Mami reached out a palm to Susie, who hesitated for a second, then tentatively put her free hand in Mami's. She held tight to Mami's and Clem's hands while the human train carried her into the cottage. Ti-Jeanne had seen her grandmother do this many times: soothe wild things, get their trust. The turtles in the lower pond would take food from her hand. Harold, the irritable goat who always tried to butt Ti-Jeanne, followed

Mami like a dog and would nuzzle his head against her leg. In return, Mami ate almost no meat. At most, the animals that were old or sick. She would ask them if they were ready to go, and Ti-Jeanne could swear that she had seen egg-bound hens and lame horses stagger gratefully toward the knife. Ti-Jeanne had once jokingly complained to Tony that the only meat she got at Mami's was old and tough. Mami and Roopsingh had even fallen out over it, because Mami refused to sell him any goats for his curry.

The children took Susie into the room Mami used to treat patients. Ti-Jeanne and Tony followed her in. Ti-Jeanne took Baby and soothed his fussing. Mami helped the children to gently lay the little girl down on the examining table.

"Now," she said to Susie, "I'm going to have to feel your leg to see if it's broken."

"W-will it hurt?"

"Yes, it'll probably hurt, but not for long. And if I have to put it in a cast, I'll give you something to sleep so that you don't feel anything. Okay?"

"Okay," she said, but she didn't release Clem's hand for an instant.

"Mistress Hunter," Tony said shyly, "I could help. Mix the plaster and like that. If you want."

Mami looked at him suspiciously. "You sure you remember any nursing at all?"

"Yes, ma'am."

"All right, then. You stay, too. But you don't touch nothing until I tell you, then you do exactly what I say."

"Yes, ma'am."

"Susie," Mami said, "I want to put a good meal in everyone's belly. You mind if the other children go into the kitchen and eat? Clem will be here with you the whole time."

Susie looked doubtful.

"Don't worry 'bout it, Suze," said Clem. "I'll be right here. Old lady tries anything, I'll pop her one and yell for the others."

The harsh words sounded strange in his high child's voice. Mami simply raised an eyebrow at him. Resentment twinged in Ti-Jeanne's breast. If she had ever said anything so disrespectful to Mami, her grandmother would have clouted her behind.

Susie agreed to let the others go and be fed.

"Make them some porridge," Mami told Ti-Jeanne absentmindedly, already concentrating on Susie.

Feeling somehow left out, Ti-Jeanne sullenly herded the smelly children to the kitchen in the back of the cottage. She wished she could make them all bathe before touching anything. She wondered if any of them were the ones who'd tried to pick her pocket the day before.

In the kitchen, the eldest girl said to Ti-Jeanne, "I'm Josée." Josée's voice was harsh from smoking cigarettes. Ti-Jeanne could smell the jungle breath and see the yellow nicotine stains on the young woman's teeth. "I look after them. I'm, like, their mum."

"Why? It must be hard enough to survive alone on the street. Why take on the responsibility for other lives, too?"

"B'cause somebody did it for me. Old Gavin. So I show

them. We stick together, we can watch out for each other, Old Gavin says. We have rules. Anybody gets out of line, they're out." She spoke louder to get the children's attention:

"Hey! Listen up! This lady's going to give us food. You remember the rule?"

The gritty gaggle just looked at her, shuffling its feet. She prompted them, "If somebody helps us . . ."

"We don't steal their stuff," they chorused glumly.

"Nothing?" whined a charmer with too many teeth missing. "Not even one little thing?" Ti-Jeanne couldn't tell if it was a boy or a girl.

"No, and whatever it is, you put it back right now."

The child grimaced, produced Mami's good kitchen knife from out of its shirtsleeve, and tossed the knife back into the sink. He or she handled it with the ease of long practice. Ti-Jeanne tried not to think about it. The sooner she got them fed, the sooner they'd be gone.

"Allyou sit at the table." She went to the cold storage and hauled back a basket of apples. That would hold them while she fixed them a meal. The children dove at the apples, chattering excitedly, crunching them down as fast as they could chew and slinging the apple cores at each other. Josée growled at them. They stopped the game but kept eating.

Ti-Jeanne had a look through their stores. There was plenty of cornmeal.

"Josée, you know how to cook?"

"Some things. Do it for these kids. On a fire, you know? With a strip of sheet metal over it?"

So Ti-Jeanne set Josée to stirring up a big pot of cornmeal mush. A little girl with dead straight black hair reached up and tickled Baby's leg. Baby chuckled, kicking his legs and pumping his arms. Ti-Jeanne moved Baby to her other hip, out of the urchin's reach. Dirty child probably had fleas.

The little girl asked, "Can't I hold him?" She was about eight. She had one wandering eye. There was a black line of dirt under each of her fingernails. She smelled of rotten teeth and sour milk. But Baby was playing peek-a-boo with her across the bulk of Ti-Jeanne's body. He chortled with glee.

Ti-Jeanne decided. "Go and wash your hands in the sink," she told the girl. She dipped a bowlful of water from the bucket and gave it to her. "Use the carbolic soap. And wash your face, too."

The little girl obeyed. Ti-Jeanne pursed her mouth in a grimace as she watched the water in the bowl darken with filth. She caught Josée looking appraisingly at her and smoothed her expression over. The little girl came back, presenting rough pink hands to show that they were clean. "Now can I hold him?"

Reminding herself to bathe Baby again later and check him for lice, Ti-Jeanne put him carefully into the child's arms. "Hold him good, but not tight-tight, you hear?"

The little girl nodded and started humming a half-remembered lullabye at Baby. The language sounded like Chinese. Baby often fussed when strangers held him, but to Ti-Jeanne's surprise, he seemed content to stay where he was. She took the pair out to the paddock with her while she milked the long-suffering cows. Baby and the girl rolled about happily on the straw-covered ground. She did a so-so job of preventing him from manoeuvring handfuls of dirt into his mouth.

When Ti-Jeanne brought the full buckets of milk into the kitchen, Tony had taken over stirring the porridge. Baby took one look at him and started wailing.

Ti-Jeanne sucked her teeth in exasperation. "Lord, child. Is what do you today?" She put down the milk, took Baby from the little girl, and carried him, screeching, upstairs to their room. She put him in his crib. He kept crying. She rapped on the side of the crib to startle him into silence. Instead his cries became screams, his little tongue curled and quivering in his open mouth, tears squeezing themselves out from his screwed-shut eyes. Feeling helpless, Ti-Jeanne patted and stroked his chest for a few moments. "Ssh. Ssh. Is only your daddy. You don't need to 'fraid he."

It didn't help much. Finally she just pulled the blanket up to his chin. Under her hands, his small body was stiff with indignation. She patted his chest once more, then went downstairs, hoping he would tire and stop eventually.

Tony was grating a whole stick of Mami's precious cinnamon into the porridge. "Susie's leg was broken all right," he told her. "Greenstick fracture. She's sleeping now."

Josée had her hands full, trying to keep the pack of kids from investigating every corner of the house, playing tag around the kitchen tables, jumping up and down on the sofa. She looked apologetically at Ti-Jeanne.

"They don't get to be in houses much," she said.

Ti-Jeanne scowled. "Call them into the kitchen."

She and Josée organised the washing of many dirty pairs of hands, then she gave everyone a job: cutting up apples to be stirred into the cornmeal; sprinkling in handfuls of raisins (Josée had to explain to young Clem what they were); spooning in maple syrup (Ti-Jeanne stopped one little boy after the tenth tablespoonful had plopped into the mixture); laying out bowls and spoons for everyone. She stirred the fresh milk right into the cornmeal, trusting the boiling mixture to scald the milk free of bacteria. Her eyes met Tony's over the steaming pot. His upper lip was beaded with sweat from the heat of the kitchen. It was strange to see him so at ease caring for the children. She'd never seen him at work, never experienced him as the type of person who could tend to another's needs. She touched his hand.

"You have to stir it slow," she said. "Slow enough so it won't splash over, but fast enough so the heat don't burn it. Keep it simmering."

"You know I could do that," he said with a grin. In a few minutes it was ready. They served it up at the long picnic table that served as a kitchen table. The children slurped down their porridge, chattering excitedly to each other.

Mami came out of the examining room. She was holding a bloody scrap of bleached cotton to her finger. "The child resting," she said to Josée. "She's going to wake up in two, three hours."

Ti-Jeanne asked her, "What happen to your hand, Mami?"

Gros-Jeanne shook her head. "The scissors slip and cut me."

Tony hurried to her side. "Here. Let me wrap that up for you."

Mami stared at him a moment, then held out her hand. He carefully took the scrap of cotton off the cut. "This dressing is soaked through. I'll get another one." He went into the examining room.

"Hmph," Mami muttered. "Just trying to get on my good side."

• • • •

In the examining room, Tony glanced back at the door. No one had followed him. The little girl was fast asleep, curled up under a blanket. He'd taken off his jacket to help Mistress Hunter. It was still hanging behind the door. Quickly he fumbled in the jacket pocket, took out the blood test box that the hospital had given him. He thumbed the wad of bloody cotton into the depression in the box, pressed the button for the display. AB positive. Dismay and excitement washed over him in equal proportions. Ti-Jeanne's grandmother had the right blood type, the right body dimensions. If her crazy scheme to save his ass didn't work, he might be forced to an extreme solution to his problem.

• • • •

Tony came back out with an alcohol swab and a fresh bandage. He cleaned and dressed the cut. "There. Should be healed in no time."

Mami turned and walked into the kitchen without answering him. Ti-Jeanne could see the distress plainly on his face. She gave him an exasperated shrug. Mami was being hard, as usual. Tony was only trying to help. Ti-Jeanne followed Mami into the kitchen. Mami set the children to washing up their dishes, then gave Tony a machète and pointed in the direction of the wild part of the farm. "Go and cut a pair of crutches for Susie."

When she turned her back, Tony gestured for Ti-Jeanne to follow him. Baby was in his crib, having finally cried himself to sleep. Ti-Jeanne caught herself thinking that he couldn't see them and alert Mami with his squalling. It was odd to think of the helpless child doing something so deliberate, but that's how it felt. She pushed the thought away. Feeling guilt and excitement in equal parts, she went quietly with Tony.

They walked along the Upper Road, saying nothing at first. The wind swept fall maple leaves across their path in splashes of purple, deep red, and yellow-orange. Ti-Jeanne caught Tony looking at her out of the corner of his eye. She glanced shyly away and pointed out the downhill trail to the Lower Road. "Down so," she said. "It have a stand of young trees there. Probably some of them could cut into good crutches." They went that way, but when they got there, Tony just stood on the pathway, looking at her. His glance warmed her, despite the cold wind.

"It's been a long time since I've been alone with you, Ti-Jeanne. You been avoiding me."

"Just go and cut the crutches, Tony."

Instead he walked back up the path to where a wild rose-bush was making its last windblown stand against the cold. Its branches were covered in fat rosehips, but there was one blossom left. Tony wadded up one of his gloves and used it to pick the prickly rose. Seriously he presented it to Ti-Jeanne, glove and all. Blushing, she took it from him. She dared not put her nose to it; like everything that Tony had ever given her, this gift had thorns.

Tony made as if to reach for her free hand. Ti-Jeanne felt herself leaning closer to him. But he lowered his hand and said, "Why'd you leave me?"

There it was. She'd finally given him the opportunity to ask the question. "What else I was to do, Tony?" She was about to tell him all the fears that had plagued her, all her worries about whether Tony would have been able to help her provide for the child. He interrupted her:

"I would have let you keep the baby, no matter whose it is. I love you, Ti-Jeanne."

Ti-Jeanne blinked in shock. He would have "let" her keep the baby? The moment had passed. She gave Tony the glare that always threw him off balance. "Don't talk foolishness. You going to cut the damned crutch, or you want me to do it for you?"

"Ti-Jeanne . . ." He sighed. "Is that where you want me to go? Into the bush there?"

The "bush" was nothing more than a straggly clump of trees. Ti-Jeanne sucked her teeth in mock disgust at him. He smiled. "You going to show me the way?"

"Come." She beckoned.

He reached for the beckoning hand, held it in his. She made to pull her hand away but knew she couldn't do it if her life depended on it. They entered the clump of trees. Trying to act casual, she pulled him toward a sapling that seemed a likely one. "Chop that one."

Still holding her hand, he pulled his arm in against his chest, compelling her to come closer to him.

"Tony, let me go."

"What, dry-dry so?" he asked, a laugh in his voice. "A man going off into the bush to do dangerous work with a machète, and you can't even give he a kiss for good luck?"

Ti-Jeanne couldn't help herself. She giggled. She looked up into Tony's eyes and saw the pleading there that his merry tone masked. She put her hand on his shoulder, stood on tiptoe, gave him a quick kiss on the cheek.

He let the machète fall behind him, took her face in his hands. "You call that a kiss?"

The taste of his lips and tongue against her was sweet, sweet as she'd remembered. She relaxed into the kiss, put her arms around him. A sound came to her, blown on a stray breeze. Was that Baby she heard crying? Ti-Jeanne pushed Tony away.

He frowned. "Now what?"

"Just leave me alone, all right? Cut two crutches out from the blasted tree, and leave me to go about my business." Not waiting to see what he would do, Ti-Jeanne quickly climbed the hill back up to the house. Mami was waiting for her on the porch. She scowled as she saw the rose. Ti-Jeanne thrust her chin out defiantly. She held on to the flower, ignoring the bite of its thorns.

"Go and see to your child," Mami said. "He hungry."

• • • •

Gal, hug and kiss your partner, tra-la-la-la-la,
For you look like a sugar and a plum (plum, plum).

—Ring game

It felt like a lifetime before night finally fell. As soon as little Susie was awake from the anaesthetic, Josée had herded her brood away, even though Mami had said they were welcome to stay overnight in the old Meeting House.

"Naw, lady," Josée had said. "You make them nervous already, eh? Some of 'em still think you're a witch. Come nighttime, they'll go squirrelly on me. Kids." And they'd trooped off through the dusk, groggy Susie manoeuvring shakily on her handmade crutches.

Ti-Jeanne felt as though she'd been doing a dance all day, swerving one way to avoid her grandmother, then swinging around another way to stay out of Tony's hands when they grasped for her. A few times he'd caught her, though. And she hadn't pulled away immediately. They'd exchanged a few more sweet, sweet kisses. Ti-Jeanne felt sticky and feverish, her skin sensitized by Tony's touch. She was sure that Mami noticed. The old woman became more and more sullen and short with her as the day wore on. And Baby had been driving Ti-Jeanne to distraction. He was colicky and cranky. Whenever she was gone from his side for more than a few minutes, he would start screaming. Once, Tony went into his room to try to comfort him. The baby's screech had held so much outrage that Tony had had a hard time persuading her and Mami that he hadn't pinched the child or something. Ti-Jeanne was almost thankful when the sun went down. Now Mami would do whatever it was she had in mind, and Tony would be on his way.

But to Ti-Jeanne's dismay, Mami told them that she wouldn't do the ritual until well into the night.

"'Bout two o' clock or so," she said.

"Why so late, Mami?" Ti-Jeanne asked.

"I ain't know if . . . how Osain go hide he from the posse." Mami jerked her head in Tony's direction. At some point during the day, she'd stopped addressing him directly. Ti-Jeanne guessed that it was because her grandmother could see the flirting that was going on between them. "Is best if he leave while it still dark, and most people gone to bed. Fewer people to see what going on."

That was eight hours away! "Mami, what we go do in the meantime?"

"All of we should get some sleep. It go be a long, hard night."

Mami didn't put up with any arguments. They had a cold supper, then Mami gave Tony a blanket and a pillow and told him he could curl up on the living room couch. Tony looked at the love seat that was too short to allow him to stretch out his six-foot frame, but he said nothing. Mami bustled Ti-Jeanne upstairs and sat with her while she gave Baby his nighttime feeding. Mami said nothing, just sat, staring at the flickering candle on the windowsill. Her face was set hard as stone. She clutched her arms around her and rocked her tiny body back and forth.

When Ti-Jeanne couldn't stand the silence any more, she said, "Mami, I want to thank you for helping Tony for me."

The old woman kissed her teeth, a sound of exasperation. "I ain't doing it for you, you know? I want his good-for-nothing Black ass out of here. Nothing but trouble."

She couldn't argue with that. "Yes, Mami," she said meekly.

"Doux-doux, I have to tell you right now: I ain't know if this going to work."

Ti-Jeanne felt fear threading itself ice cold through her veins. "Mami, you is Tony last chance. It have to work!"

"It ain't Tony I 'fraid for," she said absentmindedly. "I ain't really business with what happen to he, oui. But is so long Papa ain't come to me. To tell the truth, doux-doux, I ain't call he, either. He and me had a falling-out. If I ain't call he and he ain't come, that not too bad. But suppose I call he tonight, and he refuse me? What I go do then, Ti-Jeanne? What I go do without Papa?"

Ti-Jeanne had no idea what her grandmother was talking about, but the lost loneliness in Mami's voice was plain enough. Ti-Jeanne pitied her for whatever it was that caused her to sound so. She reached out and patted Mami's shoulder. "Sshh, Mami, sshh. I sure things go work out."

But she wasn't sure at all.

After they had all gone to bed, Ti-Jeanne lay in her narrow bed, staring into the dark. Her mind was a storm, her skin on fire. All her senses focused on where she knew Tony was, curled up just downstairs on the couch in the parlour. Was he asleep yet? Was he thinking about her? She tossed and turned, imagining his lips softly kissing the back of her neck the way he used to do, moving down her back to the hollow of her spine, that place where the lightest touch could make her shiver. She could almost feel his hands on her breasts, gently tugging at her nipples until they stiffened, the areolas crinkling with pleasure. Her body flushed with warmth. She sat up in bed, pulled the flannel nightgown off over her head. The cool night air on her skin was like the exhaled breath of a lover. She ran her hands over her body, arching her back at the sensation.

What was she doing? Her baby was in his cot in this very room, and this was how she was carrying on? Shamed, Ti-Jeanne got up and tiptoed over to where Baby lay, fast asleep, his thumb in his mouth. It would be another two hours before he demanded to be fed again.

Her skin was burning with its own heat. She went and knelt on her cot, opened the window just above it, and leaned out into the cool night air, feeling it slide like a tongue down the front of her body. A full moon rode the clouds, bucking. Was that a noise she heard from downstairs where Tony was, a foot treading on a creaky floorboard? Ti-Jeanne closed the window so Baby wouldn't catch a chill. She pulled her nightgown back on and left the bedroom, tiptoeing down the stairs. At the bottom, Tony stepped out from the shadows. Ti-Jeanne gasped, giggled, looked at him full on for the first time in months. Moonlight traced his body, his arms strong enough to wrap her round, his chest broad enough to rock her on. His waist, nearly as narrow as her own. The devil! He was naked as God had made him, erect and ready for her. Ti-Jeanne smiled and stepped into his embrace. It was like coming home. She put her arms around him, slid her hands down over his ass, feeling the hollows that muscle made in the sides of his buttocks. Tony tried to kiss her, but she put a finger to his lips instead. Taking his hand, she quietly led them both out the front door and headed for the Francey barn. "It warm in there," she whispered. "And Mami can't hear we."

He smiled.

Mami's eyes weren't what they used to be. Standing at Ti-Jeanne's window, she could just make out the white of Ti-Jeanne's nightgown, practically dancing along the path to the barn. At moments, the dark blot of Tony's body hid the sight of her grandchild from her. When they reached the barn door, the nightgown was suddenly ruched up into a ball. It went sailing out over the grass to land in a heap on a fence post. The barn door creaked open. Then shut. Mami thought she heard a faint giggle on the wind.

"Eshu," the old woman muttered to the night, "the crossroads is you own. Help my granddaughter safe across this one, nuh?"

• • • •

Ti-Jeanne woke up, absently brushing something away from her face that was tickling her. Straw. In the dark, she inhaled the warm, rich smells of hay and dung and remembered where she was. She could hear the snuffling of the sheep and goats. Tony's arm was thrown around her neck. She'd fallen asleep with her head pillowed against his hand. For a second or two, she relaxed into the hollow between his arm and his body, her remembered place. What time was it? Had they slept too late? Ti-Jeanne leapt to her feet, creaked open the barn door. It was still dark in the house.

Tony's voice came softly out of the dark: "Ti-Jeanne?"

"We should go back in, Tony. Don't want Mami to find we out here."

She heard him getting to his feet. She stepped outside, found her nightgown where she'd thrown it. A rush of guilt swept over her: how could she have done something so stupid? She pulled the nightgown over her head, looked backward to where she could hear Tony coming toward her. "Hurry up, nuh?" she said impatiently. "Come on."

Something moving past the front of the house caught her eye. She stiffened in surprise as she saw a tall figure outside in the park, heading up the pathway that led to the cemetery. Its long legs stalked eerily. She hissed, "Tony! Tony! Come fast! The posse people reach!"

"Fuck!" Tony was at her side in a second. With a trembling hand, Ti-Jeanne pointed the man out to him.

"Where, Ti-Jeanne? I don't see anyone."

"How you mean? Look, he right there, walking bold face towards the Necropolis!" The man stopped, slowly looked over to where she and Tony stood. Terror made gooseflesh rise on Ti-

Jeanne's arms. The man's face was a skull. It grinned at her. The thing tipped its top hat to her and kept walking. As it crossed in front of the house, she could no longer see it. Another vision. Ti-Jeanne swallowed hard on a cold lump of fear.

Tony shook her shoulder. "Where are they?"

"Never mind, Tony. I make a mistake. Was a branch blowing in the wind, or something."

Quietly as they could, they walked back up the path and into the house. "You stay here on the couch and pretend as if you sleeping," Ti-Jeanne instructed Tony in a whisper. "Mami go probably come and get we soon." She kissed him once more.

She took the stairs up to her own room, remembering at the last instant to step over the creaky one, third from the top. When she reached her room, Baby was just beginning to stir, ready to be fed again. He yawned, knuckled his eyes with a little fist, began to whimper. At the sound, her milk started to come. The let-down reflex made her breasts ache. She remembered Tony's mouth on them earlier, the game he'd made of licking the drops of milk that arousal had squeezed from her nipples. She sighed and picked Baby up, took him over to the bed, and sat down, shrugging off one shoulder of her nightgown so that Baby could suck.

Mami found her like that a few minutes later. "Is time," the old woman said. "When he done eating, it have a bucket of water in the kitchen for the two of you to bathe. Have to be clean to meet the spirits."

"Mami," Ti-Jeanne asked, "it go be all right to take the baby with we?"

"Yes; it ain't have nothing in what I do to hurt he, doux-doux."

Ti-Jeanne wasn't much comforted by her grandmother's response. The one time Mami had persuaded her to attend a ritual in the palais, she had fled screaming from the sight of Bruk-Foot Sam writhing purposefully along the floor, tongue flickering in and out like a snake's.

Mami sat down beside her, just looking. The old woman's face was sad, resigned. Without saying a word, she reached over and removed a piece of straw from Ti-Jeanne's hair, then patted the hair back into place. Her hand was gentle. Ti-Jeanne felt her face flaring hot with embarrassment.

CHAPTER FIVE

Duppy know who to frighten.

—Traditional saying

It was finally time for the ritual that Mami had promised Tony. Ti-Jeanne had Baby cradled against her chest in a Snugli. Mami had changed into a brown dress and tied her hair into a bright red headwrap. The colours she was wearing were the same as those on the necklace that was always around her neck, except when she bathed: tiny brown and red beads.

Mami took Ti-Jeanne and Tony into the kitchen, where she filled a basket with all kinds of odd things: three bunches of dried herbs that had been hanging in the kitchen window; two white potatoes—those were hard to come by, and Mami usually hoarded them; a margarine tub into which she had poured cornmeal; some of her homemade hard candy; her sharpest kitchen knife; a pack of matches; and a cigar, which she took from a cookie tin on the topmost shelf.

Tony asked, "What's all that for, Mistress Hunter?"

"You go find out."

Mami gave the basket to Tony to carry, then lit kerosene lamps for herself and Ti-Jeanne.

Tony said, "I could carry a lamp, too."

"No. In a little bit, both your hands going to be full."

Tony looked nervously at Ti-Jeanne, but what could she do? She gave him a tentative smile, tying to reassure him.

Mami led Ti-Jeanne and Tony out of the house, down the back steps, and into another barn, the one that held the chicken runs and the pig pens. Their upheld lanterns threw swaying circles of light. The animals stirred, blinking their eyes at the brightness. The chickens clucked irritably at being awoken.

Mami peered through the wire mesh of the doors of the chicken run.

"That one, Tony. The white sensé fowl with the curly-curly feathers. Go in there and catch it. We go bring it with we."

"C-catch it, Mami?" Tony stuttered. Ti-Jeanne knew that he was a city boy, had been born in Port of Spain, Trinidad's bustling capital, and had come to Toronto when he was five. He'd probably never handled a farm animal. She said:

"I could do it, Mami."

"No, it have to be Tony. Is he asking the favour; he have to do some of the work. Quick now, Tony. Just dash inside and grab the hen by it two feet before it could get away. But mind the rooster, you hear?" She pointed out the feisty little bantam rooster, red and green plumage gleaming. He had his jaunty tail feathers held high and was cocking a belligerent eye at these intruders to his domain. "If you don't move fast, he going to try and rip you with he back claw-them." Mami chuckled. The own-way old woman was probably enjoying putting Tony through this. She stepped away from the coop, then held up the lantern so Tony could see.

84

With his foot, Tony cleared the straw from a patch of ground and put down the basket. He looked hesitantly into the coop, marked where the sensé fowl was, then quickly snatched open the coop door and stepped inside. His shadow blocked Ti-Jeanne's view. There was a flurrying sound, a squawk, feathers flying. The hens screeched and chided, scurrying around inside the coop. Tony made a desperate leap for the bird. He missed and cracked his head on the lantern that swung above the coop. Mami chuckled. Tony made another rush and this time grabbed the screeching sensé fowl, holding her tightly by her feet. The rooster crowed a challenge and flew at him, its claws scratching, its beak striking.

"Fuck!" Tony swore, trying to shake the rooster off his arm. "The bastard bit me." Before he could get outside the coop, the enraged bird made another swipe at him. "Ai!" Tony leapt out, slamming the coop door behind him. Just like one of her own chickens, Mami cackled at the sight of him.

Ti-Jeanne could see blood running from a gouge in his forearm. "Oh, God, Tony, you get hurt! You want me get a bandage for you?" she asked anxiously.

"No, I'll be all right." He brought his arm up, sucked at the gash. Ti-Jeanne felt a flare of anger. She wished she could give the old woman a good slap, wipe that grin off her face.

"Mami, all of this best help Tony for true, oui!"

"Lord, don't give me no umbrage here tonight, Ti-Jeanne. Is because of you I helping he at all. Stupidness." Mami knelt so that her face was level with the screeching, flapping hen that was trying to twist out of Tony's hands. She soothed the

85

distressed bird, closed its wings, stroked her hands along its body. "Shh, darling, shh. I realise it ain't your time yet, but we need great. Pardon what we go do to you tonight."

Ti-Jeanne's skin crawled at her grandmother's words. The bird stopped fighting and simply hung in Tony's hand, making anguished croaking noises. Frightened and uncertain, Ti-Jeanne followed Mami as the old woman led her and Tony out of the barn, across the street to the little chapel and crematorium that stood at the entrance to the Necropolis, the old cemetery.

The Toronto Crematorium Chapel crouched sullen as a toad in front of the gates to the Necropolis. As Mami shone her lamp on its heavy oak doors, Ti-Jeanne could see the ornate cement mouldings that decorated the chapel and the gleam of the brass plaque dedicated to Henry Langley, the architect who had designed it in 1872. When Langley died, he'd been buried in the Necropolis. Mami still put flowers on his grave, in thanks for the use of the chapel. She called it the "palais."

Mami swung open the curlicued black iron gate, then the heavy oaken doors. Ti-Jeanne hovered at the entrance. She hated the place. She didn't take part in Mami's rituals, but many was the morning that Mami had set her to cleaning up the blood-and-rum-soaked cornmeal from the floor.

When Ti-Jeanne had been a child living with her mother and grandmother in the apartment building on Rose Avenue, Mami Gros-Jeanne would regularly go off in the evenings, dressed all in white and carrying food for some kind of religious celebration. Sometimes she stayed away all night. Ti-Jeanne's mother, Mi-Jeanne, had never wanted to accompany Mami, and she absolutely refused to let Ti-Jeanne go, so Ti-Jeanne had no idea what happened at these ceremonies. Ti-Jeanne had once asked her mother, who had responded disdainfully, "Is one set of clap hand and beat drum and falling down and getting the spirit, oui. Stupidness!"

The answer hadn't explained much. After the Riots, when Mami had moved herself and Ti-Jeanne into the Riverdale Farm buildings, Mami was soon leading regular rituals in the chapel. At nights, people dressed in white would troop past the front door of their house, carrying food and drums. Ti-Jeanne could hear them speaking. Mostly Caribbean English, but some spoke Spanish and others the African-rhythmed French of the French Caribbean islands. One or two were White, and there was Mami's friend Jenny, who was Romany. Ti-Jeanne had joined them that one time, but after being frightened away, she'd refused to join them for any more ceremonies. Mami tried to explain what went on in the chapel, but Ti-Jeanne had become so agitated that Mami soon stopped talking about her work there altogether. Her grandmother had been hurt but hadn't tried to command her. Many nights Ti-Jeanne would lie on her little cot, awake and restless from the compelling sound of the drumming and singing coming from the back house. The occasional screams, grunts, and moans frightened her.

Now she was going to have to witness a complete ritual. She hugged Baby to her for comfort. It had been a long, exhausting day for him. He had dozed off again, even sleeping through the screeching of the indignant chickens. In the moonlight, she could only partially make out his sweet little face, soft and innocent in sleep. This was when she loved Baby best, when he was quiet and she could admire the beauty of the being that had come from her body.

"Ti-Jeanne, you coming in?"

Ti-Jeanne took a deep breath for courage and stepped inside. The rows of tall wooden pews ranged on either side of the chapel, facing the raised dais where coffins used to be placed during funeral ceremonies. After the funeral, a mechanism in the dais would lower the coffin and its contents into the high-powered ovens to be burnt to ashes. The walls all around the crematorium were lined with what Ti-Jeanne had once thought were small marble tiles. They were in fact marble boxes, packed tightly in rows against the walls. The face of each box had a different name and dates etched on it: "Maisie Belmore, 1932–1995"; "James Cover, 1896–1942." Ti-Jeanne looked at the boxes of ashy remains and shivered.

Mami took both lamps, climbed up onto pews to hang them high on looped wires suspended from the ceiling. The flickering light danced, illuminating the centre pole in the middle of room, running up into the ceiling. The wood of the centre pole was untreated, the axe marks standing out sharply against its grain. Mami had got some strong men from her flock to chop down a poplar and install it in the middle of the chapel. Ti-Jeanne had never been sure exactly what it was for. The ceiling was sound. Her sense of unease deepened.

She stayed near the door, thinking that she could always dash outside and get away. Tony looked just as frightened as she did. His eyes were wide. Mami was preoccupied, bustling around the room. She pulled a piece of string from one of her pockets, tied the poor sensé fowl's legs together while Tony held it, then hung the fowl by the string from yet another hook in the ceiling. There were many of them. The hen dangled helplessly, twisting slowly in the air and clucking forlornly to itself. Mami went into a back room, came out with a small, clumsily moulded cement head that just fit between her two hands. It had cowrie shells for eyes and mouth. She put it at the foot of the centre pole. She got the cornmeal out of the basket. Taking a handful at a time, she dribbled it in intricate designs around the centre pole. Ti-Jeanne had seen her do this once before. She marvelled at how quickly and neatly Mami created the filigreed designs. Then Mami opened the flask of rum, took some of it into her mouth, and blew out, spraying it onto the effigy she had put at the foot of the pole. Reverently she laid the cigar and the bowl of candies in front of the effigy. Then she got out the potatoes and the three bundles of herbs and placed them on the ground on top of one of the cornmeal designs. She went back into the room, came out wrestling a stool and a deep drum with a long neck. Tony jumped to help her with the drum, but she shook her head, handed him the stool instead. "Put it over beside Eshu."

"What?"

"Beside the stone head. Eshu."

He did so, taking care to avoid smudging the cornmeal patterns. Mami put the drum in front of the stool. The head of the drum was made of stretched leather, held on with wooden pegs all around its barrel.

Mami straightened up and looked at all she'd done. She nodded to herself, took her kitchen knife and a pack of matches out of the basket, and knelt on the ground, facing the altar she had created. She then turned and bowed down low to the chapel's images of Saint Francis and Saint Peter. She remained kneeling on the ground. "All right. We ready now. Allyou come and sit beside me."

Hesitantly they went over to her. Tony took off his jacket and balled it up into a cushion for Ti-Jeanne to sit on. He took Baby while she did so, then sat cross-legged beside her on the cold ground.

"What to do now, Mami?"

"Bow allyou heads to the ground like me."

They watched as she made another deep bow, then did the same.

"Now, from here on, listen and watch. If I start to talk like somebody different, and move different from how I does normally move, I want allyou to ask me what message I bring you."

Tony's voice was almost a croak: "What?"

"Yes, say it just like so: *'What message you have to give we tonight?'* And ask who it is you talking to, for allyou ain't going to know."

Ti-Jeanne ventured: "Papa, maybe?"

"Maybe. Maybe it go be Osain for true," the old woman said wistfully. "But I don't really think so, oui? Long time now, Papa Osain ain't come to me."

Osain. That name again. "Who he is really, Mami?" Ti-Jeanne asked.

"The healing spirit. My father spirit." She sighed. "Never mind. Allyou just watch, and do what I tell you."

And Mami closed her eyes and whispered a prayer. The lamplight danced on her face, filling it with shadows. She looked at the cement head.

"Eshu, is we here tonight: me, Gros-Jeanne, and my granddaughter, Ti-Jeanne, and she baby with no name, and she baby-father, Tony."

Tony started; looked over at Ti-Jeanne, who ignored the surprised question in his eyes. It made Ti-Jeanne mad. What Mami have to go and tell her business for?

Mami kept talking: "Eshu, we ask you to open the doors for we, let down the gates. Let the spirits come and talk to we. Look, we bring food for you, rum and sweet candy."

She took one of the candies out of the bowl, crunched it, and swallowed.

"We bring a cigar to light for you, Eshu, to sweeten the air with the smoke."

She picked up the cigar and put it to her mouth. She lit it, cheeks sucking in to draw it to life. She took a deep drag of the cigar and gently blew the smoke in Eshu's face.

"Eshu, we ask you to bring down the doors so the spirits could be here with we tonight. Spirits, please don't do no harm while you here; is we, your sons and daughters."

Mami balanced the still-burning cigar on the candy bowl. She got creakily to her feet, hooked the chicken down from the ceiling. She put the chicken on the floor in front of Eshu and motioned to Tony to hold its wings and body. She stretched its neck out long, so that the pinny neck feathers stood up, revealing the pink pimpled flesh beneath. Then she took her kitchen knife out of the basket and before Ti-Jeanne could warn Tony, sliced clean through the sensé fowl's neck. Blood spurted in gouts from the headless body. Its legs kicked. It was no worse than the way they killed the fowls for their supper table, but Tony made a sick noise in the back of his throat and looked away.

"Hold it, Tony," Mami hissed. "Don't make it run 'way! Here, give it to me."

Tony watched the grisly rite, curling his lips away from his teeth in disgust and fear. He seemed quite happy to relinquish the twitching, gushing body into Mami's hands. Mami directed the blood over the stone head. "We give you life to drink, Eshu, but is Ogun wield the knife, not we."

She laid the chicken and its head in front of Eshu. The hen's body jerked again feebly, once, then was still. The air was heavy with the stench of chicken flesh and blood.

Mami took her place on the stool, put the drum between her knees. With her fingertips and the heels of her hands, she began to beat out a rhythm. Ti-Jeanne recognised the pattern of sounds. She'd often heard that rhythm in the loud drumming coming from the chapel at nights. She hated it; it tugged at her blood, filled her head with sound until she thought it would burst from within, her skull cracking apart like an over-ripe pumpkin to reveal the soft, wet interior. Although Mami was rapping out the rhythm softly, the sound beat at Ti-Jeanne as loud as drums. It made her bones vibrate, her teeth ache. The small chapel was saturated with the rhythm, dripping with it. And still Mami kept drumming. Ti-Jeanne felt as though the chapel bell was chiming and gonging in time, her heart pounding to the drum, the shadows in the chapel leaping to it. Mami was rocking from side to side. So was Tony, not even seeming aware that he was doing so. He rolled up his sleeves to his forearms. Yes, it was hot now in the chapel. Ti-Jeanne could see the buff slashes on his arms. Two of them looked hardly healed. She sighed, sadly. Tony was still using. Same thing they fired him from the hospital for.

In Ti-Jeanne's arms Baby was wide awake, his eyes alert. He looked as though he were listening, hard, with his whole self. Ti-Jeanne realised that she was swaying to the drumming, too. She tried to stop herself, but her attention would waver and she'd find her body moving again.

Ti-Jeanne's focus shrank until all she could perceive was the sound of the drumming, the sight of Mami's water-chapped fingers beating and beating their rhythm. The cadence caught her mind in a loop, spun it in on itself, smaller and smaller until she was no longer aware of her body, of her arms cradling her child. She barely knew when she stood up.

• • • •

Trying not to retch from the thick stench of raw chicken and fresh blood, Tony sat hunched between Ti-Jeanne and her crazy grandmother. He was terrified. He could still feel the warmth of the chicken's body on his hands. He wanted to run out of there and never come back. But if he did, he'd probably run straight into the arms of the posse. His time was up. And Rudy was even crazier than Mami Gros-Jeanne. If Tony didn't get out of Toronto, Rudy's vengeance would probably make Tony wish for a death as quick as that of the throat-slit hen. Mami was his only chance. So he stayed, wrapping his arms around himself. He began rocking, rocking, praying this would be over soon.

Beside him, Ti-Jeanne giggled, a manic, breathy sound that made Tony's scalp prickle. She rose smoothly to her feet and began to dance with an eerie, stalking motion that made her legs seem longer than they were, thin and bony. Shadows clung to the hollows of her eyes and cheekbones, turning her face into a cruel mask. She laughed again. Her voice was deep, too deep for her woman's body. Her lips skinned back from her teeth in a death's-head grin.

"Prince of Cemetery!" Mami hissed, her eyes wide. She kept her rhythm going, but even softer.

"You know so, old lady," Ti-Jeanne rumbled. She pranced on long legs over to Mami, bent down, down, down; ran a bony forefinger over the old woman's cheek. "Good and old, yes? Like you nearly ready to come to me soon, daughter!"

To Tony's surprise, Mami Gros-Jeanne spoke sternly, drumming all the while, to the spirit that was riding her granddaughter. "I ain't no daughter of yours. Stop the foolishness and tell me what you doing with Ti-Jeanne. You know she head ain't ready to hold no spirits yet."

Ti-Jeanne/Prince of Cemetery chuckled, a hollow sound like bones falling into a pit. He danced over to Eshu's stone head and used a long, long finger to scoop up some of the chicken blood thickening there. Slowly he licked and sucked it off his finger, smiling like a child scraping out the batter bowl. Tony's stomach roiled.

"But doux-doux," Prince of Cemetery said, "your grand-daughter head full of spirits already; she ain't tell you? All kind of duppy and thing. When she close she eyes, she does see death. She belong to me. She is my daughter. You should 'fraid of she."

The old woman sucked her teeth in disgust. "Man, don't try to mamaguy me, oui? You only telling half the story. Prince of Cemetery does watch over death, yes, but he control life, too, when he come as Eshu. So why I should be frighten?"

The spirit grinned wide, did a pirouette. "Well, if you know that, old lady, tell Ti-Jeanne. Tell my horse to open she eyes good and see the whole thing; death . . ." He stopped, seemed for the first time to notice Baby strapped to his chest. Baby stared up at him, no fear in his face. Prince of Cemetery chortled. He pulled open the Velcro, took Baby out of the Snugli, and held him up in the air, grinning and cooing at him. Baby cooed back.

"And life," Prince of Cemetery continued. The words were now coming from Baby's lips. The booming deep man-voice lisped with the effort of forming words through the baby's underdeveloped vocal apparatus. "Tell she when she go out tonight, she must carry something she man give she. She must conceal it somewhere on she body. I go hide she halfway in Guinea Land, where flesh people can't see she. So long as she carrying Tony gift on she, nobody go see he, either. But only till sunup. Tell she that," the baby cooed, then laughed, a sound too deep and knowing for its young body.

• • • •

"Tell she that. . . ."

Ti-Jeanne came back to herself. She was standing, holding Baby up toward the ceiling. He was speaking in a man's voice. Shocked, she nearly dropped him. He laughed. Gaping, she brought him back down to chest level, but his mouth was closed now. Had she had another vision? But she didn't remember anything. "Mami? Tony?"

"Sit down, doux-doux," her grandmother said. The rhythm she was beating had changed. "You go be feeling tired."

She did feel tired. She handed Tony the baby so she could sit. He flinched back from her touch, then all but snatched Baby out of her hands. Why was he looking at her like that? She lowered herself to the ground, feeling her leg muscles tremble.

Mami's body started to jerk. Her eyes closed, fluttered. She took in little gasps with each jerk of her body. Eerily, her fingers kept tapping the beat, as though someone else were controlling them.

"Help she, Tony! She having some kinda fit!"

Tony handed Baby back to Ti-Jeanne and crawled over to Mami, but as he reached a hand toward her, her eyes snapped open. Her hands stopped moving on the drum. Ti-Jeanne felt as though the rhythm had continued, though, in the very cells of her body. Mami glared at Tony. "Don't touch me. So long you ain't use your hands to heal. Don't touch me. You not my son any more."

She seemed even older than her years, one eye scarred shut, her voice raspy. She fumbled a stick from the shadows behind her and began to clamber awkwardly to her feet. The stick was as gnarled as she appeared.

Where that come from? Ti-Jeanne thought. *I ain't see she bring it out with the other things.* Then she gave a little cry as Mami stood up her full length. One sleeve of Mami's dress flopped empty, and only one foot showed beneath the hem of her dress. One arm was missing and one leg! "Oh, God!" Ti-Jeanne wailed.

Mami looked at her and answered in the voice of an old, old man. "You calling on God Father, but he ain't go answer. Me now, I right here. Gros-Jeanne send for me, and I come." Mami hopped over to the altar, leaned her cane against it. She picked up one of the potatoes, took a bite out of it, chewed, and swallowed with relish.

Tony nudged Ti-Jeanne, whispered, *"Ask he!"*

"He who? Ask he what?" she hissed back.

Tony cleared his throat, tried to speak, stuttered, tried again: "I—is who you is, spirit? Who we talking to?"

Mami looked at him disdainfully. "You used to be one of mine. Me, Osain. But I ain't come because of you. I come because my daughter Gros-Jeanne ask me."

Osain! It was the name Mami had said. Papa Osain. Ti-Jeanne realised that the person she was looking at wasn't exactly her grandmother. Mami/Osain hobbled forward, using his stick for balance. He leaned down toward Ti-Jeanne, until she thought he would topple. "I mad at Gros-Jeanne, you hear? So many years now I telling she what she have to do to get rid of that Rudy, and she ain't listening to me."

Rudy? What Mami have to do with he? The wrinkled old face looking down into hers was softer in feature than Mami's, but its glare was even more fierce. Ti-Jeanne swore she could see the bump of an Adam's apple in its throat. She really was talking to a man, a man far older than anyone living. She remembered Mami's instructions, found her voice. "What message you have for we, spirit?"

The old man sighed, as though he'd been waiting years to hear just that question. "Tell Gros-Jeanne is past time for she to do my work. Is too late for she and for the middle one, but maybe the end one go win through. Ti-Jeanne, she have to help you to get Rudy dead bowl and burn it. Is the only way to stop he from catching shadows in it. The spirits vex at he too bad for all the evil he cause. Prince of Cemetery arms getting weary from carrying all Rudy dead across the bitter water to Guinea Land. Tell Gros-Jeanne is time and past time for she to play she part."

"And me," Tony burst out. "What about me? All of this mumbo-jumbo is supposed to help me get out of this damned city!" Baby writhed irritably in Tony's arms, whimpering. Roughly, Tony handed him back to Ti-Jeanne.

Osain swivelled on his one good heel to look at Tony. "You? I ain't business with you! Look at you; why you arms cut up like that?"

Tony looked defiant. He rolled down his sleeves over the half-healed buff slashes.

Osain waved his cane in Tony's direction. "If I had my way, them would catch you and make a end of you, oui? Farmer must know when to grow, and when to prune. You is a branch I woulda chop off one time!" Osain sucked his teeth in disgust. "Healer turn to dealer. What I business with you?"

There was a tremor in Tony's voice. "But Missis Hunter said you would help me!"

Osain looked at him, made a face, sighed. His badly scarred cheek made him look stern. "Yes, is my daughter ask me this favour. I wouldn't have grant it, oui? You lucky that Prince of Cemetery decide to help you instead."

What was he talking about? Ti-Jeanne spoke up timidly. "Papa Osain?"

"Yes, child?"

Ti-Jeanne shuddered as she looked at Mami's skirt flapping emptily around the space where her leg should be. "I ain't understand. What we supposed to do to help Tony get out of here?"

The old man didn't answer at first. He hobbled back to the altar. He picked a few leaves off the bundle of dried mint that Mami had put there, rubbed them between his fingers, sniffed at them, touched them to his tongue. "Somebody dry these good. The taste still fresh, and the leaves ain't mouldy or damp. Is who do this? Gros-Jeanne?"

"No, Papa," Ti-Jeanne replied. "Is me. Is spearmint I pick and dry from out of the garden."

"Ah, child . . ." He smiled. "You know how to treat the herbs-them. You granny teach you good. It make me wish you was my daughter, instead of Prince of Cemetery own."

Prince of Cemetery? Why would the old man give such a horrible name to her father? Ti-Jeanne had never known her real father.

Osain jerked his head in Tony's direction. "That one give you any presents lately?"

Ti-Jeanne blushed. "Yes, Papa. A rose."

"Well, do like the Prince say. Carry it on you and lead Tony out of the city. Nobody go see allyou until dayclean. Them will look right through you. But, Mister Healer-Turn-Dealer"— Osain turned baleful eyes on Tony—"once the sun rise, we ain't go hide you from eyes no more. We want you gone, oui."

Gone. Tony gone, never to come back.

"Remember now, Ti-Jeanne: tell Gros-Jeanne everything I say. Allyou have to see to Rudy."

Without any warning, Osain's eyes rolled back in his head and he crumpled to the ground, stick clattering away into the shadows. Ti-Jeanne and Tony rushed over to help. Mami's eyes were fluttering, her breathing fast. Tony checked the pulse in her wrist, pulled up one eyelid to look at her eye. Ti-Jeanne realised that the old woman had two arms again. She felt through Mami's long skirt. Yes, both legs were there. Had she imagined what she'd seen? She looked around for Osain's cane, but it was gone.

Tony helped Mami into a sitting position. She seemed a bit disoriented, but fine otherwise. She grabbed at Ti-Jeanne's shoulder. "He come? Papa Osain come?"

"Yes, Mami."

The old woman's smile lit up the chapel. "Papa come back to me, after so long. What he say? Tell me what he say!"

• • • •

The young man's eyes rolled in fear as, knife in hand, Rudy approached the table where he lay immobile. His body jerked only a little as Rudy drew the knife across his throat, catching the blood in a large calabash bowl. "Drink," Rudy said to the bowl, "then make me know what the rass that Tony up to now."

• • • •

Three man went to mow (went to mow),
Went to mow a meadow,
Three man, two man,
One man and he dog,
Went to mow a meadow.

—Traditional song

Tony helped Mami into a sitting position against the centre pole, made sure she was all right, then proceeded to loudly accuse her of trying to play tricks on him.

"Oh, so you think I mamaguying you?" Mami asked acidly. "Then how you explain the spirit that come and ride Ti-Jeanne?"

"What spirit, Mami?" Ti-Jeanne's scalp prickled with fear. What had just happened to her, really?

"Later, child." Mami turned to Tony again. "Ain't is obeah you come here tonight to ask the spirits for, Tony? A way to hide from the posse so you could leave the city? Ain't is you

101

self stand up in my house and tell me I is a obeah woman? What happen; like you don't believe no more?"

Tony spluttered, "But . . . but . . . it was just a bunch of playacting, wasn't it? All of that couldn't really have happened, your leg disappearing, Ti-Jeanne growing seven feet tall."

"What?! Mami, you going to tell me what happen?"

"Later, I say." Mami waved Ti-Jeanne into silence.

Tony was still fuming. He was completely rattled. "Fucking fool I am, letting you talk me into doing this shit. And Ti-Jeanne?" His look was hurt. "You too? How you could do me so, Ti-Jeanne? Prancing around in the dark, playing duppy. I really needed your help, love. Don't you understand? Rudy's going to kill me if he finds me!"

"Tony . . ." Ti-Jeanne didn't know what to say. What did Mami mean, a spirit had been riding her?

"Well, mister, is you ask the favour, and from what I see, you wish get grant, for all I think you don't deserve it. Now you just go have to trust Prince of Cemetery, that is all."

That didn't satisfy Tony. He paced around the chapel, grumbling to himself. Ti-Jeanne knew he was desperate, but she had other things on her mind at the moment. "Mami," she asked again, "what happen to me just now? Who is Prince of Cemetery? What allyou talking about?"

Her grandmother reached for the boiled potato that Osain had bitten into and calmly took another bite out of it. She looked at Ti-Jeanne, considering. "Prince of Cemetery claim you for he own," she said, "just like Osain is my father spirit. No wonder you does see death."

In the shadows, Tony kicked at a pew, slammed his hand against it for good measure. Then he sat down, chin in hands, muttering.

"But what that mean, Mami? I going to dead?"

"No, child. Prince of Cemetery is a aspect of Eshu, who does guard crossroads. Prince of Cemetery does see to the graveyards." Ti-Jeanne didn't like the sound of that.

Mami continued, "It mean you could ease people passing, light the way for them. For them to cross over from this world, or the next. But I go have to train you." She smiled in triumph. "And the baby, too, for Prince of Cemetery did ride he for a few seconds before he leave."

"What? Baby too?"

"Yes, doux-doux. So it look like you go have to stay with me a little while more."

"But Mami, Tony going away for good!"

Baby chuckled, probably just at the way the coal-oil lamp flame was flickering above his head.

"And so? Ain't you done left he already? Best thing you ever do. Live here with me and give your baby a good home. You could help me more with the healing and so. I go teach you what you need to know. For if Prince of Cemetery decide to ride you again before your head ready, I 'fraid you go go mad for true."

Just like her mother. Ti-Jeanne's heart felt like cold lead in her chest. She had known it would come to this. Do what Mami said, or be lost, like Mi-Jeanne.

Tony stood up. "I'm gonna do it," he said. "I'm gonna go,

obeah or no obeah. I just have to make sure they don't see me, that's all."

"Nobody ain't go see you," Mami said. "Not so long as you take Ti-Jeanne with you."

Ti-Jeanne frowned at her, confused.

"Is true," Mami told her. "Prince of Cemetery promise that when you walk out this door, he go hide your living body halfway between here and Guinea Land. That way nobody go see you."

"Guinea Land?"

"Every time a African die," Mami intoned, "them spirit does fly away to Guinea Land. Is the other world, the spirit world. You carry that flower that Tony give you, and nobody go be able to see he, either. Until the sun come up, the Prince say."

"No, she can't come, it's too dangerous. You stay here with your baby. My baby." Tony reached out and patted Baby's head. "Why couldn't you tell me, Ti-Jeanne?"

The child twisted away from his hand. It was obvious he didn't like his father.

Mami said, "Either she go, and keep you safe from eyes that way, or you take a chance and go by yourself with no protection. Don't matter to me which."

Ti-Jeanne still didn't fully understand what Tony and Mami were talking about, but she understood that she had to accompany Tony for him to be safe. "I coming," she told him. And that was that.

"Then go and get the flower he give you," Mami said to her.

Ti-Jeanne wished she had the time to ask her grandmother what exactly she'd done and said while under the spirit's influence. She had to come back to Mami. Just long enough to find out how to control the dreams, keep the spirits out of her head. Then she'd be free.

Ti-Jeanne gave Baby to her grandmother. She stepped out into the clear night. Mami said, "Hold Tony hand!" A fog sprang up from nowhere. It crept quickly up over her and Tony and gave a soft blur to everything they looked at. Mami stepped out, dandling Baby. She peered around her. "Ti-Jeanne? Tony?"

"We right here, Mami." But her grandmother appeared to neither see nor hear them, even when Ti-Jeanne waved her hand right in front of her face.

"Jesus," Tony breathed. Ti-Jeanne's scalp prickled.

Baby reached for her, a pleading look on his little face. Ti-Jeanne asked, "I wonder how come he could see we?"

"I don't know, man. That fucking kid's weird. Just don't let my hand go."

Mami noticed the direction in which Baby was looking. She addressed them: "Take the bicycles from the Francey barn, allyou. You could go faster that way." Her gaze was a little off, too high, too far to the right. She really couldn't see them.

Holding tight to Tony's hand, Ti-Jeanne went back into the house and got the wilted rose from her bed where she'd left it. Mami'd said it had to be hidden on her body. She released Tony's hand to reach for some of Mami's gauze bandage. He gasped. "Fuck, now I can't see you."

Ti-Jeanne wrapped the rose's thorns in the bandage, then tucked the rose inside her jacket. Tony sighed in relief.

"There you are. Shit." He looked grim.

Ti-Jeanne's eyes were burning from lack of sleep. They got the bicycles from the barn and set off through the fog.

The foggy night air had a clean, sharp smell to it, like biting into an apple. They moved cautiously through the dark streets, ducking out of sight of any passersby. They were still afraid to trust in the spell that kept them only partially in the real world. Soon they were in the heart of Cabbage Town. Every so often they would pass a big Victorian home that was still inhabited. The smells from this part of the city were not as fresh: woodsmoke from fireplaces, rotting garbage, stale piss from the poorly built outhouses. These used to be elegant tree-lined streets of large heritage homes, all stone walls, stained glass, and deep, wooden-banistered porches. Now, many of the homes were gutted or were being used as cramped squats. In the summer, the flies and the stench of shit from the outhouses was almost unbearable.

The rose was scratching at her skin. "Hold on, Tony." She stopped her bike and adjusted the flower under her jacket. That helped a little.

There were still one or two people about; the nightlife of the Burn was pretty active. A few people looked their way, then looked away again, but that didn't prove anything.

Then they saw two men approaching.

"We'd better hide," Tony said, getting off his bike and starting to pull it into a nearby alleyway.

But Ti-Jeanne was curious. "You go ahead. I want to try something."

"Ti-Jeanne! Come on!" Tony hissed.

"Just now, just now. You go."

The men got closer. Tony hid. The two had their arms around each other, singing. Ti-Jeanne stood in their path. They simply separated, walked around her, still singing, then rejoined again once they'd passed her. The skin on Ti-Jeanne's forearms rose in gooseflesh. She turned to Tony, not bothering to keep her voice down. "Look like it working, oui. Them look at we, but is like we image don't stay in their minds!"

"Jesus," he muttered. "This is too fucking weird." He scowled and leapt onto his bike, then pedalled furiously off down the street, leaving Ti-Jeanne to catch up as best she could.

Every time Ti-Jeanne's knee rose with the upswing of the bicycle pedal, the stem of the rose inside her parka pricked at her belly button. She pumped the pedals hard. Puffing, she finally pulled level with Tony. He glanced over at her briefly but didn't say anything. He just kept going, lips pursed, his face set. After a few minutes he said, "Why didn't you tell me the baby was mine?"

"Now is not the time, Tony."

He grabbed her handlebars and yanked them both to a halt. He glared at her. "So when was supposed to be the right time, huh?"

"Lord, Tony!"

"No, really. Were you just gonna let me leave town? When were you going to tell me that I have a son!" He slammed his hand down on her handlebars, making the bicycle shudder in her grasp. Furious, she grabbed his arm, shoved the sleeve of his jacket up to his forearm. He winced as the fresh scabs tore open. Tiny beads of blood popped up along the slash tracks on his arm. She yanked the arm up to his face so that he was forced to look at them.

"You see that? Eh? That is where all your health going, all your strength, all your money. What you could keep child with? Eh? You go feed he buff when hunger pining he?" She let his arm drop. She sucked her teeth in disgust. "Worthless," she pronounced him.

"I would have stopped slashing," he said in a low voice. "Bruk-Foot Sam, he—"

"Tony, I don't want to hear it no more. Is the same story you been telling me for years now. Look, just make we go, eh?"

As she mounted the bike again, he heard him say to himself, "But he's my son." She didn't check to make sure he was following.

They made a left off Parliament Street onto Dundas. As they turned, Tony had to swerve wildly to dodge a pedicab runner who was about to smash into him. His bicycle skidded, slammed into the sidewalk verge, toppled. Tony went down with it, skidding a few feet before he came to rest on the sidewalk. "Hey!" he shouted at the runner. "Watch what you doing, nuh, man?"

But just like the other people they had passed, the man kept on running, oblivious, pulling the empty carriage behind him. Ti-Jeanne pulled up to the sidewalk, got off her bike, and went to help him. "You all right?"

"Yeah. I'm sorry, Ti-Jeanne."

"Me too." Bending gingerly so as not to crush the rose, Ti-Jeanne helped Tony up, an instant before the foot of a running street kid would have smashed down on his hand. The child ran on, thin body curled protectively around something that writhed under his jacket.

"Mothercunt—!" Tony leapt to his feet. In two steps he'd reached the little boy, grabbed him by one thin arm. "You can't even say sorry? Eh? You nearly mash my hand just now!"

The boy looked briefly at the hand that was clutching his arm, attempted to brush it off as though he were shooing a fly, and when that didn't work, simply stood still, his face blank, his body relaxed. Even though he was being restrained, he couldn't keep the idea of his captor in his mind long enough to react.

"Answer me!" Tony demanded.

"Tony," Ti-Jeanne called, but he didn't answer her.

The child looked Tony full in the face for a brief instant, then his eyes skittered away, glancing everywhere but at Tony. Ti-Jeanne felt the goose bumps come out on her arms again. The boy was oblivious to them. He looked down at the squirming front of his shirt. He was still supporting whatever was inside it with one hand. He made a clucking noise. "Lightning. You okay in there, Lightning?" A furry face poked out between his shirt buttons. A ferret. It hissed at Tony, bristled up to twice its size, and lunged. Tony released the boy and leapt back. The boy caught at his pet. "What's the matter with you, boy?" He turned around. He started walking away. "Been keepin' half a peanut-butter sandwich for you. Hid it with my blankets in that old Hyundai on Gerrard Street? I'll pick off the mouldy bits for you, okay?"

Tony came back to her, picked up his bike. "This shit is freaky, you hear?" he grumbled at her. "I keep thinking that people could damn well see and hear me, them only ignoring me for some reason."

Ti-Jeanne could see his hands shaking. She felt pretty shaky herself. She checked to make sure that the rose was okay, then got back on her bike. They rode on in silence. After a few more minutes Tony said, "Say something, Ti-Jeanne, or I go think I turn invisible to you, too."

"Is all right, Tony. I seeing you. I hearing you." *I don't see nothing but you. I don't hear nothing but you.* She felt the tears coming down. They kept heading east through the early morning dark.

They were almost at the Dundas Street turnoff for the unused Don Valley Parkway. Dug into the heavily wooded valley that marked the eastern boundary of the city core, it ran northward out of the city into the 'burbs. Toronto no longer maintained its section of it. Where the Parkway ran into civilization again, Ti-Jeanne had heard that the police in the five satellite cities had set up guard posts at their borders to keep Toronto out. "How you going to get past the blocks at the other end?" she asked Tony, huffing as she pedalled.

"The closest . . . guard post is at . . . Pottery Road," he replied, lungs working as hard as hers. "I'll come off the highway just before it . . . ditch the bike . . . hike through the woods. That goes into East York. Bingo, I'm out of Toronto and into the real world."

Ti-Jeanne took her eyes off the road long enough for a doubtful glance at his thin-soled dress shoes. "You don't think the police does look out for people trying to get in through the bush there?"

"Jesus, what do you want me to do, then? Stay here? Go organ hunting?"

She pursed her lips. The Guinea Land fog made it hard to see into the distance, so they stopped at the corner of Bayview to make sure it was clear. "What you going to do when you reach East York?" No one coming.

He smiled a little as he stuck his feet back in the toeclips and mounted up again. "Catch a bus. No, really. Into North York. Remember when you could just jump on a bus down here? Find a rooming house. I have a little money. Then look for work. I hear they're building an extension to the subway station out in North York there. Maybe there's some job there I could do."

The thought of the 'burbs scared Ti-Jeanne. She knew it was safer. She knew that there were hospitals and corner stores and movie theatres, but all she could imagine were broad streets with cars zipping by too fast to see who was in them, and people huddled in their houses except for jumping into their cars to drive to and from work. It had been years since she'd seen any cars actually running, except for Mercy Hospital ambulances and Rudy's elegant grey Bentley.

"It'll be great," said Tony.

And what you going to do for buff? she thought, but she knew better than to ask. He'd say that he took the drug for pleasure; that he wasn't addicted.

There were three figures milling around the turnoff to the highway. They had lit a small fire on the gravel verge. Two crouched in front of it, hands held out for warmth. The third sat on the low aluminum railing that marked the beginning of the long, narrow turnoff that dipped down onto the Parkway. Seen in the dark through the Guinea Land fog, their faces appeared smudged. One of them spoke, his words indistinct. The other two laughed. Ti-Jeanne and Tony were closer now. The men were Jay, Crapaud, and Crack Monkey. "Shit," Tony muttered. "What're they doing here?" Ti-Jeanne and Tony stopped their bicycles.

". . . duppy bowl, my ass," Crapaud was saying to the other two. "That blasted thing he have in there only stinking up the place."

The exit ramp was only the width of one car. Trees and thick undergrowth lined it. Tony would have to pass the men; there was no way around. "We have to go to another exit," he told Ti-Jeanne. "Queen, maybe."

Crapaud continued, "One day I leaving here, you hear me? Going out to the 'burbs to find a rich White woman to keep me. Rudy and he posse shit get to be too weird sometimes."

Jay said, "True, man. You see the woman Rudy holding now: Melba? Man, the things that man does have she doing does turn my stomach sometimes."

Ti-Jeanne whispered, "No time, Tony. Sun coming up soon."

"Shit, yeah. Maybe I'll try to go through the bush, then," Tony said uncertainly.

"No, them would see the trees shaking."

Crapaud shook his head. "I tell allyou, that man mad. Him and he obeah shit. Every time I see Crazy Betty, my skin does crawl."

Tony muttered, "But to just walk past them, bold-face like that? Why are they even here!"

"Is all right," Ti-Jeanne reassured him. "You know them can't see we. Go on," she urged, although it was breaking her heart. "Just go now."

He took a step toward the men, stopped, looked at her.

Crack Monkey drawled, "All me know say is since me hook up with Rudy, me got food in my belly and money in my pocket." Tony reached for her hand. She hung on to it hard, trying to remember why she was sending this man away. Tony said softly, "Will you come? If I send for you later, I mean. When I get a job, and stuff."

Leave the Burn, leave her grandmother's home and the people she knew, to live in the barren 'burbs with a man who'd rather slash buff than work. Would she do it? "When you get settled," she said, "send word for me."

"And you'll come?"

"I ain't know, Tony, and you don't have time for this! Go, nuh!"

Hanging on to the seat of his bicycle, Tony leaned forward

and kissed her. She inhaled his scent deeply for the last time then pulled away, wiping tears from her eyes. Tony was blinking, blinking. His eyes were red. He didn't say anything more, just turned away and began to wheel his bicycle carefully past the three men.

A phone rang. Crack slid his palmbook out of a back pocket, flipped it open, pressed the microphone function. "Yes, boss."

Deep as a death-watch bell, Rudy's voice issued from the palmbook. "Duppy say them there right now, in front of oonuh. Do it."

The three men actually turned and briskly walked away, Crack and Crapaud on one side of the on ramp, Jay on the other. Tony frowned. "What . . . ?"

It went too fast. In a split second, each of the three had pulled a baseball-sized lump of what looked like modelling clay out of their pockets and slammed it down hard onto the ground. Impact sent a stake sprouting a good eight feet high from each lump of clay. Synapse cordon. There was a zapping sound. "Run, Tony!"

Too late. Eyeblink fast, clear, branchlike filaments exploded from the triangle of stakes, intertwining to form a net that trapped them both inside it.

"Oh God oh God," Tony was saying under his breath. He stepped clear of the bike. "Them coming to get we now, we go dead now." He was going to let the bike go. That was a mistake.

"Tony!" Ti-Jeanne said quickly, trying to keep her voice as calm as possible. "Hold on to the bicycle. Don't let it go, or them will see it."

He was listening to her, barely. He kept his hold on one of the handlebars, turned to her, eyes wide in shock. "What the fuck difference does that make?"

The three men were peering in through the branches of the cordon. Jay asked doubtfully, "You think them in here for real?"

"You see? Them still can't see or hear we," Ti-Jeanne repeated urgently. "And them can't hold the thought of we in them heads for long. Just keep quiet, nuh? It might give we chance to get away when them release the cordon. Get ready to run."

Then came the doomsday tolling of Rudy's voice through the palmbook phone again. "Yes, she say oonuh have them. Knock them out."

Now, even Crack looked uncertain. He shrugged. "We have them? Well, all right, boss." He kicked at the cordon, activating the synapse surge of current across the gap where Ti-Jeanne and Tony stood. Ti-Jeanne's bonesshiveredteethchattered as the daze charge surged through the cordon, short-circuiting her neuromuscular system. She couldn't take her hands off the juddering steel frame of the bicycle, couldn't unlock her arms or her knees. The same thing was happening to Tony. The cordon shrank back down into three lumps of clay. The cessation of the shock was sweet release, and even then they might have made it, for they were still standing, still holding the bicycles, still hidden, and the sun wasn't completely risen yet, except for Ti-Jeanne feeling the soft impact on her feet of the rose that had worked its way loose as she shook. The rose landed right in front of an astonished Crapaud. The

Nalo Hopkinson

Guinea Land fog cleared instantly, and Crapaud shouted in surprise. They were fully back in reality. He could see them.

●●●●

Crack Monkey grabbed Tony's arm. He pulled out a dazer, the portable equivalent to the synapse cordon, and put it to Tony's chest. "Stand right there so, brother. Nah move."

Fuck, they were all wearing black rubber gloves, not leather ones as he'd thought. Tony obeyed. He wouldn't risk being dazeshot. *Jesus, Jesus, Jesus. I'm dead now. Rudy's got me. I'm dead.* He was dimly aware of Jay pulling Ti-Jeanne away from his side. Crapaud, a sickly shade of grey, kept his dazer against her neck. His hands were shaking.

"Don't let she go, Jay, don't let she go," Crapaud said. "Oh God, look at how them just appear so out of nowhere. Hold she right there, Jay; you ain't see she is a obeah woman?"

"Crapaud, man, have some sense. Between you, me, and the dazer, how this one puny woman going to get away from we?"

"You just don't let she go, or I go zap the both of allyou one time."

"Huh."

Tony stayed still, looking right into Crack's eyes with the intensity of a lover, pleading with the man not to pull the trigger. Crack gazed back coldly, calmly. Without looking away he said, "The two of oonuh just stop oonuh arguing. Rudy only tell we to bring Tony, and look we have he good. Put the charge to maximum and just shoot the damn bitch one time, and get she out of the way."

116

I should help her. I have to help her, but God, the dazer!
Tony heard Ti-Jeanne whimper, risked looking out of the
corners of his eyes. Jay was frog-marching Ti-Jeanne over to
the bushes, Crapaud scuttling alongside, gun still held nervously on her.

And then Ti-Jeanne chuckled in a deep, rumbling voice,
the same unearthly sound that she'd made in the chapel.
"Brothers, brothers, don't fight! It have plenty of me to go
around." She suddenly seemed much taller than Jay. She
broke his hold with ease, reached to her own neck with
long, long arms, and grasped the head of Crapaud's dazer.
He fired. She shivered, apparently in ecstasy, as the power
surged through her. She smiled lovingly at Crapaud. "Ah,
me brother; you know how pain could be sweet, ain't? You
want to go first?"

Crapaud released the dazer, took a step back. Ti-
Jeanne/Prince of Cemetery took a daddy-long-legs step over
to him, put a hand on his shoulder. The man did the crazy
dance of the dazeshot and fell twitching to the ground. Jay
rushed Prince of Cemetery, who picked him up like a baby
and *cradled* him to its bony chest. "Jason Egbert Petrey, what
you in such a hurry for? Eh? You will come to me in time,
but not yet. You must ask my horse about that. She know
your life story. Sleep, brother." Gently Prince of Cemetery
lowered the now unconscious man to the ground. The spirit
picked up the fallen rose, kissed its petals. They withered
instantly to brown. It dropped the dead rose on Jay's chest,
then straightened up, up, up to its full height and turned its

gaze on Tony and Crack Monkey. Crack stepped behind Tony, using him as a shield.

"Go 'long, woman, or I shoot he dead right here so."

"Crick Crack Monkey," came Prince of Cemetery's voice like rattling bones, "left the man and gone. Tell Rudy is me say so."

"And who the rass is you to be giving Rudy orders, woman?"

"Woman, man, child? Is all one when them come to me in the end." The spirit was at their sides in an instant. It put two fingers under Crack's chin, tilting the man's head upward so they were eye to eye. Crack's body went limp, but he remained upright, supported by Prince of Cemetery's two fingers under his chin. Tony's gorge rose at the smell of rotting flesh that the spirit exhaled from its mouth. He slid out of the way.

"Tell Rudy him know me," the spirit said to Crack, "the one him call so long now and never send away. Tell him this horse is my daughter. Him not to harm she. You go remember my name." It didn't sound like a question. "Legbara. The Eshu da Capa Preta."

Ti-Jeanne is as mixed up in this shit as Rudy is! Tony didn't wait to see what would happen next. He turned tail and ran.

• • • •

Ti-Jeanne came back to herself as her arm gave way from the weight it was supporting: Crack Monkey's body. He crashed to the ground, and Ti-Jeanne jumped back with a little scream, but he didn't move. His eyes were open and he was breathing, but he didn't seem aware of her. He just lay there. Crapaud and Jay were slumped nearby. Crapaud looked really bad. His face was spasming. He'd wet himself. Where was Tony? She looked around for a few seconds, called his name. She didn't see his body anywhere. Maybe he'd got away, headed up the highway already? But his bike was still there where he'd dropped it. What had happened? Tears began to cloud Ti-Jeanne's vision, but she knew she couldn't stay where she was. She picked up her bicycle and rode away.

• • • •

Hiding in the bushes, Tony watched her go. He didn't dare let her see him. She was as dangerous as Rudy. Better if he just got on his bike and rode out of this city.

He was picking up his bike when he heard the car engine. He fled back into the undergrowth. He heard the car pull up, the sound of a door slamming, then footsteps moving around the scene. A man's voice called out, "Crack? Jay? Oh God, look at Crapaud! Boss, come and see this!"

"What happen, Barry?" The voice was Rudy's. Tony heard the car door slam again, the sound of the posse boss cursing. Fear made his entrails curl tighter around eachother. No way he could get away right now. He stood trembling in the bushes, hoping that Rudy would leave soon. He heard Rudy say, "Load them in the back of the car. And put something under Crapaud nuh, so me good car seat leather nah get spoil."

The sound of heavy footsteps came closer and closer to where Tony was hiding. "Tony boy, you best had come out, for otherwise I just send some people in there to get you."

● ● ● ●

Ti-Jeanne dropped the bike at the foot of the Simpson House front stairs and ran sobbing through the front door. "Mami! Mami!"

Mami Gros-Jeanne came out onto the upstairs landing, cradling Baby in one arm and feeding him from a bottle with the other. "Is what do you, child?"

"Oh God, Mami, Tony gone, I ain't know where, and I black out again, and when I wake up, it had Crack and Jay and Crapaud lying on the ground, and the rose dead, and Crapaud . . . Crapaud . . . Mami, everything go wrong." Ti-Jeanne sat hard on the floor and wept.

Mami was down the stairs in an instant. Ti-Jeanne felt her grandmother's arm encircle her. Mami still held Baby in the other arm. Ti-Jeanne reached out and hugged them both, rocking. "Mami, I don't know if Tony gone, or them kill him. I don't know what happen to me out there. Is what I is, Mami? Is me do that to them three men?"

"Sshh, Ti-Jeanne, hush, doux-doux." Mami kept up the soothing noises and the rocking until Ti-Jeanne's sobs subsided.

By and by, Ti-Jeanne felt a little more in control of herself. She took Baby from his grandmother, picked up his bottle from where Mami had dropped it on the floor. But Baby didn't want any more milk. He was wide awake and alert, watching the two women intently.

Mami said, "You feeling better now?"

"Little bit."

"All right. I want you to tell me everything that happen after you and Tony left here this morning. Don't leave nothing out, you hear?"

Ti-Jeanne looked into Baby's eyes, focused on the child's calm, steady gaze, and told her grandmother the story of how she and Tony had reached the highway safely, only to be trapped. The old woman's eyes got hard as stone when she heard how Rudy had seemed to know where they were. "That mean another life gone," she said in a harsh voice. "Deathblood is the price you pay to get the duppy to spy into Guinea Land for you."

"What is that, Mami? That duppy everybody keep talking about?"

An ancient pain hollowed out her grandmother's features. "Doux-doux, Rudy is a shadow-catcher. He got the spirit of someone dead in that calabash, that does do he work for he. Rudy does work the dead to control the living. Is that he probably use to track you and Tony."

Ti-Jeanne's skin crawled at the words. She remembered the men at the highway talking about how Rudy controlled some woman named Melba, made her do horrible things. Ti-Jeanne remembered what Osain had said to them in the chapel: *Tell Gros-Jeanne is past time for she do my work.* "Mami," she said softly, "what Osain mean when he say you ain't take care of Rudy like he tell you?"

To Ti-Jeanne's surprise, stern Gros-Jeanne looked down at the floor, refusing to meet her eyes.

"Mami," Ti-Jeanne persisted, "what business you have with Rudy?"

Gros-Jeanne refused to meet her eyes, for all the world like a child being scolded. "Is me teach he how to serve the spirits, but he take the knowledge and twist it." Mami's eyes finally met hers, sorrow and regret brimming in them. "Rudy is my husband. Your grandfather."

Shock leached heat from Ti-Jeanne's skin. "What? But how . . . Mami, Rudy is a young man!"

The old woman shook her head sadly. "Rudy fourteen years older than me. That is other people youth he wearing, youth he steal from them when he catch their shadows to put in he duppy pot."

Suddenly Baby screamed, twisting and fighting in Ti-Jeanne's arms. Had a pin from his diaper stuck him? No. Baby howled as though he'd lost everything in the world he'd ever loved. Ti-Jeanne rocked him and rocked him, trying to soothe him, but he was inconsolable.

"Give he to me," Mami said. Ti-Jeanne gratefully handed him over.

Mami cradled Baby, looking right into his eyes. "Little soul, little soul, is what vex you so? Like you need a healing bath to soothe your spirit, child. Eh? Is what do you?"

Baby sobbed and sobbed. It sounded as though he were crying, "Bolom! Bolom!" over and over. He looked so lost and miserable. A bolom was an unborn child. It was Ti-Jeanne's private name for Baby, the one she'd started calling him while he was still in her belly. Past time to give him his own name now. She leaned over her baby, ran a hand over his head. Mami's eyes on his little face were worried. "Ti-Jeanne," she said, "when this child learn to talk, I feel he go have plenty to tell we."

"How you mean?"

"Like I tell you, is not just you Legbara did ride last night. He visit your baby, too, just for a second. Baby talk to we while Legbara did riding he."

Ti-Jeanne's heart sank. She had hoped that she had imagined coming back to her senses in time to hear Baby talking in an adult's voice. *Them spirits following he and all?* She had to leave this place as soon as she could, get away from the balm-yard and Mami and Rudy and all these beings she couldn't see who were trying to control her life. "What he make Baby say, Mami? What words he put into the child mouth?"

Gros-Jeanne relayed the odd message to her. Ti-Jeanne just found it confusing. Death and life? What did any of it have to do with her?

"Don't worry about Baby, doux-doux. Maybe Legbara just come to he because Legbara love all children, and they love him back."

"No, Mami! That skull-and-bone *thing*?"

"Oh, yes. Remember what he say: he does watch over the crossroads between death and life, too. Dead people precious to he because he does shepherd them across one way, but children precious to he because he does shepherd them across the other way."

"I go study that later, Mami. Right now, I need to know what happen to me out there by the highway."

Mami frowned. "I feel we start something when we had that ceremony last night. What happen to you is part of that. Tell me, doux-doux, what Osain say to allyou last night? I couldn't hear, because is me he did riding."

"He say he vex with you. He say he done tell you already to find Rudy duppy pot and break it. He say . . ." Ti-Jeanne tried to remember the spirit's odd words, "He say to tell you that it too late for you and the middle one, but maybe the end one go win through. I ain't know what that mean."

Mami's face was bleak. "The middle one is Mi-Jeanne. He telling me it too late to help she. God, God; my child gone for good."

Fear settled like lead in Ti-Jeanne's stomach. "My mother? And the end one?" she whispered.

"The end one is you. It look like you did dreaming true, doux-doux. I must be the one to set the trap for Rudy, but is you go have to stop he."

Ti-Jeanne remembered Rudy's voice ordering their doom from the phone. "Mami, this ain't my fight. I never do anything to get in Rudy way."

"Except today. He not going to forgive you for damaging his three generals."

"But that wasn't me!"

"I know. It was Legbara." She looked at Ti-Jeanne. "He is

a Eshu, you know, one of the guardians of the crossroads.
When you black out, he must be did riding you. You never
know what Legbara going to take it into he head to do. Him
is a trickster. The Eshu-them too love to play games."

"Games?" Ti-Jeanne pulled away from her grandmother's
hands. "Is game allyou think this is? Eh, Mami? Is game you
been playing with me and Tony all this time? With we *lives*?"

"Ti-Jeanne, you know better than that."

She did, but it felt better to have someone familiar to
accuse of all this. *Legbara.* That was the word she had been
saying when she woke up with Crack's chin in her hand.
"Mami, I need to know how to deal with this. I need to
know who is all these spirit names you does call all the time,
and what it is does happen to me when I black out." *And
how to make all of it go away,* she thought, but she didn't say
it out loud.

The old woman looked grim. "But ain't is that I been trying to teach you all along? And is now you want to learn, eh?
When is your man involved. Well, sweetheart, look like you
have to learn your lesson now. Your Tony probably run away
already to the 'burbs" (the words seared Ti-Jeanne's heart like
a new wound) "and leave you here. Well, good. I hope you
learn your lesson."

Despair settled on Ti-Jeanne's shoulders. Mami could
always cut her down to size. But maybe Mami had the key to
freeing her of the spirits that were haunting her. Let the old
woman think Ti-Jeanne was feeling chastised. Mami was
always more forthcoming then. She slumped her shoulders,

put on a glum expression. "Yes, Mami. I sorry, Mami. I ready to learn from you now."

"Now you talking sense, sweetness. We go start right now. No time to waste." The old woman settled herself comfortably on the floor, pulling her skirt up above her knees so she could sit cross-legged. As ever, Ti-Jeanne marvelled at Mami's trim, strong body. Despite her small, almost child-like frame, Mami was as tough as a workhorse. "Now, doux-doux," Mami said, "to start off, it have eight names you must know." She ticked them off on her fingers. "Shango, Ogun, Osain, Shakpana, Emanjah, Oshun, Oya, and Eshu."

Ti-Jeanne tried to memorise the sounds. "And explain to me exactly what them is, Mami."

"The African powers, child. The spirits. The loas. The orishas. The oldest ancestors. You will hear people from Haiti and Cuba and Brazil and so call them different names. You will even hear some names I ain't tell you, but we all mean the same thing. Them is the ones who does carry we prayers to God Father, for he too busy to listen to every single one of we on earth talking at he all the time. Each of we have a special one who is we father or mother, and no matter what we call it, whether Shango or Santeria or Voudun or what, we all doing the same thing. Serving the spirits."

"Osain and Eshu I hear already today, Mami. And Legbara."

"Yes. Legbara is your spirit father, like Osain is my own. I already tell you what that mean."

"Yes, but I don't understand. I supposed to watch over people dying, or something? I don't like how that sound, Mami!"

"Doux-doux, the spirits don't call we unless we ready to accept the call, so you must be ready, even if you don't want to accept it. Legbara is your guardian. He will watch out for you, if you is a good daughter."

And a good daughter single-handedly hunted down obeah-wielding gang lords, Ti-Jeanne supposed.

CHAPTER SIX

Rudy was pissed off. Tony had blurted out his story to him in the limousine ride back to Rudy's office. Only three more days left to collect the heart for the hospital, and this pissant boy had been wasting time. He'd even found a match, but he was too cowardly to do what had to be done. On top of it all now, Tony had put his three best generals out of commission. Rudy didn't even know if Crapaud was going to live, and Jay and Crack were only lying there like babies, talking foolishness about how Tony's girlfriend beat them up. He scowled at Tony across the oak dining table. He touched the linen napkin to his lips, put it down. The waiter moved in quickly to clear the table, glancing fearfully at Tony from time to time. Rudy watched him in silence, then, "All right. You could go now."

Tapping the fingers of one hand on the tabletop, Rudy glared at Tony again. *I have a mind to just feed him blood to the calabash one time,* Rudy thought. Lately the thing in the duppy pot had been demanding to be fed more often. And what about that message that Crack had brought him from Eshu? The Eshu in the Black Cape. The one that had shown him the way to control people, to work the dead.

Rudy thought about it. Now that he knew where to find a match for Uttley, he could get some of his boys to beat the woman up, then just call the hospital to come and collect, and claim his finder's fee. Less money, but still profitable. Maybe not yet, though. He still had a chance to use Tony to get the full fee. Rudy was sure he could give the man the right incentive. And it would get those blasted women and their nicey-nicey balm-yard spirits out of his way once and for all.

"I figure," Rudy said to Tony, "you must be did see what happen out there by the highway? You see the spirit that appear to Crack?"

Of course, Tony couldn't reply. He was flopped limply in the armchair in Rudy's office, head flopped to one side. Only the panicked look in Tony's eyes betrayed any awareness.

"Some people call that spirit the One in the Black Cape, seen? Him does always dress in funeral colours. Him is the one you call when somebody work a obeah 'pon you and you want revenge. I call him. Twelve years ago. I wasn't nobody then, you understand? Just a poor man who get kick out of he house by he ungrateful wife. Motherass woman take up with a next man behind my back. Them days, I was living in a flophouse, and I had one little problem, same like you. Buff. Used to spend all my money on it, then steal to get more. And just like you, I make a mistake. I steal from the posse."

Tony's eyes were watering.

"But your eyes must be stinging you, eh, Tony? It does burn when you can't blink them, right? Is so the toad poison does take you. Temporary paralysis. Is them kinda things could happen when people cross me. Never mind, though," he said in mock friendliness, "I go get Melba to fix you up, all right? Melba, take your hand and close that man eyes for him. Gentle, now. Don't poke him like you jook the last one."

Melba shuffled out of the corner where she'd been standing. She'd been bathed, but the boys hadn't known what to do with her hair. It hung matted and snarled from her scalp. She had lost a lot of weight. Her clothes sagged on her body, and her skin was grey and flaky. She wouldn't last much longer. She went toward Tony, who started making "uh, uh," noises. She ignored them, slid his eyelids down over his eyes, then stood where she was.

"Now," Rudy said, "what I was saying?"

Tony's noises took on a more desperate tone. Rudy chuckled. "What, Master Tony? Me think say you would prefer if you could see what me a-do, eh? All right, brother. If you could stand the burning, who is me to tell you no? Melba, open up he eyes again." She did.

"Move away now, Melba. Go back to your corner." The woman obeyed.

"So yes, brother, me was telling you: me steal from the posse, and them find out, and the boys come for me. Me did slash all the buff one time. Me was flying high when them bruk down me door. I don't like to tell you how bad them do me that night, me brother. Them nearly kill me." He shook his head, remembering. Cool breeze, though. That was a long time ago. And the two men that had done it had lived to see their error. He went and stood over Tony. "Them break me one leg, here so," he said, laying a hand on Tony's thigh. Tony's eyes were wild with terror. "And me hand, and them crack open me cheekbone, here so." With his index finger, he touched a spot just under Tony's left eye. A tear dripped down. He smiled and flicked it off his finger.

"Oh, I know you can't see no scar or nothing on me face now. Me does keep meself young and good-looking nowadays. No scar, no scratch, that me duppy don't fix it for me. And it take away the craving for buff, too.

"So yes, posse do for me that night. And them wasn't the first one to do me bad, no, sir. From I born, people been taking advantage. Poor all me born days. Come up to Canada, no work. Me wife and all kick me out of me own house. Blasted cow. If it wasn't for me, she woulda still be cleaning rich people toilets back home, and is so she treat me. Just because me give she little slap two-three time when she make she mouth run away 'pon me." Anger at the injustice of it all burned again in Rudy. But it wasn't like that now. Nobody took advantage of him now.

"So lying there in me broken bones that night, me decide nobody nah go get nothing from me no more. Time to get my due back from them, you understand?"

A line of spittle ran from Tony's mouth to drip down his chin onto his shoulder, mixing with the tears that were now running freely from his tortured eyes.

"Me face did swell up, the two ends of break bone in me leg rubbing every time me try to move. And me call the Eshu. The One in the Black Cape, just like me wife did show me.

Me soul did already flying free from all the buff what me slash, and me reach out from them heights there, and me call, drumming the rhythm on the ground with me one good hand that leave. Me ain't know how long me call, but me swear me see the sun come up and go back down again. And me ain't stop. Mouth dry, leg a-pain me, and me ain't stop for nothing. Finally him come, and me tell him me want him to kill everybody that do me bad. And imagine this: blasted Eshu tell me no! Him tell me say revenge is one thing, but him nah go help me to kill, for nobody I vex with ain't kill nobody of mine. *But killing is that me want,* me say to him. *And if you don't give it to me, I go keep drumming you back here until you do it.* And me do it, seen? So him go 'way, so me drum him back. Three times. The buff wasn't keeping away the pain no more. Plenty times me nearly faint from it, but me bite me lip to keep me awake, and me keep on drumming. The third time him come back, him did vex, you see? Him say all right, if is death I want to deal in, he go tell me what it take for a man to deal in the dead. Stupid spirit. Him think say I woulda frighten at what I have to do, and I would back off with me tail between me legs. But I listen, and I learn. Him tell me must find a dead in the cemetery, somebody who just cross over. Him tell me must call the dead man duppy, and make him serve me. Him tell me how to keep the duppy by me, and what to feed it. He tell me if I do alla that, neither him nor the rest of the ancestors go want nothing more to do with me. Well, me didn't business with that; what the ancestors ever do for me before?" Rudy chuckled, half to himself. "Is long time I had to wait till me leg heal good enough to follow he instructions. But you know what? I is a patient man." He fell silent for a minute, remembering the smell of carrion and grave dirt on the night he'd gone to the cemetery. "Sometimes I wonder is what Eshu think when he watch me doing everything he say, and he see the duppy rise. It heal me, Mas' Tony; heal me good good like you see me now. Then each day after that, one of my enemies dead. On the third day, was Dunston turn. Blasted man who steal my woman. When them find him, him had no skin left on him body, and his heart did rip out. Dogs, them say. Me know better. Then me tell the duppy me want more than that. Me want to run things in the posse. And so I ask, is so it go. Inside of a year, I was posse boss. Funny thing that, eh?"

Tony made no sound.

"What you think Eshu want now, eh, Tony? Why you think he warn me away from your woman? Ti-Jeanne, Mi-Jeanne, Gros-Jeanne; them fucking women been giving me trouble from since when!"

Rudy turned Tony's chair to face him. He reached out a big, powerful hand and closed the man's eyes with a deliberate tenderness. "See now? Don't that feel better?" Tony made a mewing sound. Rudy looked down at Tony's body and chuckled. Funny how many of them this happened to. "But see how you pay me back for my kindness," he told Tony. "You gone and piss up my good good chair. Is a good thing the seat make out of leather. Melba, get a damp cloth and clean up this chair."

Easily as he would a doll, Rudy lifted Tony out of the

chair and lowered him to the floor. He removed Tony's shoes and socks, undid his belt buckle, and began taking off the sodden pants. Tony's moaning started up again, like a weak sobbing.

"But what a way this man could fret, ee?" Rudy inquired gently. "Don't you want to have fresh, clean clothes? I go get Melba to bring some for you."

Once the pants were off, Rudy sat back on his heels and looked at the helpless, half-naked man. Maybe he should have robbed Tony of his volition when he'd had the time to, the way he had done with Melba. Then the man would have done anything he told him to. But the mindless slaves could only follow simple instructions. He needed Tony to be aware so that he could use his medical training to transfer the live heart into its container.

The paralysis must have begun to wear off a little. Tony had managed to open his eyes and was blinking slowly through his tears. His eyes seemed to beg. It was Rudy's power alone to answer that plea. Or not. Rudy felt the familiar tightening in his crotch that that sense of power always brought him.

"Well, boy, look at you. The time come to pay the piper. You been bringing me one set of trouble. You had a match for the heart all along, but you been wasting time? Boy, what wrong with you? Me a-go show you what me do with people who make me vex, then me a-go give you a choice: either you bring me the blasted heart by tomorrow, or you turn duppy food."

• • • •

Barkodey, me buddy,
Barkodey
Them send me to shave you,
Barkodey
With me ten pound razor,
Barkodey
And if you laugh me go cut you.
Barkodey

—Call-and-response chant

Sensation was returning to Tony's feet in the form of an almost unbearable prickling. He'd been able to move his upper body for a few minutes now, to turn his head away from the ritual that Rudy was performing in front of him, but with his arms shackled to the chair he was sitting in, he hadn't been able to shield his ears from the sounds of a knife ripping through skin or his nose from the smells of blood and human waste. Melba had been allowed to scream only once. After that, Rudy had told her to keep silent, and impossibly, she had. The drug that he had been feeding her had that much power to place her will under his control, though her muscles trembled and twitched with reaction from the pain he was inflicting on her. Most horribly, since Rudy had ordered her to lie perfectly still on the dining table, she had made no attempt to escape over the last minutes as Rudy methodically flayed her alive.

Tony whimpered as he stared transfixed at the living anatomy lesson that Melba had become. Insanely, he remembered a lecturer at college informing them, "The average human has about twenty square feet of skin weighing about six pounds." Tony's medically trained mind persisted in identifying the structures that Rudy had exposed with his knife: anterior tibialis of the lower leg; the long bulge of the rectus femoris muscle of the thigh; external obliques covering the stomach region; flap of the platysma myoides muscle layered over chin and clavicle; sterno-cleido mastoid just visible behind the ear. The fat pads and gland tissue that had been her breasts had come off with the skin covering her torso. Lips, eyelids, and hair had come away, too. Her exposed eyeballs goggled, and lipless, her exposed teeth and gums gave her a ghastly grin. The drug that incapacitated her must also do something to delay shock. Deprived of their skin, the largest organ of the human body, any other human being would have died by now. Tony clenched his eyes shut and prayed that the ordeals both he and Melba were suffering would soon come to an end.

Rudy said, "Look at me, my brother." Tony didn't dare disobey. He opened his eyes, feeling the tears start unbidden as he looked at Melba's body again. Arms gory to the elbow, Rudy smiled happily at Tony from the other side of the table. "This is what I go do to your Ti-Jeanne if you nah get that heart for me."

"No!" Tony had control of his vocal cords again.

"No? All right, Master Tony, tell you what. Me just decide a next thing, yes? You know say me can't make word get out that a man try to cheat me and I make he get off scot free, right? I wouldn't be able to keep no discipline if I carry on like that."

Tony stared at him, chest heaving.

"So. You have to get punish. You go kill your Ti-Jeanne for me, boy. Is the price for your own life. Kill she clean, or I go do it like this."

Tears started down Tony's cheeks again.

"Like you nah like the sound of that, neither. Look like I go have to set my watchdog 'pon you to make sure you nah try to cheat me again. Me soon come back, Tony." He disappeared through a door that led to the back of his office, returned wheeling a small, black-painted metal gurney, just wide enough for the bowl that was balanced on its top. The bowl appeared to be unvarnished wood, about the size of a watermelon. It had designs incised on its surface. Its bottom was round. It was sitting inside a ring of cloth that held it steady. "Look my watchdog here," Rudy told him cheerfully. "My duppy. It need lifeblood for it to have the vitality to do what I go ask it, and you go get to watch me feed it."

He wheeled the gurney to the head of the dinner table, positioned it beside Melba's left ear. "Melba, sweetness," he cooed, "your punishment nearly finish now, darling. You is a strong woman, Melba. Almost two years you last. See what does happen when people defy me? But when you dead, darling, you go be free. Soon now. Just stretch out your left side neck for me there."

Wet, red muscles glistening with fluids, Melba presented her neck to the knife. Tony thought he was going to be sick. Rudy tilted her chin toward the bowl. Melba's eyes were now staring straight at Tony. He couldn't read the expression on the weaving of muscles that were her face.

With a quick slash, Rudy slit the woman's jugular vein. Bright blood gouted into the bowl. An appalling sound came from it, like someone guzzling great amounts of liquid as fast as they could. Melba's body relaxed into death.

"Yes, me duppy, yes," Rudy crooned at the bowl. "Drink it all. Then me have a special job for you. Me want you to follow this man here, this Tony. Make sure him reap a heart out of a living body for me. Then make sure him kill the one named Ti-Jeanne."

Rudy looked up at him briefly. The man's eyes were inert lumps of coal, empty of emotion. He looked back down into the duppy bowl. "And if he ain't do it, duppy? Well, first you feed on Ti-Jeanne, then you feed on him."

The slurping noises from the bowl stopped. In its ring of cloth it rocked around and around, fast, then was still. A red mist seeped out of it and hovered in the air. Shapes coalesced from the mist, then melted back again: grasping, clutching hands; a rictus of a mouth, lips pulled back into a snarl; deranged eyes that appraised Tony like so much meat on a hook. Petrified, Tony was the monkey transfixed in the tiger's frozen stare. Nothing in his world had prepared him for this creature from another reality. He was looking at a thing that must have died and never stopped dying, a thing that Rudy would not allow its natural rest, that he kept barely appeased with the blood of the living. Tony's heart hammered in his chest. He could not endure another moment of that gaze.

The thing looked away, focused on Rudy with such malevolence that Tony didn't understand how Rudy was still standing. Rudy sighed. For the first time that evening, he looked tired, older than he seemed. But he gave no sign of fear or fatigue, just stared calmly at the red, hovering mist. Then, butcher knife still in his hands, he strode casually over to where Tony was tied. Tony scrabbled his heels desperately against the floor, trying to shove the chair he was shackled in out of Rudy's reach. The chair almost went over backward. Rudy reached out his free hand to right it. "Steady, brother, steady." He knelt in front of Tony. "Good thing this material so dark, eh? The stain won't show." And he wiped both sides of the bloody knife clean on one leg of the pants he had given Tony to wear. "So tell me now, nuh? You go do this little job for me, or you go join Melba?"

Tony felt his throat closing. He couldn't, he couldn't. He made an inarticulate noise.

"What, Tony? You have to speak up loud so me and the duppy could hear you."

"I, I'll do it."

"Good. I feel say we finally understand each other, me brother." He freed Tony from the chair.

Tony stood carefully, on wobbly legs. His eyes kept being drawn to the body on the table. Two days ago he'd been a whole man. Now he felt as though his protective skin had been removed along with Melba's. He would never feel so sure of himself again.

"Barry go give you back the hospital equipment," Rudy said.

"Yes." A sun in torment, the duppy whirled before his gaze.

"Go 'long, boy. Just know it go be following you."

Tony nearly ran from the room.

Rudy wiped a gory hand on the leg of his pants. He'd need a new suit. He said to the duppy, "Never mind what I tell you before. Once he give the heart to the hospital, I want you to kill all of them: Ti-Jeanne, Tony, everybody."

It didn't make a noise, exactly. More something like the remembered sound of a wail of agony. Then it sharpened into an arc and poured itself at speed right through the wall to the street outside.

CHAPTER SEVEN

Give the Devil a child for dinner!
One!

—Derek Walcott, *Ti-Jean and His Brothers*

The soup bubbled fragrantly on the stove. Mami knew that Ti-Jeanne hadn't eaten since the night before. She would make some bitter melon, fried up and served on the side; that would strengthen her blood. Ti-Jeanne loved bitter melon. Mami pulled a few leaves of sage and rosemary from the bunches drying at the kitchen window and added them to the soup. She missed the tropical herbs she could no longer get in Toronto, both for healing and for cooking, but no help for that. Romni Jenny and Frank Greyeyes were teaching her about northern herbs. In time, she'd have a more complete arsenal.

She looked sidelong at Ti-Jeanne. She was sitting at the kitchen table, clutching Baby resentfully, like a boulderstone that someone had given her to hold, and drumming with her free fingers on the table. Ti-Jeanne was pretending obedience, pretending she was dutifully learning all that Mami had to pass on to her, but Mami knew that look. It masked resentment. Mami kissed her teeth in frustration, too late realising that Ti-Jeanne would just hear more scolding implied in the noise. Why was the girl child so sensitive?

"Stupidness," Mami muttered. Ti-Jeanne scowled at her. Mami didn't know what to say. Silently she pursed her lips and busied herself making Ti-Jeanne's favourite cornmeal dumplings, cooking in the love she couldn't express.

Silence sat thickly between them.

There was a loud knocking at the door. It was beginning, the thing Mami had been dreading. She didn't know what was going to happen, but it would change her and her grandchild's lives forever.

"Go and see who that is, Ti-Jeanne. Here, give me the baby."

Mami dusted the cornmeal from her hands so she could take Baby. She rocked him a little in her arms as Ti-Jeanne went to get the door. Things were moving fast now, too fast for her to control them. She feared for Ti-Jeanne. She hadn't given her granddaughter all the knowledge she would need to be able to do as the spirits had commanded them.

Ti-Jeanne was back, looking nervous and frightened. "Mami? Is Crazy Betty out there. I think she asking for you. She just standing out there, saying, 'Mami, Mami, Mami,' over and over."

All these years Ti-Jeanne had been telling her about Crazy Betty, Mami Gros-Jeanne had never encountered the street woman. She began to have a horrible suspicion. Oh, spirits. It couldn't be, say it couldn't be. Wordlessly Mami took her granddaughter's hand. They both went to the front door.

Gros-Jeanne opened it and looked full into the face of the shrunken woman standing there, muttering softly to herself.

It was Mi-Jeanne. Oh God, it was her daughter. Gros-Jeanne cried Mi-Jeanne's name, started forward, but the baby in her arms prevented her from hugging Mi-Jeanne. "Here, Ti-Jeanne, take he. Don't you see is your mother?"

"My . . . ?" Gaping at Crazy Betty, Ti-Jeanne took Baby.

Mami Gros-Jeanne felt her tears spring hot as she gathered her daughter into her arms after so many years. "Mi-Jeanne, you come home at last?"

Mi-Jeanne started at her touch, then stood still. She was whispering to herself: "It have hearth in this home? Or it heartless? Worthless. Worthless girl child. No sense nor manners! Stupidness!"

Gros-Jeanne held her tightly as she dared. She didn't want to let go. She could feel Mi-Jeanne's bones through the thin rags she wore, smell the sour sweat of her. Mi-Jeanne pulled her arms out of her mother's embrace, batted awkwardly at her own face, as though trying to banish voices whispering in her ears.

Mami took Mi-Jeanne's hands in her own. "No, doux-doux, no. Don't hurt yourself. You ain't worthless." Then she said the words she'd welled up inside herself all these years. "I do wrong to ever tell you so. You hear me? I do wrong."

Ti-Jeanne asked quietly, "Mami? Is she in truth? Is Mummy?"

"Yes, doux-doux." Gros-Jeanne led Mi-Jeanne into the parlour, sat her in a chair at the warm fireplace. Mi-Jeanne kept muttering, batting at her ear with her free hand.

"But, Mami," Ti-Jeanne continued, "why she never come home before? All this time? Why she been living in the street like that? And what happen to she eyes?"

What *had* happened to her out there? Mi-Jeanne looked older than her years, about the same age as Gros-Jeanne herself, but nowhere near as healthy. Her body was stooped and frail, her hair dull, matted into clumps. The sockets where her eyes had been were sunken holes. Her pretty Mi-Jeanne, a mad, blind street woman, living off filth.

"She wanted to go and live with she daddy," Gros-Jeanne admitted. "He was living in some little break-down room in town, stoned out of he mind all the time. She tell me he wouldn't have leave if I had been taking care of he."

"Take care of he," muttered Mi-Jeanne. "Watch out for he."

"I did have a new man by then. Dunston. She ain't like he. She tell me I horning she father. She call me all kinda names. She own mother, imagine! I tell she to go then, if she love she worthless daddy so bad. Go, but don't come back."

"Go," said Mi-Jeanne distractedly. "Go, and don't come back."

Someone else was pounding at the door. Ti-Jeanne just stood there, looking stunned.

"You best had go see who it is, doux-doux," Gros-Jeanne told her.

At this, Mi-Jeanne blindly grabbed at her mother's arm, held on tight. "No! Sly mongoose! He stealing the chicken, you don't see? He name full of shame!"

Gently Gros-Jeanne took Mi-Jeanne's face in her hands.

"Is all right, my darling. Is probably just someone who need some medicine." She mouthed the words "Get the door" at Ti-Jeanne and took the baby from her.

Mami Gros-Jeanne sat down beside her daughter. "Mi-Jeanne, you know you have a grandchild? A boy, Mi-Jeanne!" She took Mi-Jeanne's hand and led it to Baby's face, holding on tightly in case her mad daughter tried to hurt the child. Instead Mi-Jeanne's face went soft and gentle as she felt the baby's face. That was almost a smile on her lips. Baby blinked at her touch but didn't seem to object.

"Dort, dort, petit popo," Mi-Jeanne sang in a cracking voice, running a hand over his fat cheek. *Sleep, little baby, or the tiger go come and eat you up.*

Ti-Jeanne came back into the kitchen, Tony behind her, looming above her with his greater height. Ti-Jeanne's face was trembling between smiles and tears. "Look, Tony come back," she said. "He come back for me!" Trustingly she reached her hand behind her, groping for Tony's.

Tony looked scared to death. He took Ti-Jeanne's hand just long enough for her to pull him into the room. Mami noticed that he let go almost immediately. "Crazy Betty?" he said. "How'd she get here?"

"She is my mother, Tony. She just tell me. She is Mi-Jeanne."

"What? What nonsense you talking?"

"Never mind that," Mami Gros-Jeanne snapped at him. This masquerade was making her vex now. "Is what you come back for? I thought you reach Scarborough by now."

"I, ah, Rudy said I could stay. They got the donor they need. Some woman head-shot in a fight last night."

Ti-Jeanne's face could have lit the sky like the sun. "But Tony, that good! Everything all right now, ain't?"

He looked at her, glanced at Mami, then lowered his eyes to the ground. "Yeah, everything's great." Mami could see his hands shaking. Lying brute. He was up to something.

She asked, "What happen to the three men what Rudy send for you?"

Tony flicked guilty eyes at her, then at Ti-Jeanne. "Ti-Jeanne, you told her about that?"

"Of course I tell she, how you mean?"

"Well," he said with a nervous laugh, "I don't know what you did to them, but Rudy had to have an Angel of Mercy ambulance pick them up. They don't know if Crapaud's going to live."

"He go live," Ti-Jeanne replied. "Is booze go kill that one."

"What? How d'you know that?" The fear on Tony's face was obvious.

"Is one of the things I see, Tony. I does see things sometimes." Tony seemed to accept the explanation, distractedly. Gros-Jeanne could hear the fatigue in Ti-Jeanne's voice. So much her granddaughter had had to face in these past few hours.

Suddenly Mi-Jeanne flew at Tony, mad hands scrabbling like claws for his face. "Sly mongoose! Slying, lying mongoose!"

"Hey!" He grabbed the crazy woman's wrists, immobilized them effortlessly. "Ti-Jeanne, call she off, nuh?"

Mami just watched, noticing how easily her daughter had found her way over to Tony. Blind she might be, but obviously she hadn't lost all of her Sight.

Hesitantly Ti-Jeanne touched her mother's shoulder. "Mummy? You go come with me and sit down?"

Something in Ti-Jeanne's voice seemed to reach Mi-Jeanne. Her scrabbling hands relaxed. She turned to the sound of Ti-Jeanne's voice. "Ti-Jeanne? My baby?"

"Yes, Mummy."

"Brown skin gal stay home and mind baby?"

"Yes, Mummy. Come and sit with me and I go let you hold the baby."

Ti-Jeanne led Mi-Jeanne back to the chair where she'd been sitting. She took the chair next to her mother, signalled for Mami to give Baby back to her. She murmured to her mother, let her pat Baby's small body for a while. Crazy Mi-Jeanne's twitching became less as she felt the baby under her hands. "Dort, dort, petit popo," she sang again in her fading voice. Mami noticed that Ti-Jeanne was biting her lips. She always did that when she was nervous. Ti-Jeanne put Baby into her mother's arms but didn't let him go. Mi-Jeanne's cracked, trembling hands moved automatically to support Baby's head and his back. She had been, after all, a mother. Mami watched the two women cradling the baby and managed a small smile. Her granddaughter was learning, learning how to reach out a healing hand to others, despite her own cares. She would make a good seer woman.

"You think it's a good idea to let her get so close to the baby?" Tony's voice reminded Mami that this drama hadn't played out all the way yet. Rudy never let people off so easily. Probably he'd sent Tony back here to spy on them. Mami stared at him in disgust. He couldn't hold her eyes. "Why're looking at me like that?" he asked.

"I think I looking at a tool, not a man," she replied. "And I think I know is who hand on the handle."

"I don't know what you're talking about." His hand moved nervously to the pocket of his jacket, patted at it.

Then Mami felt something change in the air around them. She thought she could just barely detect the difference, a misty redness that seemed to centre around Mi-Jeanne. Used to seeing into the spirit world, Mami briefly glimpsed something that might have been eyes burning with longing and loss, clutching hands. The mistiness faded, seeming to melt into Mi-Jeanne's flesh. Was it real, Mami wondered, or had she imagined it?

Mi-Jeanne released Baby back into Ti-Jeanne's arms. She clasped her hands to her head, groaned as though she were in pain. Ti-Jeanne touched her shoulder. "Mummy? You all right?"

Mi-Jeanne collapsed from the chair onto the floor. Ti-Jeanne jumped to her feet with a little scream. "Oh God, Mami, what wrong with she? Mummy!"

What now, Osain? Quickly Mami moved to kneel at her daughter's side. Mi-Jeanne's pulse was fast, faint, and irregular. Her breathing was shallow. *What it is I see?* Mami wondered. "Tony, quick. Carry she into the examining room for me."

"No!" Ti-Jeanne said. "Put she in my bed."

"Doux-doux, she might have something catching. . . ."

Silently Mami cursed herself for not having thought of it sooner.

"She's my mother. Put she in my bed, I say."

Too late to worry about spreading disease now. Mami nodded at Tony. He bent and picked up the sick woman. Mami and Ti-Jeanne followed him up the stairs to the little bedroom. *Osain, pray you,* Mami thought to herself, *don't make she have passed anything on to the baby.*

Tony laid Mi-Jeanne down on the bed. She lay like the dead, barely breathing.

"Tony," said Mami, "go back downstairs and bring me some smelling salts. They in a bottle in the big cupboard in the examining room." Maybe that would revive her.

Ti-Jeanne put Baby in his cot, then came and knelt at her mother's side. She put a hand to Mi-Jeanne's neck. "She ain't have no fever, Mami. So what wrong with she?"

"I ain't know, child." Mi-Jeanne's skin looked bluish. Her hands were cold. She was muttering something under her breath. What was keeping Tony? "I soon come, Ti-Jeanne." As Mami went down the stairs, she heard Baby start wailing, wailing. Poor little soul. She hoped he wasn't becoming colicky again.

She found Tony in the examining room, pacing back and forth, patting and patting at his jacket pocket. He still looked frightened. Mami pursed her lips in irritation. Why had he gone into the healing profession? He obviously didn't have the stomach for it. From the open door Mami said, "Like you can't find the smelling salts?"

Tony started at the sound of her voice. "Um, no, Mistress Hunter. I don't see the bottle." His eyes were big in his head, like a spooked sheep.

"Boy, is what do you? Like duppy riding you, or what? The smelling salts in the cupboard just by you left hand there."

Tony leaned into the cupboard, rummaged around. Irritated, Gros-Jeanne kissed her teeth. She knew the bottle was right in front. "Here, let me get it." She bustled into the room. Tony stood back to let her into the cupboard. There was the bottle, just where she'd told him. "Stupidness," she sneered. She reached for the bottle. She never saw Tony pull the hammer out of his pocket and slam it into the top of her head.

• • • •

Give the Devil a child for dinner!
One, two little children!

—Derek Walcott, *Ti-Jean and His Brothers*

Baby screamed, then started sobbing as though his heart were broken. Ti-Jeanne rushed to pick him up, but all her rocking and shushing didn't help. His clenched fists punched at the air. The sorrow on his pudgy face made him look older than his years.

The noise had no effect on Crazy Betty. With Baby cradled in one arm, Ti-Jeanne sat on the edge of her bed and stroked Crazy Betty's forehead. The woman moaned a little. Was this really her mother? Ti-Jeanne stared at the ruined face, trying to see some resemblance to the beautiful, vibrant woman who had left her twelve years before. Funny how eyes defined a face. With them gone, the rest of her features seemed to have lost their definition, too. The nose looked a little like she remembered her mother's. Maybe. The mouth, too, but it was hard to tell. Some of Crazy Betty's . . . Mi-Jeanne's teeth were missing, and her lips caved in around the spaces, shrinking her face.

Mi-Jeanne's hands jerked, then her feet. Alarmed, Ti-Jeanne stood up, ready to go to the top of the stairs and yell for her grandmother. An ambulance howled by, very close. Then the noise stopped. Seconds later there was a pounding at the door. Had someone called an ambulance for Mi-Jeanne? But who would pay for it? Couldn't Mami help her? Ti-Jeanne put a still-weeping Baby back in the crib and ran downstairs, but Tony had already answered the door. He was pointing the visitors toward Mami's examination room. He looked ill. Six men brushed by him and went into the room. They were Vultures. All were wearing hooded, floor-length bulletproofs in Angel of Mercy black. Two of the men had Glocks. One more was carrying a telescoping stretcher.

"Why you going in there?" Ti-Jeanne asked them. "She upstairs."

The Vultures hesitated, looked to Tony for confirmation.

Mutely he shook his head. The glance he gave Ti-Jeanne held all the sadness of the world. She could almost weep just looking at his face. He went outside.

"Leave the door open, sir," one of the Vultures called. The small speaker grid in the beak of his bulletproof magnified and distorted his voice.

Ti-Jeanne didn't understand. She followed the men into the room. For a second, her mind rejected what her eyes saw. The body on the floor was recognizable only by its small frame in its patched black housedress. Mami's necklace of beads had broken. The brown and red beads were scattered over the floor and her body. Tony's funny square knapsack lay beside her, open. A machine of some sort hummed inside it, fat red tubes extended like claws into Mami's neck, arms, chest, thigh.

Her head was the wrong shape. Someone had smashed the back of her head in. In the room above her head, Baby's screaming reached a crescendo.

Two of the Vultures knelt at Mami's side, began checking the machine's connections.

"Looks good," one of them said, checking the readout in his hand from the wand he was running over Mami's chest. "BP falling a bit. Kurt, step up the dopamine some, will you? And Jamie buzz the hospital. Tell 'em to meet us at the airlift out front. We'll fly the heart straight to Ottawa General."

Dimly Ti-Jeanne's mind registered two shocks of pain as her knees hit the floor. She choked on the word "Mami," then she screamed it. "Mami! Oh God, Mami!" She crawled over to her grandmother's body, reaching to touch. Hands pulled her away, dragged her to her feet. She resisted. "Let me go! Mami!"

"Please stay out of our way, miss. That woman is a bio-material donor." Ti-Jeanne kicked back with her heel, connected with someone's kneecap. She ignored their howl of pain. She was free. She fell at Mami Gros-Jeanne's side again. Sobbing, she touched her grandmother's face, still warm.

The pulse at Mami's neck was still beating. Incredulous with joy, Ti-Jeanne looked at the Vultures down on the ground with her. "She ain't dead! She heart still beating! Quick, make we take she to the hospital; maybe we could save she!"

One of the Vultures raised the beak off its face. It was a woman. "I'm sorry, miss. She's dead all right. That's not a pulse. It's just the CP bypass machine keeping the blood circulating. I'm very sorry."

"Dead? Mami really dead?" Ti-Jeanne felt as though her own heart were being turned inside out. The words came out without thought: "How she get like this?"

Another of the Vultures with the weapons raised her to her feet again, gently this time. "We don't know, miss. Maybe she fell or something."

"No!" Ti-Jeanne looked at one, then the other, searching for the faces behind the Shattertite beaks. "Allyou ain't understand. She did fine when I leave she. Somebody must be . . . Oh God, where Tony?" Ti-Jeanne rushed out, flung herself through the open front door. There was no sign of Tony. "Is he do it." The words fell from her lips. "Jesus Jesus Lord, is Tony kill she?" She ran back into the examination room. The Vultures had activated the stretcher. It was telescoping to its full size, Mami's body on it.

"Miss, we're going now." The words came faster, like a litany: "Angel of Mercy Hospital offers its condolences for your loss and thanks you and your family for making this life-giving donation of your loved one's biomaterial. Your address has been entered into the hospital's data banks and you will be compensated for your donation. Good day."

Ti-Jeanne grabbed for the side of the stretcher, took her grandmother's hand. She willed the fingers to close around hers, but there was no response.

"Miss, I'll have to ask you to step aside." They were pushing the stretcher quickly, almost running. Ti-Jeanne ignored the words. She kept pace with them, holding Mami's hand all the way to the ambulance. They had to pull her away, prevent her forcibly from entering the ambulance with Mami's body. They all climbed in the rear. The doors slammed shut, hollowly. The ambulance started off down the gravel pathway that led to the road.

"Mami!" Ti-Jeanne wailed. "Oh God, Mami; I sorry!" She ran after the ambulance, screaming, begging, crying. The ambulance sped away, kicking pebbles into Ti-Jeanne's face. She barely felt them. She stood in the road, howling, wailing, until her breath was gone and her desolate eyes were swollen nearly shut.

CHAPTER EIGHT

duppies of dust and ululations in light
vortexed around her.
Ritualist, she tried to reduce the world,
sketching her violent diagrams
against a wall of mountains which her stare made totter.
Her rhythmic ideas detonated into gestures.
She would jab her knee into the groin of the air,
fling her sharp instep at the fluttering sky,
revise perspectives with the hooks of her fingers,
and butt blood from the teeth of God.

She cooked and ate anything. But, being so often busy,
she hardly ever cooked or ate.

—Slade Hopkinson, "The Madwoman of Papine"

In the calabash duppy, regret, hunger, remorse, and anger had merged into one howling need. When it killed, or each time it was fed blood, the essences of terror, pain, blood, and death appeased the hunger for a little while. But whenever it brought sweet death to another, it knew that it did murder, that it would once have abhorred its own actions.

And it knew that it was denied the rest it had given its victim. Then, fuelled by guilt, the hunger and fury would rage again, stronger. Always stronger. It hated the man who kept it bound, neither alive nor dead. Rudolph Sheldon. One day its chance would come, and then, Rudolph Sheldon, then. But for now, it was compelled to do Rudy's bidding. This time its captor had set it to a task more complex than the rending of flesh from bone. Watch Tony. Make sure he killed. And the thing Tony didn't know: once that was done, kill him, too. There was something else about the task, something that gave it joy. Yes. For the first time since it had been bound, Rudolph Sheldon was letting it go home. The spell it was under compelled it to follow Rudy's orders, but he had made a mistake now. He had given it a chance for freedom.

How to warn them? How to tell them what they must do to free it? It had hovered in the air above the city like a fine mist of blood, considering. A gull had flown heedlessly into the mist. A squawk, a gulping sound, then a clump of skin and feathers had dropped to the ground below, followed by a clatter of small bones, picked clean.

The duppy had realised that it needed to find the woman, the bodily part of itself that wandered the city while its mind was trapped in the calabash. Crazy Betty would give it the voice with which to speak. Where . . . ?

Ah, there she was, toasting filth on a brick to eat. But it hadn't been able to take the time to go into her yet, had had to obey Rudolph Sheldon's orders, had to follow Tony.

Screaming silently with frustration, the duppy had seized

the crazy woman's awareness, turned her toward the little fa-cade house on the farm, had driven her on gibbering ahead of it like that monkey that sees the tiger. No need for Crazy Betty to have sight. It could see.

Soon. Almost there. Soon. Tony had walked so slowly! The duppy had been tempted to reveal itself to him, herd him, too, but men had died with fright before at the sight of it on the hunt. So, patience. Hunger. Sorrow. Anger. Rudolph Sheldon.

It had felt the mad woman-body arrive at the farm, had felt her try to communicate the message of danger. Tony was danger. But Crazy Betty had no intellect to drive her tongue. She had only babbled half sentences that they hadn't understood.

It could have wept with relief when Tony had finally reached the door of the Simpson House. It had swept into the parlour with him; had filled up Crazy Betty's eye sockets; let itself be sucked up through her nostrils; slid into her ears; crawled past gappy teeth and then her tongue to glide down her throat; had sunk like mercury in through her pores; had layered itself directly into her bloodstream. Body and mind, they had fallen to the ground, stunned by being reunited. It had always been like that, the few times they had managed to be together.

Now, lying where her family had put her on her old bed, Mi-Jeanne fought her way up from coma synapse by synapse, regaining control of her body that was Crazy Betty.

And awoke. Oh God, to feel again! She lifted! an arm! to her face, feeling the remembered, intricate play of muscles, will, and joints that made such a miracle possible. She touched a bruise on her forehead. New, that one. The brief pain it gave her was pleasure as strong as anything she knew. Her own touch sent a thrill of sensation through her fingertips. She giggled. Breathing. She was *breathing* again after so long, pulling the sweet substance of air through her nostrils into lungs that obligingly swelled to hold the gift.

She remembered why she'd come. "Jesus! I ain't have the time for this. Anybody there?" No answer. Just a soft sobbing and a sucking noise. She remembered that sound: a hungry baby suckling its own fist. Her daughter's child.

Mi-Jeanne swung her legs over the side of the bed (tension in the lifting thighs, trembling stomach muscles clenched to counterbalance; her body was in bad shape). She stood shakily, groped until she found the baby in its crib. "Well, child," she said, patting his tummy, "it look like everybody gone and leave we." And that wasn't good. Where were they? Had Tony got to them already? The baby just whimpered.

• • • •

Tony sat in the cold mud on the bank of the duck pond and washed and washed his hands. The cold water made them throb and burn. He didn't really care. He'd dropped the hammer with its load of blood and hair into the pond. He couldn't see for weeping. One more. He had to kill one more, or the horror from the calabash would come after him.

• • • •

Give the Devil a child for dinner,
One, two, three little children!

—Derek Walcott, *Ti-Jean and His Brothers*

More than the cold, it was her aching, milk-swollen breasts that finally brought Ti-Jeanne to herself as she knelt in the middle of the road. Baby was still back at the house. He would be hungry. He would need to be changed. Mi-Jeanne was sick. Mundane things, they seemed now. How could she think about those things when Mami was dead? Killed. By Tony. Betrayal and grief almost overwhelmed her again, but despite that, her feet took the path back to the house and up the stairs.

To her shock, Mi-Jeanne met her at the bedroom door, holding Baby in her arms. "Who's there?" the blind woman called out.

"Mi . . . Mummy?"

"Ti-Jeanne, is you? Where Tony?"

Mi-Jeanne was aware! Stunned, all Ti-Jeanne could think to ask was, "You feeling better now?"

"Never mind that. Where Tony?"

Ti-Jeanne registered her own keening as that of someone far away. "I don't know where he gone! But I think he kill, he kill Mami!"

"Jesus, I come too late. Look, girl, he go be looking to kill you, too. Is that Daddy . . . Rudy send he to do. You have to stop he."

"Tony? Tony want me dead? How you know?" she challenged the madwoman.

"I know everything Daddy doing." Grief and pain twisted Mi-Jeanne's too old face. "I is the duppy that Daddy does keep in he calabash. I could only inhabit my own body when Daddy let me out to do he dirty work for he. Is my soul he bind to get he power. Is my sight he twist into obeah, into shadow-catching for he."

It was too much. Ti-Jeanne felt herself move beyond hysteria into an odd, shaky calm that she knew wouldn't last. Nothing in her world was what she'd thought. "Motherscunt bastard," she muttered, unsure if she meant Tony or her grandfather. She pushed past Mi-Jeanne, strode into Mami's room, and started opening drawers and cupboards. "I know it have a gun in here somewhere." She heard Mi-Jeanne groping her way to the bedroom behind her. Mi-Jeanne barked her shins against the bed, felt to see what it was she had bumped into, then sat down on the thin, narrow mattress.

"Mami tell me is a dead that Rudy have in he duppy bowl," Ti-Jeanne said.

"Used to be a dead. Then he come to find out the obeah does work stronger if he ain't kill the body, just steal the spirit. What Tony do to Mami?"

Ti-Jeanne described what she'd seen. "How come you taking the news cool cool so? Is your mother."

"Child, if you only know how much suffering and death I see these past few years, eh? And how much of it I cause. Mami gone . . ." Her voice trailed off to a whisper. "Maybe it better so."

"So, if killing come in like cool breeze to you, why you ain't help we?" Anger. That's what she should be feeling now, not this vague, distanced resentment. "Why you ain't do for Rudy?"

"I could only do what Daddy order me to do," her mother replied. "If he hadn't tell me to come here to watch and make sure Tony carry out he orders, I couldn't even self pass the door. And to talk to allyou, I had was to come back inside my body. When I do that, is like having a fit. It does take time for body and mind to come back together again. That's why I couldn't warn Mami in time. I do what I could, doux-doux. I not going to be able to fight Tony for you," Mi-Jeanne said. Her voice lowered in shame. "Truth is, I supposed to kill Tony, but only after he kill you."

"Oh, is so it go?" Ti-Jeanne replied. Her world had frayed into tattered threads. She felt almost detached as she listened to herself calmly discuss her own murder with her long-lost mother. "Let Tony come then, nuh?" Ti-Jeanne said to her. "Bastard. Say we going to move from here. Say we going to settle down. I go shoot he lying mouth right off he worthless face."

"If you did have to see what Tony watch Rudy do, you woulda be same way. After you see what Rudy capable of, you would do anything he tell you, so you don't end up on that table, feeling Rudy knife strip the skin from off your body."

Ti-Jeanne's body went cold. Was this what she was up against? Her knees wouldn't hold her. She sat down hard on the bed. Mi-Jeanne must have felt the mattress give. She groped along the bed until she found Ti-Jeanne's leg. She held it hard and continued: "Feeling he slit your throat, Ti-Jeanne. Feeling your lifeblood running into he duppy bowl for the monster inside to drink. For *me* to drink, Ti-Jeanne. Is that Tony see last night. You have to free me. You have to find Daddy duppy bowl and break it."

Ti-Jeanne pulled away from her mother's grasp. She got up and continued searching through Mami's belongings. "Allyou ain't want plenty, oui?" Her tone was bitter. Good. It would hide her fright. "Mami want me to turn bush doctor; Tony want me to dead; you want me to save your wicked soul. What I go help you for? After you abandon me from small?"

She heard Baby's thin, hungry cry from the other bedroom. Her milk let down at the sound, dampening the front of her shirt. "God, not now, child. You ain't see I busy?"

Busy. Ti-Jeanne almost laughed at the inadequacy of the word.

"Turn around, Ti-Jeanne," said Tony from the doorway, in the voice of someone who had looked into hell and seen his own face. "Turn around so I can see your hands."

Holding up her empty palms, she turned to face Tony. His face was swollen with weeping, but he looked determined. He had a gun of his own pointed at her. He kept glancing back and forth between her and her mother. "I have to do this, Ti-Jeanne. After what you did to Crack and Jay and Crapaud, Rudy wants you out of the way."

"It wasn't me. Is Legbara do it. You saw."

"Don't give me that! You and Gros-Jeanne been playing me from the start!"

"For what, Tony?" Mi-Jeanne asked sadly. "You ain't see how the two of them been trying to stay out of posse business? You is Ti-Jeanne baby father, but she leave you when she realise that posse more important to you than she. Man, even your own baby does cry when it see you coming."

That startled Ti-Jeanne. She hadn't thought of it that way. Mi-Jeanne was right. Every time she had started to get close to Tony again, Baby had demanded her attention.

"Too late for everything now," Mi-Jeanne said sadly. "Ti-Jeanne, I sorry. The only way to prevent me from doing what Rudy tell me is to break the duppy calabash and free my spirit. And you not go get to do that now." She stood up, looking in the direction of Tony's voice. "Tony, none of we ain't want nothing to do with you. So do your business, or don't do it. Is all the same to me. Daddy say I must kill you either way. Stop me if you could stop me, nuh?"

She took a step toward him. He swung the gun in her direction. "Stay there," he ordered her. She ignored him. She kept walking.

"Tony, don't shoot," Ti-Jeanne said. He risked a glance at her, swung the gun back at her. Mi-Jeanne reached him. She touched his arm. He turned and shot her full in the chest.

"No!" Ti-Jeanne's calm vanished. "Mummy!"

Mi-Jeanne fell like a sack of bones. A red mist rose from her crumpled body. Ravening jaws, mad eyes, and clawing hands swirled in it. It slammed Tony to the floor. He screamed. The gun discharged into the ceiling.

The thing sat on Tony's chest, gibbering. Almost lovingly

it licked his cheek. A strip of skin came away at its touch, disappeared into the swirling mass. The thing made a harrowing moan of pleasure. Terrified, Tony batted and clawed at it, but his hands just wafted through it and came away bloody.

"La Diablesse. Soucouyant," Ti-Jeanne muttered. This was her nightmare. Her own mother. And it was up to her to stop Mi-Jeanne. She threw herself to the ground, level with the duppy, and shouted, "Mummy! Stop this! Stop now!"

For answer, the duppy dove at her face. Ti-Jeanne pulled back just in time. The hot wind of its attack swept by, millimetres from her cheek. Three of her plaits fell to the ground, sheared off clean. Her mother's duppy had no choice. It was bound to do what Rudy told it to do. "Mummy, wait," Ti-Jeanne begged hopelessly.

To her surprise, the duppy held off for a moment. It was like watching a hurricane rage in a small space. Ti-Jeanne had the impression of a frenzied howling, although she heard nothing. But the duppy's claws were already scrabbling at Tony's whimpering throat. Its daughter's plea held it for now, but in a second it would have to do its master's bidding. *It had to do what Rudy said.* Ti-Jeanne thought fast, opened her mouth before she quite knew what she was going to say.

"Rudy tell you to kill we, yes?"

The maddened red eyes seemed to agree with her.

"But he ain't tell you *when,* Mummy, and he ain't tell you *where?* Ain't?"

Had the duppy's crazed swirling slowed down a little? Desperately Ti-Jeanne started talking again, hoping that some kind of plan would emerge from her babbling. "That's right, that's right. You could take we anywhere, kill we there, you still go be doing what Rudy tell you. Right, Mummy?"

The duppy's claws pulled back from Tony's neck. It seemed to be waiting for Ti-Jeanne to say more. What could she say that would draw out their lives a little more, give them a chance?

"You want, you want me to . . . free you, ain't it? Find Rudy dead bowl and break it, so you don't have to kill no more? Well, take we there before you kill we. Take we to Rudy place."

Tony grabbed her wrist. His eyes were wide. "Woman, like you mad, or what?"

She felt his grip warm on her skin and looked into the eyes of this man she had loved beyond sense or reason. She thought of her grandmother's body lying there with its head broken in, looked at Mi-Jeanne's cooling body lying beside them on the ground.

"Yes, I mad," she answered him, firmly pulling her wrist from his grasp. She stood up. The duppy lifted itself off Tony's chest and coalesced into a red fireball. It hovered above them, waiting. "I mad like France," Ti-Jeanne said. "Mad like that old woman jumbie thing who used to be my mother. I mad at all of allyou for making me run around trying to save allyou, but allyou just digging yourselves in deeper, each one in he own pit."

"But Ti-Jeanne," Tony protested, getting to his feet, "you can't go to Rudy's. He'll just kill you. What's that going to help?"

"I tell you, I going. But me ain't business with what you want to do, oui? You could try to run away again, I guess. But I bet you the duppy go find you."

Tony's eyes slid to the fireball that was now tracing an impatient, sizzling orbit in the air.

"Mummy," Ti-Jeanne addressed it, "let me just go get the baby. He hungry. I could feed he while we walk."

The fireball moved out of the way. Refusing to look at the body of her mother lying on the floor, Ti-Jeanne went into her own room to get Baby; Tony and the fireball followed her as if attached to her apron strings. She stared down at her child in his crib. Leave him here alone, perhaps to starve to death, or take him with them? Baby looked at her, reached for her. Another life tied to her apron strings. She picked him up, put him into his Snugli, and slung it onto her body. "Let we go then, nuh?"

The strange procession filed down the stairs and out into the night.

Mi-Jeanne's body was dead. If Ti-Jeanne did manage to free her mother's soul from the calabash, where would it go now?

CHAPTER NINE

The operation was routine. It was their patient who was unusual. Margaret Wright was well aware that she was known for being an unflappable surgeon. During the next few hours, that reputation would be at stake. The media were following Premier Uttley's heart transplant like hawks. They were expecting Dr. Wright to give a news conference as soon as she was out of the operating room. And they'd be talking to everyone who'd been in the OR, too. Every move Dr. Wright made would be on a newscast within hours. If she had snapped at a nurse, if she had made a crooked suture, all of Canada would know.

Nothing could go wrong. She wouldn't allow it. She had to make sure that her patient was smiling for the camera within days.

Everything was going fine so far. Uttley had already received a portion of her donor's bone marrow. Uttley's leucocytes had not attacked the donor marrow; that was a good sign. When Wright transplanted the heart, white blood cells from Uttley's bone marrow should migrate smoothly into the foreign organ, and vice versa, a chimerism that would trick her immune system into accepting the foreign organ so that body and heart could coexist peacefully.

Now it was time for the transplant.

Prepped for the surgery, Dr. Wright watched Dr. Fang do his part on the unconscious form of Premier Uttley. The surgical resident had never seen this operation done with a human heart. Wright knew that he wanted to be as involved as possible.

The ventilator was already breathing for Uttley. Her entire body was covered in sterile white sheets, leaving exposed only her chest area: the surgical field. As always, the area of flesh that Wright could see didn't look human. Best that way. Now was not the time for the people in the OR to focus on who their patient was. They needed to concentrate on what they were doing. Don Fang and Jim Nesbit, Wright's associate surgeon, had already cut through the sternum and pried open the ribs with chest spreaders. They freed Uttley's heart from its pericardial sac. Nesbit leaned closer to inspect the heart.

"Hang on, Jim," Wright said to him. "Let me get a look, too." Jim made room for her. Yes. A clear case of cardiomyopathy. The flabby, distended sack that Uttley's heart had become was about twice the size it should have been. It beat sluggishly.

Jim made a "tsk, tsk" noise. "Whoo. Not a moment too soon, eh?"

"Yup. Let's get that baby out of there."

Wright stepped back out of the way. Jim sutured the ascending aorta and the right atrium, cannulated, injected the heparin to prevent blood clotting. Then he connected Uttley to the heart-lung bypass machine. He made the last few cuts and lifted Uttley's heart out of her chest cavity. The perfusionist and the anaesthesiologist checked their readouts. Doing fine.

"Okay, Margaret."

Dr. Wright stepped up to her place at the operating table. She took a deep breath, looked at the faces around her. "Here we go, guys." She lifted the donor heart from its basin of sterile fluid. Through her gloves, it felt firm and chilled from having been kept cold.

"So that's what a healthy human ticker looks like," muttered Dr. Fang. "Not so different from pig hearts."

"That's all we are," Jim chuckled. "Long pig."

Fang asked, "How old did they say the donor was?"

"Fifty-seven," Wright replied. "A bit old for this, maybe, but we were getting desperate, and she was healthy as a horse. Pathology says she never smoked, looked like she worked hard all her life, had arteries as soft as a baby's. Suction, Jim."

As Jim suctioned the excess blood from the chest cavity, Wright lowered the heart in. *Straightforward stuff,* she told herself. Nevertheless, she anxiously reviewed the procedure aloud. She told herself it was for the benefit of her team. "Four anastomoses: fuse donor heart's left atrial to patient's left atrium; join the two right atrials; attach donor aorta to patient's aorta; attach pulmonary arteries."

Jim looked at her over his mask. He knew all this, had worked with her hundreds of times. She took another breath for calm and positioned the heart.

"Bonding stylus," Jim said. The nurse handed him the pen—the "glue gun," they called it—that would fuse the ends of the blood vessels together with fine lines of a nontoxic organic binder. The cellular growth factors suspended in the binder would promote accelerated healing.

Jim started beading the first join line. Wright maintained pressure on the join as he went.

First line done. Wright poured a bucket of ice-cold sterile saline solution on the heart. Jim finished bonding the left atrium, started on the right. Fang moved in closer to observe what he was doing. As a resident in training, he had to learn every step of the operation.

"Watch that sinus node," Wright cautioned Jim. Last thing they needed was to fuck with the heart's electrical activity.

Jim looked up at her again, eyes crinkling. "Little nervous there, Margaret?" The bastard was laughing.

"Nah," she lied with false calm. "Just got a hot dinner date. Gotta be out of here by seven."

"Tell you what: betcha we'll be done by six. News conference at six-thirty, tell 'em baby's had a change of heart and is looking fine. Pasta by seven, you and your sweetie heavy breathing by eight." He bent his head back down over the surgical field.

"You're on," Wright replied, moving in closer beside him to begin trimming the aorta of the donor heart.

Finally the heart was hooked up. Wright placed the final lines in the pulmonary artery as they began to warm up Uttley's new heart. Rich red oxygenated blood was pouring into the heart, feeding the cardiac cells that had been starving for the three and a half hours of the operation. Four hours was the maximum time they could let the heart stay ischemic before it would be damaged. Wright stood back, reached for the defibrillator paddles just in case. "Okay," she breathed to the transplanted heart. "Do it, baby. Come on."

There was silence from the team in the operating room. Everyone's eyes were fixed on Uttley's new heart. Nothing happened. Then it quivered. Wright could feel her own heart thumping in her chest. Uttley's heart jumped once, then began to beat.

"Yes!" Jim said.

"Contractions regular and strong," Fang verified. "Congratulations, Doctors."

"Oh, God," Wright sighed. "For a second there, I thought it wasn't going to work. I'm getting too old for all this excitement." She was sweating with the strain of the operation. The nurse swabbed her brow. "Okay, let's close her up and get her out of here. I got a press conference to hold."

• • • •

Who stole the cookie from the cookie jar?
Number One stole the cookie from the cookie jar.
"Who, me?"
"Yes, you."
"Couldn't be."
"Then is who?"

—Children's rhyming game

"Yes, man. Tomorrow do me fine, Mr. Baines." Rudy signed off. Slipped his palmbook into a pocket. The hospital was happy with their newest acquisition, had flown it to Ottawa immediately. The operation was under way, and he would get his money, with extra compensation for his three men who had been injured in the process of retrieving the heart. Tony had done what he was supposed to. Everything was going smooth like cool breeze, except that Tony hadn't yet reported back that he'd killed the interfering girlfriend. *The women in that family been giving me trouble from so long,* Rudy thought. And the duppy wasn't back in its calabash, either. What did that mean?

"Crack!" Rudy shouted. Crack opened the office door and hobbled inside. The dark, mongoose-thin man looked like he'd been to war. He was using a cane to help him walk; he'd cracked his leg when Legbara dropped him. His arm and his side were a mass of bruises from the same fall. There were two fingerprint-shaped contusions under his chin, where Legbara had lifted him into the air. He complained of a persistent headache, for which the hospital had given him pills. And he was the best off of the three. He had insisted on coming right back to work. Gingerly, Crack stood to attention. "Yes, boss?"

"You hear from Tony yet?"

"Tony. No, boss." Crack spat out the words as though they were bitter in his mouth. He had a personal vendetta against Tony now, for humiliating him like that at the hands of a woman. Rudy didn't mind. It would make Crack more diligent in exacting retribution, if it turned out that Tony had disobeyed orders.

What was really going on? Tony had obviously had the balls to kill the old woman; what was taking so long to finish off the rest of the job? And if he hadn't done it, why hadn't the duppy obeyed its orders and returned?

"Shoulda never let she go back by she mother," Rudy muttered.

"Boss?"

"Nothing." He came to a decision. "You could drive?"

"I could drive."

"Come, then. We go find Tony weself."

Crack grinned like a dog that had been offered a steak. He hobbled out of the room ahead of Rudy and pressed the button for the elevator. "Boss, if the so-and-so ain't kill that leggo beast of a woman he have there, let me deal with the two of them, all right?"

"All right." Where the rass was the duppy?

• • • •

Lord, what a night, what a night,
What a Saturday night!

—Traditional song

"People are going to see that *thing* herding us along," Tony whispered in Ti-Jeanne's ear, jerking a thumb in the direction of the fireball duppy that buzzed through the air behind them.

"And that is all that worrying you? What they go do? Try and stop it?"

"I guess not," Tony replied in a regretful tone of voice.

Pursued by the duppy, they were stumbling toward the

southernmost end of the city as fast as they could. The streets were pretty empty, in that lull before the nightlife of the city awoke. Once or twice Ti-Jeanne had caught Tony eyeing dark alleyways as they went by. She knew he was trying to gauge the odds of running off and losing himself somewhere in the city before the duppy could catch up with him. Let him try, then, nuh? She didn't care what he did. Every time she looked at him, an image of Mami's body burned across her vision.

Night had fallen again, even colder than the night before. Winter was slowly enveloping the city. Here and there a lone snowflake spiralled to the ground. As they walked, Ti-Jeanne opened her jacket and put Baby to nurse. Her breasts were achingly full. As Baby began to suckle, the familiar draining weariness tugged at Ti-Jeanne, as always when it had been a long time between feedings.

Baby's little fist opened and closed against her skin. He looked deeply into her eyes as though he were trying to communicate something. He seemed reluctant to take her breast. He'd suck a little, then spit out the nipple and whimper, staring up at her. She was probably taking him to his death. "Child, I sorry," she whispered at him. He fussed and kicked. "She gone, doux-doux," she said to him. She'd never used that endearment with him before. But now he was the only one of her family left, unless she counted the disembodied woman who was bound by Rudy's obeah to kill her. "Mami gone." She wanted to cry, but no more tears would come, only a sort of dry, gasping noise. Baby suckled halfheartedly and eventually fell asleep.

They were out of the Burn now. They had passed Church Row and crossed Sherbourne, the boundary street that had given the Burn its name; had gone down Jarvis Street past Allan Gardens and were passing the Clarion Hotel, where Mami's friend Romni Jenny had claimed a living space on the main floor. Lamplight flickered from the first few floors of the hotel. The glassed-in main floor was covered with sacking, old curtains, and sheets to make a privacy screen. Against the jerky backlight, the shadows of the people inside moved eerily against the hangings. Outside in the driveway of the hotel, two old women and a younger man were barbecuing a haunch of meat over a fire pit. They looked at Ti-Jeanne and Tony, then up at the fireball. One of the old women crossed herself. The other two people gaped briefly, then became very interested in the precise placement of the blackened, smoking slab on its sheet of tin. In the city, it was best not to meddle in other people's business. The smell of cooking meat made Ti-Jeanne's mouth water. She hadn't even had a chance to taste the soup that Mami had been cooking for her.

Ti-Jeanne regretted that she couldn't go in and tell Jenny that Mami was dead, but the duppy wouldn't let them slow down, certainly wouldn't let her out of its sight for a moment. She wondered how long it could delay its own hunger and the task it had been commanded to do.

They were now angling through the Ryerson University campus, picking their way past the old stone buildings and the flickering lights of the tents that formed the squatters' camps on the university grounds.

They were coming up to the Strip; Yonge Street, the dividing line between the east and the west sides of the city. For some minutes now they'd been able to hear the buzz of voices and music and see the glow of light that rose from the Strip, above the city buildings. The Strip came alive at night. To Ti-Jeanne's surprise, the duppy herded them down Yonge Street, instead of crossing it and continuing down to the lake by a less crowded route. Maybe it wanted to give them the chance to escape it in the crowd? But Ti-Jeanne was determined to go to Rudy's place and make an end to this madness, one way or the other.

The noise and lights crashed on their senses. If you didn't look too closely, you could believe that the Strip was the same as it had been before the Riots. Garish storefronts flashed crazed neon outlines of naked women with anatomically unlikely endowments. Deeplight ads glowed at the doors to virtually every establishment: moving 3-D illusions that were hyped-up, glossy lies about the pleasures to be found inside. If you believed them, Shangri-la lay beyond each door, in the form of fragrant, compliant women and men, drinks that shamed the nectar of the gods, and music that would transport you to ecstasy. The Deeplight tableaus shimmered, whispered, fucked, came, beckoned.

The Strip was fuelled by outcity money. It was where people from the 'burbs came to feel decadent. The *thok-thok* sound in the air was the copter limos that bussed people in from the 'burbs to the rooftops of the Strip. From there they would descend staircases that led down inside the buildings.

With enough money, you got a taste of the city without ever setting foot on its streets.

Ti-Jeanne and Tony began to push their way through the crowds. Underdressed teenagers jittered in lineups to the clubs, both sexes trusting in the cloaking of makeup and the heat of sexual tension to keep them warm. Every few feet came a request for "spare change for a coffee," accompanied by a grimy cap or a cardboard coffee cup shoved under their noses. Those people took one look at the duppy and then fell back in silence. But other than that, surprisingly few people seemed to notice. In the fuzzy, glittering radiance of the Strip, the duppy became just one more lightflash to the eyes. She all but disappeared.

Except to one young man lounging lazily with his girlfriend against the outside of a virt arcade. He looked up as they approached, nudged his girlfriend with a smirk, and said, "Hey, check that weird shit. That ball floating up there. Bet I bust their bubble."

To Ti-Jeanne's Deeplight-dazzled eyes, he looked like all points, and she all black circles. He was spiked green hair; sharp metal points running down the outside seams of his jeans; the arrowhead hanging from a piercing through his bottom lip. She was black rings drawn around her eyes; the black thighband of fishnet stay-up stockings biting into the meat of her thighs; the black-lipsticked "O" of her mouth when her boyfriend chuckled evilly, leapt up to bat at the duppy, and came howling back down, blood-slicked palm denuded of skin. He crouched on the ground, staring at his dripping hand, too amazed to scream. Not his girlfriend, though. She ran to his side, took one look at the mess, and started shrieking for help. The duppy had brightened briefly as a result of its snack. In the confusion, it moved them onward.

They reached the Dundas intersection of the Strip. The Paramount Eaton Centre loomed black and silent ahead of them, a block-long "elite" megamall complete with coded security fence. If your biocode wasn't in the mall's data banks, you got an electric jolt rather than admittance. The crowd flowed past the structure at a respectful distance.

Just as Ti-Jeanne and Tony were about to cross Dundas, the duppy flew in front of them and hovered at chest level, so that they had to back up or be burned.

"What the rass . . . ?" Tony swore.

It was Rudy's Bentley, coming slowly west along Dundas, horn blaring as it tried to clear a path through the people milling in the streets. As the only car on the street, it stood out, and people were stopping to gawk. Its mirrored windows were a sinister camouflage, hiding its occupants.

"Shit." Ti-Jeanne grabbed Tony's arm and pulled him into the shelter of the building on the corner. The duppy followed, hovering fretfully over their heads. "You think him see we?"

"What difference does it make? You're the one who was going to march right up to his place and deal with him, right?"

"I know, but . . ." But now that she was actually faced with Rudy, some sense of reality intruded on the false bravado that grief and anger had lent her. What had she been thinking? This was the man who skinned someone alive on a whim!

"Not here. We can't meet he here, like this. I not ready."

"Not ready?!" Tony's voice climbed an octave. "Ti-Jeanne, don't you get it? You'll never be ready to face a monster like that!"

"We have to run."

"But if we do, the duppy will get us! It has to kill us if we're not going along with it, remember?"

He was right. She ignored him. Panicked, she stepped into the street and began edging through the crowd to the other side. "Pardon. Pardon, please. Pardon." There was an alleyway there. Maybe they could hide. Tony followed and the duppy, too, a little too close for comfort. Now that she was forcing it to chase them, it was going to have to carry out its orders to kill them. She heard a shout. She looked back. Crack Monkey had opened the driver's side door of the Bentley. He was standing on the running board of the car. He had seen them. Ti-Jeanne started using elbows and knees to shove through the crowd.

"Jesus," Tony panted behind her. "He get out the car."

They were on the other sidewalk now, just a few yards from the cover of the alleyway. The duppy made a halfhearted swipe at Ti-Jeanne, leaving a burning trail of blisters on one cheek. She smelled burning hair, batted at a few of her plaits whose ends had caught on fire. "Mummy," she yelled, "stop it!"

"It's not your mother," Tony hissed. "It's a thing that's hunting us down. Come on."

He grabbed her arm and started dragging her toward the alleyway, clearing the space ahead of them with powerful sweeps of his right arm. The duppy swooped at him. He ducked. When he straightened up, Crack was standing barely twenty yards from them, gun trained right on Tony, grinning like the smile on the face of the tiger. Crack fired. Tony was thrown backward into Ti-Jeanne. She staggered back, trying to hold him upright. The blast made her ears ring. Was Tony dead? People were screaming, running away. Baby was howling with fright. Tony moaned, tried to get to his feet. Ti-Jeanne saw the steps leading down to the abandoned subway. "Tony, you have to walk," she begged.

He pulled himself upright. His right shoulder was torn and bleeding, but his feet were moving. Supporting him as best she could, Ti-Jeanne staggered down the stairs to the subway.

They got only halfway down. The duppy was blocking their way. It sizzled and hissed, threatening her.

"Mummy," Ti-Jeanne said. "Try to let we pass." She took another few steps. Ravening eyes appeared in the fiery mass. Claws reached out to grab them.

"Duppy!" The deep voice was Rudy's. "Where you? Come and give we some light."

And the fireball went flying past them to its master. Ti-Jeanne hissed at the heat of it. She and Tony stumbled the rest of the way down the stairs.

It was dark. And it smelled of stale urine and rotting garbage. "Oh, God," Tony muttered, "I feel weak."

"Keep your feet moving. Just concentrate on that." Ti-Jeanne felt her way along the cool tiled wall, trying to remember how Dundas station had been laid out when there had been a functioning subway system. Ti-Jeanne could hear Rudy and Crack making their way down the stairs.

"Look fresh blood there so," came Rudy's voice. Tony's wound was leaving a trail. Baby stopped his crying almost instantly, as though he were aware that his bawling could lead their pursuers to them.

The heavy, even tread of Rudy's footsteps got closer, punctuated with the tricky triple thump of Crack navigating the steps with his cane. Ti-Jeanne prayed that Crack's injury would slow them down. She moved a little faster, kicking what felt like sheets of newspaper and old tin cans out of her way. Her foot connected with something fleshy that scrabbled at her running shoe and then fled, squeaking. Her hands touched plexiglass. The ticket collector's booth. She felt her way around it, palms hitching on rubberiness that she hoped was only old wads of gum. Her hands found the turnstiles that led to the platform. She reached to push through the first turnstile. It was chained shut. The rusty chain flaked in her palms. Desperately she groped from turnstile to turnstile.

"Shit. Tony, all of them lock off."

"Oh, God, they're gonna get us."

"Climb," Ti-Jeanne said. She clambered clumsily over the obstruction, taking care not to drop Baby. The turnstile was wet and sticky. No matter. She helped Tony over. He whimpered with the pain. She could see the glow of the duppy now, filling the vestibule. Biting her lips in terror, she started a lumbering run down the length of the platform, groping along the wall in the near darkness, pulling Tony after her. He was breathing hard through his mouth. There was a chittering noise coming from the black furrow that was the subway tracks. Ti-Jeanne imagined the tunnel filled with squirming, toothy rats. There must be millions of them living in these old tunnels. The three of them had to stay away from the edge; Ti-Jeanne couldn't bear the thought of falling into a swarming mass of rodents. Feeling along the tile wall, she kept moving. The cracks between the tiles were slimy. It smelled mouldy.

Rudy and Crack must have investigated the vestibule. They were now at the turnstile. Hovering about them, the duppy flared fire red. "I could hear them moving, boss," came Crack's thin, sharp voice. Ti-Jeanne brought them to a halt. She pressed herself against the wall, using one hand to push Tony back, too.

Rudy sucked his teeth in disgust. "Rasscloth. Enough of this. Duppy, go find them and do your job, then come back and bring we to them." Ti-Jeanne could hear Rudy and Crack climbing over the turnstiles.

The duppy flew toward them like a flaming rock from a slingshot. In a corona of fire, Ti-Jeanne could see her mother's anguished face. She stared full into the duppy's eyes while Tony whispered, "Oh God oh God."

Suddenly a sea of screaming children's bodies boiled up from the tunnel below them and fell on Rudy and Crack. The duppy pulled back, a look of surprise on its unearthly face. Ti-Jeanne felt small hands pulling at her and Tony, taking them to the end of the platform. No time to protest; she just went along.

Crack's pistol went off twice, three times. Ti-Jeanne looked back. Agile as snakes, a knot of squirming children had borne Rudy and Crack to the ground. The children were attacking them with what looked like rocks and torn tin cans. Two or three little bodies lay bleeding, but the rest kept at it, screaming with a fierce glee. Rudy shouted, "Duppy! Take we home!"

Crackling, the duppy rushed the swarm of children, growing in size as it did so. Battered and bleeding, Rudy and Crack fought their way clear, leapt into the heart of the duppy's flame, but were not burned. They hung suspended in the glow.

. . . And the illusion of a battalion of feral children winked out, leaving only a small, grimy band of eight or ten surrounding Rudy and Crack. Rudy gaped, then narrowed his eyes in fury at Ti-Jeanne. His stare washed over her like cold ice. He gestured toward her, opened his mouth to speak, but the duppy fled, taking him and Crack. In a blink it was gone.

"C'mon, lady," said Josée, the young woman who'd brought Susie to the balm-yard to have her broken leg set. "We gotta hide in case Rudy comes back."

Carrying their injured, Josée and her troupe led Ti-Jeanne and Tony down the short flight of stairs into the tunnel.

●●●●

Gal, show me your motion, tra-la-la-la-la,
For you look like a little sugar plum (plum, plum).

—Ring game

The little children carried flashlights, the older ones flares. Ti-Jeanne could see mice and rats—and a raccoon?—scurrying away from the noise and light. With every step, Ti-Jeanne's

183

shoes stuck in degenerating gum wads, fluorescent pink and green. She had to kick at squashed pop cans that rolled tinnily away. Torn subway posters flapped at them as they passed, thin men and women posturing in outmoded clothes, gesturing at obsolete appliances. NOW, they said, and TOWER, and TROJAN. Baby's eyes were wide, his head turning from side to side as he tried to take it all in.

The raggle-taggle children ranged in age from about seven to fifteen. One little girl was holding a bleeding wrist and whining from the pain. A tall young man half carried, half dragged another along, saying, "Come on, Chu, come on, buddy, you can make it." Chu held a hand to his stomach. In the reddish light of the flares, it looked like molasses was leaking through his fingers.

"He need help," Ti-Jeanne told Josée, jerking her chin toward Chu.

"Yeah, so does the guy you're carrying, and Alyson. Can't stop. We'll be home soon."

"At least wrap something snug around he waist to slow the bleeding little bit."

Josée called out for what she needed. Somebody brought forth an oversize hockey sweater and tied it around Chu's middle the way Ti-Jeanne had described.

"Alyson," Ti-Jeanne called out to the little girl, "close your hand tight around your wrist, but *above* the cut, you understand? The side closest to your elbow. . . . Yes, like so. Now, hold your hand high up against your body."

"Like this?" Alyson sounded scared.

"Little bit higher, doux-doux, higher than your heart. Yes, just like that. That go slow the bleeding down. Good girl."

Then Ti-Jeanne had a look at Tony's wound. He knew what to do, was pinching the torn edges of the hole in his shoulder closed with one hand. He didn't look good. His breathing was shallow, his eyes unfocused. His body felt cool against her side. He was going into shock. "Tony," Ti-Jeanne said, "you still with me?"

"I'm here, but I'm feeling faint."

"Hold on. Them say we nearly reach." They kept walking.

"Josée," Ti-Jeanne asked, "is what allyou do? To fool Rudy, I mean?"

Josée's grin was feral. "That was Mumtaz," she replied.

A girl of about twelve returned the grin, flicking a hank of black hair out of her eyes. Her brown face was difficult to see in the dark of the tunnel. Her teeth gleamed. Mumtaz was carrying some kind of jury-rigged electronic box, about the size of a loaf of bread, held together with patchy layers of masking and electric tape. Ti-Jeanne could just make out toggle switches bristling from the top of it.

"Listen," said Mumtaz. She flicked a switch, and Ti-Jeanne jumped as the tunnel filled with the din of hundreds of children screaming. She could discern the words "Die!" "Fuckers!" "Kill you!"

Mumtaz shut off the noise. "I layered all our voices. That way, it sounds like there's more of us than there are."

"And the visuals?" Ti-Jeanne could have sworn there'd been a good forty kids.

"Deeplight projector hooked up on the subway tracks. I rigged it myself a long time ago. Keeps people out of our space. It's a tape I made of all of us, dubbed on six waves so it looks like a lot more. You tripped my beam when you came down the stairs, so we knew someone was there. We came to scare them off, in case the projection didn't do it. Smart, huh? Then we realised it was you."

Ti-Jeanne had to smile. "Smart, yes. But why allyou save we? You coulda get away safe."

Hatred twisted Josée's face. "Because of Rudy. Wish we'd killed the bastard. He's killed enough of us." Josée and Mumtaz told Ti-Jeanne about the street children that the posse had kidnapped. They never came back.

"What they do with them?"

"We've followed them as far as Rudy's, but we don't know what happens to them in there." Her tone got sad. "But we found a body once."

"Emily," said Mumtaz in a frightened voice. "Her throat was cut. She was really, really pale."

Ti-Jeanne thought she might be sick. Rudy bled the children to feed the duppy—her mother. She remembered Mi-Jeanne's anguish and shame when she talked of the things Rudy had forced her to do. She understood why her mother was begging for death.

They had reached College Station. The double weight of Tony on Ti-Jeanne's shoulder and Baby in his Snugli was exhausting. Ti-Jeanne hauled them both up the narrow dirty stairs that led to the subway platform. They went through another creaky turnstile and up the stairs for the College Park Mall exit. Ti-Jeanne hadn't been into a mall since the Riots. Mami had told her they were too dangerous, that the squatters would attack her. Right now she'd have rather faced starved street people than spend another minute in the subway tunnel.

The swinging glass doors had been broken a long time ago. They crunched their way through little squares of shatterglass and came out into what had been the food court for the mall, with its bolted-down Formica tables and plastic chairs of institutional orange. Like everything else in the city, the food court showed the marks of the Riots. Many of the chairs had been broken, their plastic burned, melted, and blackened. A few of the tables had nearly been pulled out of the floor. They sat at crazy angles, bent bolts sticking up out of the ground like mushrooms. The stalls that boxed in the eating area used to sell fast food: GENERAL GEORGE FRIED CHICKEN, proclaimed one sign; BURGER DIVINE, another. Now, almost all of them had ash-blackened walls. Refrigerators lay crashed and broken on their sides, robbed long ago of the pop and fruit juice that had been in them. From where Ti-Jeanne stood, drooping under her charges, she could make out debris piled chin high in many of the stalls. The mounds seemed to consist of heat racks, aluminum chafing dishes, and orange plastic trays.

Something was odd. The lights were on! "It have electricity in here!" Ti-Jeanne exclaimed.

Tony said groggily, "'S a mall. They all have power."

"Yeah," Josée said. "Malls were built with their own generators in case of power failures. We can cook in here, and everything. C'mon. Let's lie these two down over here."

Not a moment too soon. Tony was almost incoherent, and Chu had gone completely unconscious at some point during the trek. He'd lost a lot of blood; the front of his body was soaked with it. His friend was now carrying him in his arms. He tenderly laid Chu down and cradled his head in his lap. Chu moaned slightly but didn't rouse. The young man stroked Chu's hair away from his face, leaned forward, and kissed his forehead. His tenderness was that of a lover. He asked Ti-Jeanne tearfully, "Is he gonna be all right?"

"I ain't know. He need medical attention."

"Hospital won't come. We can't pay. You're a healer, can't you do something?"

Panicked, she stared down at Chu. "If the bullet rupture a organ, or bust into he intestines," she told the young man, "I might not be able to help he."

The young man reached for Chu's hand, stared down at his face as though trying to imprint its features on his memory. "Josée," Ti-Jeanne called out, "I need some blankets to keep them warm with."

Josée brought two heavy, lined drapes. They'd do. To her surprise, Mumtaz handed Ti-Jeanne a battered first-aid kit, too.

"'S not much," said the girl.

It wasn't. It contained only some cotton swabs and an aged bottle of alcohol. Ti-Jeanne sniffed at the alcohol. Not completely denatured. That would be of some use. There was also a rusted pair of tweezers in the kit. At least she could use that for fishing out the bullets.

"I need plenty of cloth," she said. "Tear it into strips. Clean cloth, mind." She unbuckled the Snugli and put Baby on the ground beside her.

"Ti-Jeanne," Tony said faintly, "they're going to come after you again. Rudy and them, I mean."

"He don't know is where we gone."

"He found us at the Parkway," he reminded her.

Ti-Jeanne's heart shrank within her. He was right. She looked over at Chu. His face, where it wasn't smeared with his own blood, was pale. "I can't leave just yet, Tony."

The next half hour went by in a blur. The bullet had fragmented as it entered Chu's body. The rusted tweezers were absurdly inadequate to the job of trying to find and fish out the bullet fragments. Chu bled and bled. "I need sterile tools, and seven pair of hands, and whole blood," she muttered angrily. And now she could detect the smell of feces from the wound, which told her that what she was doing was useless. His intestine had indeed been punctured. If the damage from the bullet didn't kill him directly, peritonitis would.

Eventually she didn't know whether it was the blood loss or the rupture of a vital organ that caused Chu's death first. The other young man was still holding Chu's hand tightly. She put her hand over both of theirs. "I too sorry."

She jerked herself to her feet and went and sat at one of the food court tables, giving the boy some privacy. She realised that she was stabbing the bloody tweezers over and over again into the cracked Formica of the table.

"You tried," came Josée's voice. She put a bundle down on the table. Clean clothes. Or unbloodied, at least.

"Allyou was only trying to help me," Ti-Jeanne wailed.

"Yeah, we thought it'd be a lark. Besides, you and your granny helped us, eh?"

Ti-Jeanne realised that the girl's eyes were brimming. The tough words were just a cover-up. "Josée, I sorry."

"I know. Just change your clothes, all right?"

Ti-Jeanne obeyed. The pants were too big. The collar of the shirt was streaked with dirt, and it hung from her shoulders almost to midthigh. It would have fitted Chu. Hot tears fell on her hands as she tied one of the bandage strips like a belt around her waist. Sniffing, she told someone to swab and bandage little Alyson's cut while she checked on Tony.

"You luckier than that boy," she said bitterly to her grandmother's murderer. "In the shoulder and out the back. Some bones crack, but that go heal."

"Thank you, Ti-Jeanne."

"Don't thank me!" She wrapped up his injury, more roughly than she needed to. He didn't complain. She laid him back down, yanked the blanket up over him. Chu's body had been wrapped in his coat. Josée was organizing a bunch of kids to take him out and bury him.

The cold slicing through my shirt like knives. I find myself standing outside, no jacket or boots or nothing, just my blouse and jeans and my runners. I know this building—them used to call it the CN

Tower. Now we does just call it Rudy office. Mami tell me is the tallest freestanding building in the world. Is must be true. Anywhere you is in the city, you could look south towards the lake and see the needle shape of the tower stretching up to the clouds, with the bulge of the observation deck in the middle. One night, I see lightning strike the tip. The whole sky go white. For a hour after, every time I close my eyes, I see jig-jag lightning flashing behind my lids.

I look up, up. I almost have to crane my neck backwards to see all the tower, like I trying to look up into God Father face heself. I ain't go see He face today, though. The cloud cover so low it hiding even the observation deck. I swear, that tower reach right to the stars. It make me giddy, like I can't tell top from bottom no more, and gravity ain't have no meaning. I frighten too bad. Either I going to fall off the earth into that forever sky, or the whole tower going to come crashing down upon me.

"It long, eh?" somebody say from right behind me. I jump and whip around. The whole world do a spin with me and right itself again. The Jab-Jab standing there. Too close. I back up. It just bust a grin and say, "You coming?" It run up to one of the deep, curving walls of the tower and it start to climb up the side, digging it fingers in like the cement is cheese. It climb ten feet, twenty, thirty. Then it stop and look back down on me. "You ain't coming? Ain't is Rudy you want to go and see?"

"I have to, yes. I can't make this go on no longer. But I can't climb like that," I say. All this time it been haunting me, and now is the first time I find voice enough to speak to it.

It frown and jump back down beside me, with a sound like two-by-fours falling in a pile. It shake a wood pencil finger at me.

"And I suppose you won't even try." It sigh a big, jokey sigh, raising and dropping it shoulders-them like all the weight of the world there upon them. *"You have to stop he, you know,"* it tell me. *"Is only you leave. Gros-Jeanne dead and Mi-Jeanne get trapped. Is up to little Ti-Jeanne. So how you going to get in there? Think! Think fast and tell me, nuh? Think!"*

"No, Jab-Jab," I say. *"If I let myself think about what I going to meet up in there, I won't do it. I have to find another way."*

"So you won't use force of body, and you won't use force of will, neither," it say, smiling.

I ain't know why it smiling. Body and will. Brawn and brains. It ain't have nothing leave to use after brawn and brains, oui. But then I get a idea. *"I think I go have to trick Rudy into letting me in."*

"Yes!" The Jab-Jab start to jump and prance like a marionette on strings, dancing in glee. *"Is so the story go. Force won't work against a greater force. Rudy is Bull Bucker, so you have to be Duppy Conqueror. You must use cunning. Cunning and instinct, that's the trick, my doux-doux darling."*

"Bull Bucker? Duppy Conqueror? I ain't understand."

"Rudy tough, so you have to be tougher."

Tougher than Rudy? Jeezam Peace. *"I wish if I could be invisible, like when I try to smuggle Tony outcity."*

The Jab-Jab stop smiling. It stop dancing. It give me a disgusted look. *"Well, like you know everything already, then. You ain't need me."* And it disappear.

"Wait! Come back! I need you, yes!"

But it ain't come back. The wind spring up hard around the

foot of the CN Tower and start buffeting me about. The wind only calling my name: "Ti-Jeanne, Ti-Jeanne."

Josée had her by both shoulders and was shaking her. "Ti-Jeanne, snap out of it. Ti-Jeanne."

Ti-Jeanne put up her hands to stop the girl from shaking her. "You could stop now. I come back."

"Come back from where?" Josée crouched in front of her, looking at her with concern. "You didn't go anywhere. You was just sitting there, and your eyes glazed over, and you wasn't answering when we talked to you."

Ti-Jeanne wasn't paying attention. The Jab-Jab had disappeared when she wished she could become invisible again. Said it didn't need to tell her any more. Maybe she could do it, then.

"Ti-Jeanne?" Josée was reaching out a hand to shake her shoulder again.

Ti-Jeanne held her off. "No, no, I all right. I only thinking."

She realised that the vision had spoken true, even if its message was confusing. She'd go and face Rudy. She would take Tony's gun. Maybe she'd have time to use it on Rudy before his raggas reached her.

She'd have to sneak in. She thought about what the Jab-Jab had said. The last time she had been invisible, it was with Legbara's blessing. Mami had performed the ritual and begged the help of the spirits, and Legbara had answered, had hidden Ti-Jeanne from human eyes, midway between the real world and Guinea Land. And she had been able to extend the invisibility to Tony because she was carrying a gift of his concealed on her body.

Something about that thought was pricking at her consciousness. Extend the invisibility, extend . . . slowly the idea unfurled in her, tentative as one of Mami's wild roses opening to the sun. As her thought bloomed full, Ti-Jeanne felt a small, fierce smile creeping around her lips, like the fighters' grins she'd seen on Josée's and Mumtaz's faces. The Jab-Jab was right. Cunning, not force. She didn't have a plan yet, but maybe she had a way of getting unhurt into her grandfather's office. She would give Rudy the Bull Bucker more than he'd bargained for.

"Josée," she said, "I going to call on Mister Rudy. I need some candy. And a cigar."

The young woman looked puzzled, but didn't ask any questions. "It's your funeral," her shrug seemed to say. As it well might be. Josée polled the other children, and in a matter of seconds they produced two striped peppermint candies dotted with pocket lint. "Cigarette okay?" Josée asked, flipping one from behind her ear. "We ain't got cigars."

"Yes, I think that go be good enough." It would have to be. "You have matches?"

Legbara was an Eshu, but she had nothing to use to represent his head, no white rum to spray him with. Just the offerings of dusty candy and stale cigarette smoke. Maybe Legbara would understand that that was all she had. She gave Baby to the little girl who had asked to hold him back at the farm. No qualms this time about whether she was clean enough. Ti-Jeanne had the guilt of Chu's blood on her conscience. So who was the dirty one?

Ti-Jeanne asked the children to give her privacy for a while and went into a secluded corner of the food court. The children watched curiously but didn't approach her.

Ti-Jeanne crouched, facing the wall. How to start? Suppose she got it all wrong?

Use your instinct, the Jab-Jab had said. She looked over at the coat that wrapped Chu's body. Blood had seeped through it. She went over there and rolled a forefinger in it, silently thanking the young man for the gift of his life's blood.

Back in her corner she traced the Eshu image in Chu's blood on the bare ground: oval face, bulging eyes, and pursed lips. She waited. Nothing happened. No angry spirit appeared to strike her dead for her presumptuousness.

Mami had given the candy as offerings to the Eshu. Ti-Jeanne put the peppermints in front of the image she'd drawn. Then she lit the cigarette and, coughing, blew smoke gently over Eshu's face. She didn't dare beat out a rhythm with her fingers, for fear it would be the wrong one. All she could do was call on Legbara, her own personal Eshu:

"Papa Legbara," she whispered, feeling foolish, "I going to try and end the work that Mami and Mi-Jeanne couldn't finish. I going to try and stop Rudy." She knew that by calling the spirit "Papa," she was acknowledging a bond between them. Strangely, that felt safe and right, not the imposition on her that she had thought it would be. That gave her the courage to say a little more: "Help me, please, Papa, and I go make a proper meal for you. Send me to the shores of Guinea Land again, so I could get into Rudy office without anyone seeing me."

All right, she'd done it. She sat back on her heels to wait, then remembered the trick she wanted to play, if Legbara would accept the truth as she explained it and go along with her. "Oh! Papa, another thing: I want to extend the invisibility to someone else. I carrying he gift in secret. Papa, I carrying Rudy blood in my veins."

Ti-Jeanne smirked in satisfaction. That should give Rudy a shock, when all of a sudden no one could see him. This battle would be just between him and her. If it worked.

She waited long minutes to see if Legbara would accept her gift. Behind her, she could hear the children shuffling, mumbling. A young voice said, "But what's she *doing*?" Someone hushed the child.

It crept up silently, the fog that only she could see, around the edges of the food court at first, then slowly narrowing in. Papa had heard her! She had to move quickly. She stood, stamping the feeling back into her feet, and hurried over to the group of children. "Josée, listen. I don't have plenty time. If I lucky, I go stop Rudy for good." The fog was curling about the floor now, poking thin fingers up into the room.

"And if you're not?" Josée asked.

"Never mind that. You know Romni Jenny what live in the Clarion Hotel?"

"The Gypsy lady? Yeah. She's the one told me to bring Susie to your grandma."

"Good. Take Baby to she. Right away! Tell she to look after he if I don't come back. Promise me you go do it, Josée!"

"Yeah, sure, I promise. But . . . !?" The fog reached Ti-Jeanne's knees, climbed to her waist. Josée started to protest, to ask questions, but her eyes popped as she saw Ti-Jeanne slowly disappear before her eyes, toe to top.

"Magic," breathed Mumtaz. She put her hand to her mouth. The children backed away.

Ti-Jeanne took the first few stairs up to street level at a run. The gun! She'd forgotten it. She went back and got it out of Tony's jacket pocket. She held it awkwardly. It was heavy. Was it loaded? She didn't know how to check. Was that thing there the safety? "This is sending fool to catch the wise, oui," she murmured.

Josée was sitting on the floor, awkwardly putting Baby's coat and mittens back on.

"Where're you taking him?" asked Mumtaz.

"Um . . ." Josée frowned as though she were trying to remember something. Then her face brightened. "Um, well, he can't stay here. I just got this idea to leave him with that Gypsy woman, you know, Jenny? Maybe she can look after him for a while."

They seemed to have forgotten that Ti-Jeanne had ever been there.

CHAPTER TEN

Bloodcloth!" Rudy cursed when he felt the sting from the cold compress Crack was pressing against the burns on his face.

"Sorry, boss."

Rudy didn't bother to answer that. The duppy had transported them quickly back to the old nightclub at the top of the CN Tower, but even in those few seconds, her heat had begun to blister the exposed parts of their bodies. Crack's left palm was one angry, weeping sore where his gun had overheated in his hand. Luckily the bullets hadn't discharged.

Anger bubbled up in Rudy like a pot boiling over. To make everything worse, the duppy was probably hungry again, after the burst of energy it had used to carry them. He was going to have to feed it soon, which meant sending someone out at this time of night to hunt down some street kid or vagrant. He glared at the round-bottomed calabash sitting on its ring of cloth. The duppy had caused him a lot of trouble. He could punish it by withholding the lifeblood it needed, but he had to be careful with that. The power he had over it would only hold as long as he fed the spirit regularly and kept a container for it. He had once heard of a shadow-catcher who broke the rules of her pact with her duppy. It had turned on her. The people who found her said it looked as though she'd taken hours to die and that they'd never forget the stare of horror frozen on her dead, ruined face.

"This is war between me and that Ti-Jeanne woman now," he said to Crack, taking the compress from him to pat at his stinging face himself.

"Me understand, boss. So long as you leave Tony for me."

Rudy's burns were already healing as the duppy bowl worked its magic, sucking the death force from Rudy into itself, keeping him young and healthy. Another drain on the duppy's energy, but Rudy sighed happily as the pain eased. Crack was not so lucky. He winced every so often. The fingers of his left hand were curling in on themselves as the cut dried, but Rudy knew that the man wouldn't call attention to his own wounds until he was given leave. Rudy had trained his men so, and he demanded obedience to his rules. But he would need Crack in functioning order tonight, as they hunted Ti-Jeanne and Tony. "Go and get Barry to bandage your hand."

The man limped painfully out of the room. He couldn't use his cane with his burned hand.

Rudy's burns were completely healed now. He went to one of the windows to look down at the city that was thousands of feet below the observation deck of his tower. Toronto was in darkness now, except for the lights that picked out the malls with their independent power sources. To his left was the dark mass of Lake Ontario and the red glow of Niagara Falls on its horizon. This ruined city was his kingdom. He wasn't going to let Gros-Jeanne's brood take it away from him.

A reflection in the window caught his eye, and he whirled around. From the floor up, the room was filling with smoke.

"Crack! Barry!" No answer. He had to keep the duppy bowl safe. He picked it up, cradled it protectively to his chest, and barrelled out of the room. Then he stopped running. He wasn't smelling any smoke-reek of burning from the fog that was filling the room up. It wasn't a fire.

The odd fog was in this section of the observation deck, too. It cleared a little, leaving a dim haze over everything, as though he were seeing through the light of dusk. Crack was perched on the edge of a desk, grimacing as Barry wrapped a length of gauze around his wrist. What the ass was wrong with them? "So what," Rudy challenged them, "oonuh nah see what happening in here?"

"Band it tight," Crack told Barry, as though Rudy hadn't spoken. "I want to be able to use my hand tonight to break that Tony jaw for he."

"Yeah, man," responded Barry.

Incredulous at being ignored, Rudy strode up to Barry and put his hand on the man's shoulder. Barry brushed it away as he might a fly and went on bandaging.

The elevator pinged. "What the rass . . . ?" cursed Crack. The elevator doors slid open and out stepped Ti-Jeanne.

"Hey!" Rudy shouted. Ti-Jeanne jumped when she saw him, but neither Crack nor Barry seemed to take any notice of her presence.

"Bloodfire!" exclaimed Crack. "How the damn thing reach up here with nobody in it?"

"Idiot! Look she right there." Rudy pointed. No response from Crack.

"Like it haunted, oui," joked Barry. He jumped to hold the door open. Ti-Jeanne slid out of his way along the wall, keeping her eyes on Rudy. "Let we just go and make sure everything all right downstairs."

"Seen," Crack agreed.

Astounded, Rudy watched the two men leave. He was beginning to understand what was going on. The bitch was responsible. "Girl-pickney," he said to Ti-Jeanne, "like your granny teach you some of she antics after all."

She didn't say anything. Maybe she couldn't see him, either? Her lips were pursed tightly together. Gros-Jeanne used to do that when she was frightened. Rudy put the calabash on the desk that Crack had vacated. He took a step to the side. She could see him all right. She was tracking him with her eyes. Then, before he could rush her, Ti-Jeanne pulled a gun out of her pocket. She closed her eyes and, with one hand against her ear, shot him. Rudy staggered back from the impact, sharp pain blossoming in his chest. He gripped the edge of the desk for support, strong nails biting into the old oak. He growled, gritted his teeth, and forced himself to stay standing, broad chest thrust out proudly so that the bitch could see the hole she'd torn in it. And watch it begin to heal before her eyes. The pain was already subsiding. He could feel flesh and bone knitting, the flow of blood out of the wound slowing. Rudy smiled at Ti-Jeanne, who goggled at him and ducked behind the wall into the nightclub part of the tower.

Rudy chuckled. "The old woman tricks ain't help she, and them nah go help you. You go dead here tonight, grand-daughter." He didn't waste any more time on her. "Kill she," he ordered the duppy.

With the crackling sound of green wood in a fire, a spume of glowing sparks fountained up out of the calabash. The pleading and anguish on the disembodied spirit's insubstantial face were so plain that Rudy was struck by its expression. He hadn't known it could still feel. It howled soundlessly at him, and for a brief second he was afraid that the thing wouldn't attack its own child.

"Mummy?" Ti-Jeanne's voice was soft.

The fireball jerked at the sound. Sparks were raining off it, draining it of substance. Rudy's heart clenched in fear. The thing was nearly depleted of energy, and he hadn't fed it. He was losing control over it. Quickly he stammered the words of his ritual. "I give you she blood to feed on. Kill she!"

It made claws of its hands, raking at its own face, but it was still his. It had to obey. It rushed at Ti-Jeanne, who screamed and fired into it. It absorbed the bullet, glowed brighter, and fell on its daughter.

• • • •

I can do this, Punchinello little fellow,
I can do this, Punchinello little boy.

—Ring game

"Mummy!" Ti-Jeanne threw up her hands to protect her face. The fireball charged her again. She felt its heat, felt red-hot talons score deep trails through her cheek. She hissed at the pain. Fingers of flame tugged at her jacket as the duppy pulled her close to itself, eyes begging forgiveness, to lick the blood hotly off her torn cheek. The skin of her cheek bubbled as its touch seared her. The duppy glowed brighter still at the brief taste of blood. Screaming in panic, Ti-Jeanne batted at the thing. It clamped fiery teeth in her wrist, ripped away a mouthful of skin, devoured that. It latched on to her arm. The flesh sizzled like meat on a grill. It put the hot crimson hole of its mouth to the wound. Hysterical, Ti-Jeanne tried to shake it off. It held on, staring right at her with crazed eyes. Then it released her. Ti-Jeanne snatched her arm away. Drops of her blood spattered the floor. The fog about them lifted. Rudy's blood spilling from her veins had yanked them fully back into reality.

"Bumbocloth! What the ass is this now?" came Rudy's agitated voice.

Ti-Jeanne barely spared a thought for all that. Shuddering, nearly out of her mind with pain and fright, she waited for the duppy's next attack. In a shaking hand, she pointed the gun at the duppy, knowing it would do no good. But instead of pouncing on her, it lowered itself to the ground and licked up the drops of her blood, one by one. Rudy loudly ordered it to finish the job, but it kept licking, one drop at a time. It was obeying him, but at its own speed. Ti-Jeanne had shown it that trick. It looked up at her pleadingly. It was trying to convey something to her.

"What, Mummy?"

Only a few drops left on the ground. One more. Last one gone. The duppy snarled soundlessly at her, gathered itself cat-like to leap at her again. That thing wasn't her mother. It was a Soucouyant, and it was going to suck her dry of blood.

It was a *Soucouyant.* Suddenly Ti-Jeanne remembered how you delayed a Soucouyant. Praying that the old-time stories had it right, she shook her bleeding arm, scattering more drops of blood. The Soucouyant hovered over them again, licking them up one by one, like the Soucouyant in her dreams had been compelled to pick up single rice grains at a time. Duppies could be delayed by tricks like that. She had dreamt true.

Rudy snarled in exasperation and rushed at Ti-Jeanne.

Intuitively she fired past him at her mother's prison. *Instinct. Don't think.*

The calabash exploded into shards. Noxious things flew from it: reeking clumps of dirt; a twist of hair; white knuckle bones; the black, mummified body of what looked like a dead cat. The duppy swelled, flared to incandescent, its freed hands outstretched in thanks to Ti-Jeanne. It dove at Rudy, who backed away, hands beating ineffectually at the roaring flame. Ti-Jeanne thought her troubles were over. Her mother had turned on Rudy. But then the duppy shrank to the size of an ember and winked out. Gone. Her mother was finally fully dead, and Ti-Jeanne was alone with Rudy.

Rudy screamed, fell to his knees. A network of wrinkles was stitching itself over his face. Swollen veins wormed their way over the backs of his hands, while the knuckles bunched like the knobs of ancient roots; he put his arthritic hands to his mouth, spat his teeth into them. His lips sank in on themselves; a ray of fine lines etched themselves around his pursed, trembling mouth; his hair blanched to grey; his shoulders rounded as his spine curled. Ti-Jeanne gasped. Old; he was old!

Pain exploded in Ti-Jeanne's hand as Barry kicked the gun out of it. Ti-Jeanne hadn't heard the two posse members come back up in the elevator. "Lord Jesus," breathed Barry. His gun was trained on Ti-Jeanne, but, eyes the size of dinner plates, he was staring at Rudy. Ti-Jeanne started toward him.

"Don't move, sweetness," drawled Crack. She stood still. Neither his gun nor his eyes wavered from her. "Look like we not going to have that chance to get to know one another better after all."

"No, don't shoot she," came Rudy's querulous voice. The words were mushy in his toothless mouth. He pushed himself painfully to his feet. "Hold the bitch. Me can't stay old so. Me need a new duppy."

CHAPTER ELEVEN

BOLOM: *Ask him for my life!*
Oh God, I want all this to happen to me!

TI-JEAN: *Is life you want, child?*
You don't see what it bring?

BOLOM: *Yes, yes, Ti-Jean, life!*

—Derek Walcott, *Ti-Jean and His Brothers*

As the duppy bowl cracked, another soul than Mi-Jeanne's flew free of it. Rudy had reserved a special agony for this victim. He had forbade him full death, had ordered the duppy to chain and torture his soul down inside the microcosmic hell that was the world of the duppy bowl. For nearly twelve years, divorced from sense or logic, he cowered and gibbered in his purgatory, was chased endlessly through his nightmare existence by a yowling cat, a ball of fire, and a hand that clawed with no arm or body. Cats must howl and hands must clutch, but he knew that the fireball would have left him in peace if it could have. Sometimes, even as he fled his goads, he could see deep into Guinea Land, see what would be the fate of the woman he had *loved, if he couldn't warn her. He cried out for help. It had taken nearly twelve years for his call for help to worm its way through the duppy bowl world to his spirit father. Unable to reach the soul in torment, Legbara had provided a bodily housing for his soul, then set events in motion to have him freed from the duppy bowl. But too late, too late. His earthly body had tried its best, but she was gone again.*

Oh, the sound of that calabash finally cracking was a world exploding, a heart breaking twice. Flying to join its body, the soul ember took comfort that the union would bring forgetfulness. The still-growing brain wouldn't have room for the memories.

Sleeping fitfully in Romni Jenny's arms, Baby jerked once, hard. Dunston's soul and his new body finally were truly one. Then he fell into a peaceful, coma-deep sleep. No longer Gros-Jeanne's doomed second husband. Nothing but a baby now.

CHAPTER TWELVE

*Egg don't have no right
at rockstone dance.*

—Traditional saying

Held down on the table by Barry and Crack Monkey, Ti-Jeanne glared defiantly at Rudy. Inside she was quailing in fear, but she refused to show it. She watched as Rudy came out of what had been the restaurant on the observation deck level of the CN Tower. He was bearing a large pot. His newly old body walked with a stoop. He bent painfully and scraped the grave dust that had been in the calabash into the pot. Grimacing, he straightened, put the pot on top of the console that displayed the world's weather. "This pot for you," he told Ti-Jeanne in his breaking octogenarian's voice. "For your spirit when I catch it." He reached into a cupboard under the console and came to stand over her. He held a calibrated phial of buff powder. Tremors in his hand made the cobalt blue crystals slide restlessly back and forth. He asked Crack and Barry, "How much I should give she? How much oonuh think she weigh?"

"'Bout one forty, boss," Barry replied. "And hard, too, you see? No fat on she bones." He gave her a slimy grin.

"I hope you did enjoy feeling me up," Ti-Jeanne taunted him. "For I go be the last woman you touch. I is a seer woman, and I *dream* it."

Lies, pure lies, but she had the small satisfaction of seeing a look of doubt and unease creep over Barry's face. "Shut up," he told her.

"You go make me?"

He released her arm, hauled back his hand, and slapped her face hard. Stunned, she nevertheless swung out with her free arm, felt it connect with his jaw.

"Ow! Bitch!"

"Barry!" Rudy's voice still had the sound of command, although it shook with the weight of the years that had fallen on him in seconds. "Mind me, man! If you only get me vex tonight, me will take you out and shoot you myself. Just hold she. And ignore what she say." Barry sucked his teeth but grabbed her arm again, slamming it down to the table harder than was necessary.

Not to think, not to think. Instinct alone. Ti-Jeanne had been using the words as a mantra ever since she had set out for Rudy's this night. But her heart was trying to fight its way out of her chest. If she were truly to obey her instincts, she would be begging for mercy, promising anything, if only the three men would let her go free. She bit her lips and just breathed, in and out. The need for breath was a deeper instinct than even fear.

"Hold she good now, Crack," Rudy instructed the man restraining her legs. No need to reinforce the order. Crack's grip on her was already hideously strong, his fingers digging into each leg just above the knee. But she would not cry, she would not speak.

Rudy picked up the butcher knife, turned it from side to side, inspecting it.

Ti-Jeanne found she couldn't keep her promise of silence. "What you going to do?" She followed the glinty twists of the knife with her eyes, unable to look away from it.

"Let in the poison, my darling," quavered Rudy. He picked up one of her plaits, gently touched the knife to it. The blade sliced clean through. "You ever slash buff, granddaughter?"

"Uh-uh." Her voice came out high and childish. She would not cry, she would not beg.

"Is Haiti people first make it, you nah know? From poison toad and some herbs. Bufo toad. Is that name that buff come from." He rotated the phial in front of her face. Crazily, all she could think was what a beautiful shade of blue they were.

Rudy picked up the rubber gloves he had placed on the table and snapped them onto his hands. Even through the gloves it was obvious how veined and arthritic they were. He scowled at them.

There was another measured phial on the table, a molasses-thick liquid. He carefully poured a measure of it into the buff crystals, using one hand to still the tremors in the other. "When people slash buff," he said, swirling the phial to mix the two substances, "them only use little bit, cut it with crack. It make them feel say them flying. We go give you a different mixture of it, though. Buff with some other Haiti medicine mix in. You know what buff does do you, Ti-Jeanne?"

"Nerve and muscle paralysant," she whispered through clenched teeth. She'd seen the deceptively relaxed bodies of people who'd OD'd on buff.

"Yes, my darling. Your grandmammy teach you good. So you know why I have to be careful how much you get. Nah want your heart and lungs to stop working, right? Want you to be awake and know what we a-do to you. And the other things I mix in? They go lower your emotional resistance, make you more suggestible. For you see that paralysis, Ti-Jeanne? Is the first stage in making a zombie."

Then he took the knife and slowly made a deep incision in the meat of her thigh muscle. Ti-Jeanne arched her back as the knife traced a line of agony up her leg. The trembling of his hand made the pain even worse. The grunting sounds issuing past her teeth weren't sobs, not quite.

"It stinging you, nuh? Good. I coulda give a injection, but I want you to feel me make the cut. For all the trouble you cause me today." She tried desperately to heave herself free of the restraining arms, but it was no use. Rudy poured some crystals from the phial into the gash on her leg, checked the level in the container, poured some more. Then he used his thumb to work the mixture deeply into the wound. Her leg began to go numb immediately. With every beat of her heart, the poison was moving deeper into her body.

"Yes, the first stage for making a zombie. Combine the paralysis and the suggestibility with the right kind of um, *indoctrination,* and the zombie go do anything me tell it. Sometimes me want little help 'round here, you understand? To keep the place clean and so."

Both legs were numb now. An eerie sensation of cold creeped over Ti-Jeanne's trunk as the superficial nerves went dead.

"A zombie can't do nothing complicated," Rudy continued, "but if you tell it to wash the dishes, it go wash every dish in the place."

"Clean ones and all," Crack sniggered, "if you don't say different." Rudy smirked at the comment. Ti-Jeanne found she couldn't turn her head.

"Sometimes me only want to teach somebody a lesson. Like that Melba, holding back some of she earnings from me. But for you, sweetness," Rudy said, holding her by the chin to look deeply into her eyes, "me have more than that in store for you. If you could convince a spirit from out a dead body to serve you, then you nah have to fear nothing again. Not enemies, not bullets, not age, not death. The duppy could kill your enemies, trap them souls in it duppy bowl, if you want. It could stop bullets, eat death. If you only have the balls to kill somebody and trap their soul in bowl to serve you. Is Legbara tell me that."

Not Legbara! Ti-Jeanne tried to shout. *Him woulda never tell you how to do this!* But all that came from her flaccid mouth was a vague, grunting noise.

"Stupid spirit." Rudy chuckled. "Him think say I woulda find that so horrible, I wouldn't do it. Him think wrong."

He slapped Ti-Jeanne in the face, right where Barry had just hit her. She felt involuntary tears start to her eyes. She couldn't blink them away.

"And I come to find out something him nah tell me. A duppy from a dead somebody not too smart. Smarter than a zombie, but you still can't give it nothing too complicated to do, seen? But if you split off the duppy from it body while the body still alive! Well, then you have a servant for true. One that could teach you everything it did know in life. You know your mother was a seer woman, right?"

He slapped the other side of her face. "Ah, like you ain't feel that one, granddaughter?" She hadn't. Her head had rocked to the side with the force of the blow, but there was no pain. Her tears flowed freely for her mother and for the man who had trapped his own daughter's soul in a container so that he would never have to die.

"All right, she ready now," said Rudy. "Let we start."

Start? She had thought they'd already started.

They lifted her inert body from the table to the floor. She couldn't help but see what they were doing. She couldn't control the muscles that would close her eyes. Rudy produced an old, fire-blackened knife, on the blade of which he heaped a few mounds of some kind of powder. "Gunpowder," he said conversationally to her. "Me know say your body can't speak, but when your spirit agree to serve me, this gunpowder go burst into flames. The body could lie, but when your spirit ready to accept my bond, it go tell me true." They put her in a black sack. She could smell the white rum that was being sprinkled on it. Some of it dripped through the sack and made her open eyes burn.

She heard Rudy grunt as he eased his old body onto the ground by her head. Then he spoke to her once more. "Ti-Jeanne? Me know say you could hear me, granddaughter." Coming from Rudy's lips, the word "granddaughter" sounded as obscene as a curse. Ti-Jeanne prayed that he'd given her too much of the bufo poison, that her heart would stop of its own accord. But she remained stubbornly alive.

"I go tell you a little something, Ti-Jeanne." His voice sounded companionable, as though they were sharing an intimate secret, just between the two of them. "Is your mother sheself ask me to put she duppy in the bowl."

You lie, Ti-Jeanne thought.

"A-true, me tell you," Rudy said. "Mi-Jeanne come running to me for help. Your grandmother did putting visions in she head, trying to control she. Trying to make Mi-Jeanne stay with she. Making she see things to frighten she."

Ti-Jeanne remembered that night so many years ago when her mother had woken up screaming. Mi-Jeanne hadn't wanted Mami's comforting. She and Mami had been arguing a lot. Dunston had moved in and Mi-Jeanne was talking about leaving, taking Ti-Jeanne and finding their own place to live.

Rudy's words echoed in Ti-Jeanne's head. Maybe he was telling the truth, and Mami was at the root of all their problems. Maybe Mami had tried the same trick on both

Ti-Jeanne and Mi-Jeanne; caused the visions and made them feel that their only chance for being rid of them was to stay with her and receive her help. Ti-Jeanne was confused. The drug made it hard to breathe, hard to think clearly. Rudy's voice came again:

"Think about it little more, sweetheart. You nah see the power I did give Mi-Jeanne? Knife couldn't cut she, blows couldn't lick she, love couldn't leave she, heart couldn't hurt she. She coulda go wherever she want, nobody to stop she."

His voice flowed soothingly over her. *Heart couldn't hurt she.* What if Tony hadn't been able to slide into Ti-Jeanne's heart like a thorn from a rose and stick there, aching and aching? She probably wouldn't have got pregnant. There would be no Baby constantly demanding her attention and her energy. *She coulda go wherever she want, nobody to stop she.* Suppose she could have chosen her own way, instead of trying to tear herself in three to satisfy Tony, and Baby, and Mami?

"Mi-Jeanne beg me to help she live only in she spirit, for she didn't want the pains of the body no more. The only part of she flesh that she take into that calabash with she was she eyes, so she could see for me. She gouge them out sheself and put them in the duppy bowl, Ti-Jeanne."

Ti-Jeanne's mind reeled at the image of Mi-Jeanne digging her own eyes out of her head. She must have been desperate to become a duppy!

"And, granddaughter," came Rudy's soft whisper, "if you hadn't break she bowl, she woulda never dead."

Rudy was right. She had killed her own mother. "Uh, uh," Ti-Jeanne moaned through her paralyzed larynx. She couldn't feel the tears that she knew were rolling down her face.

"Granddaughter, I giving you a chance to be free of all this right now," Rudy told her. "That body don't have to be your home no more. You don't have to feel pain no more, sweetheart. Your granddaddy could help you. After I speak the right words, the powder you take will give your spirit strength to act on it own, without the body. Let your spirit talk to me, Ti-Jeanne. Let it light the gunpowder."

He started mumbling the words of a ritual in a language she didn't recognise. The mumbling went faster and faster, the words running together into a gargling noise. A gurgle. A thumping like a low drum tattoo, as though Rudy's body were jerking about on the floor.

The effect of the bufo powder on Ti-Jeanne was increasing. She felt herself floating free of her body. She lifted clear of the black sack. She could see Rudy quivering on the floor at her head as his lips moved in the words of the ritual. He was in some kind of trance. Crack and Barry stood nearby, watching the knife blade. She could feel the bonds parting between herself and her body. The ants-under-the-skin feeling had become distant. The pain of her distended belly had eased, and the burning in her body's fixed-open eyes. Her astral body saw clearly through Guinea Land eyes instead, saw the spirits of the three men sitting like slipcovers over their corporeal bodies. Rudy's fluttered and shuddered in synch with the quivering of his tranced flesh. She could still feel her body, nothing but an aching weight dragging her back to the pain of her life. If she said yes to Rudy, she could fly. She could burn bright as fire and never hurt. It was what she'd always wanted. Something clenched and released in her astral form, like an unfamiliar muscle flexing. The first mound of gunpowder on the knife burst into flame, sizzled instantly to black, and died out, leaving the rest of the gunpowder untouched. Barry pounded Crack on the shoulder, pointed at the knife. Crack nodded, his narrowed eyes holding satisfaction. Rudy kept up the incantation. Ti-Jeanne made the strange inner motion again, almost just to see if she could do it consciously. Gleefully she watched the second mound of gunpowder flare. Two more to go.

Ti-Jeanne did an experimental roll through the air, a full 360 degrees. Her flesh body always got dizzy easily, but her duppy body had no sense of disorientation from the spinning. She dove down toward the floor and, to her delight, went right through it to the level beneath. Moving through the solid surface tickled, like swimming through bubbles.

She was hovering above the CN Tower's famed glass-bottomed floor. The sight of the 1,800-foot drop to the city below her would have made her flesh body queasy and afraid, but her duppy body claimed air as its home.

Knife couldn't cut she, blows couldn't lick she. She could go wherever she want, nobody to stop she.

Yes, is this I want for true, Ti-Jeanne thought. She flowed back up to the observation deck level, mentally reaching out as she did so to flame the third mound of gunpowder. One more mound left.

The Jab-Jab was perched on the deck, knees crooked upward, feet flat on the surface. It hugged its angular knees and peered at her through the branches of its limbs. "Having fun, daughter?"

She heard the censure in its voice. Somebody else trying to make her do what they wanted, not what she wished. "You can't stop me," she told it sullenly.

"You right, doux-doux. And I can't stop the shadow-catcher, neither," it said, jerking a pencil-point chin in the direction of Rudy. "He did make up he mind long time to turn to the dark side. We lose he now. We can't talk to the ones who won't talk to us."

Rudy's mumbling had taken on a rhythm. It seemed to fill the air. Its cadences pulled at Ti-Jeanne's duppy body. Her gaze kept being pulled to him.

The "scree, scree, scree" of a noisemaker jerked her attention away from Rudy. The Jab-Jab was smiling its jokey smile at her and swinging its hand around on its wrist. The hand whirled round and round on its unnatural joint. The three men didn't seem to hear the racket. The Jab-Jab steadied the swinging hand with the other, stopping the screeching noise. "You ever ask your grandmother what she was?" the Jab-Jab said.

"She was a seer woman," Ti-Jeanne replied. Even the memory of her just murdered grandmother caused her little pain. She was impatient for the Jab-Jab to stop its chatter. She had business with Rudy.

"Yes, it have plenty names for what Gros-Jeanne was. Myalist, bush doctor, iyalorisha, curandera, four-eye, even obeah woman for them who don't understand. But you what she woulda call it, if you had ask she?"

"What you want, Jab-Jab?"

"Gros-Jeanne woulda tell you that all she doing is serving the spirits. And that anybody who try to live good, who try to help people who need it, who try to have respect for life, and age, and those who go before, them all doing the same thing: serving the spirits."

Ti-Jeanne remembered all the slaps and whippings she'd received at her grandmother's hand. How was that "living good"?

As though she'd spoken, the Jab-Jab narrowed its eyes at her and nodded. "Yes, Gros-Jeanne was a hard woman. Now Rudy, he does try and make the spirits serve *he*."

And the visions flashed around her, *through* her, invading sight, smell, sound, touch:

A blow to the side of her face jolted her, sent her flying back into a cheap aluminum folding chair. She was Gros-Jeanne as a younger woman, and Rudy had just backhanded her. He stood over her, fist pulled back for a second blow. He roared, "You think say is money me make from? Eh?" Through tears and the blood in her eyes, she could see her young daughter, Mi-Jeanne, watching, fist jammed into her frightened mouth, from the bedroom doorway of the run-down apartment.

Hunger. It filled her, burned her up. She would die of it, kill for it. She was Mi-Jeanne's duppy, looking up at Rudy from the little world of the calabash. From that angle, shadows limned the underplanes of his face, made him look otherworldly. He tipped a

*cup into the calabash, and blood poured over her, intoxicating in
its heat and smell. She drank eagerly, but the cupful was not
enough. "You could have more," he told her, "when you kill
Dunston for me. Kill he and trap he soul in there with you, and
you could have all he blood." She railed silently at him, but the
hunger was too much. It made her a thing without a will of her
own, obedient only to Rudy's commands. She knew that she would
murder her stepfather.*

*She was slumped in a chair in this same room, belly painfully
swollen and eyes fixed open from the effects of the zombie drug. She
couldn't move. She was Tony, watching Rudy tear a strip of living
skin . . .*

"Ai! Stop, Jab-Jab, stop." The images of Melba's last
moments were too much to bear.

Rudy had lied to her. And she had wanted to believe it.
Her grandmother had abused her offspring and had suffered
for it, in her own heart's pain as she watched her daughter and
her granddaughter reject her. *Love couldn't leave she.* Rudy
cared nothing for love or loss. What would she be if she
became his creature? Hesitantly she said to the Jab-Jab, "I can't
keep giving my will into other people hands no more, ain't? I
have to decide what I want to do for myself." No answer. It
wasn't going to tell her. "But Jab-Jab, how I go stop someone
as powerful as he?"

"Rudy is Bull Bucker," it said quietly, "so you have to be
Duppy Conqueror."

She looked up, but the Jab-Jab was gone. She had to figure out how to stop Rudy herself.

She remembered her grandmother's words: *The centre pole is the bridge between the worlds.* Why had those words come to her right then?

Ti-Jeanne thought of the centre pole of the palais, reaching up into the air and down toward the ground. She thought of the building she was in. The CN Tower. And she understood what it was: 1,815 feet of the tallest centre pole in the world. Her duppy body almost laughed a silent *kya-kya*, a jokey Jab-Jab laugh. For like the spirit tree that the centre pole symbolized, the CN Tower dug roots deep into the ground where the dead lived and pushed high into the heavens where the oldest ancestors lived. The tower was their ladder into this world. A Jab-Jab type of joke, oui.

She was halfway into Guinea Land herself. She could call the spirits to help her. She wouldn't have to call very loudly.

What were the names Mami had told her? "Shango!" she called in her mind. "Ogun! Osain!" Her flesh body moved its lips slightly, trying through the paralyzing effect of the drug to form the same words. "Shakpana, Emanjah! Oshun, Oya! And Papa Legbara, my Eshu! Come down, come down and help your daughter!"

With a flash of instinct, she knew that the call to the heavens should be mirrored by a call to the earth. "All you children; every one Rudy kill to feed he duppy bowl—come and let we stop he from making another one! Dunston! And Mami! And Mi-Jeanne! Is Ti-Jeanne calling you! Come up, come up and help your daughter! Melba, you come, too! Climb the pole, allyou; climb the pole!"

She wanted to wait in her duppy body to see what would happen, but her flesh body was reeling her in again. Its pain was descending upon her. Like tumbling headfirst into mud, she rejoined her flesh body, which had worked itself partway out of the bag. The drug was beginning to fade. She could move her head a little and blink her eyes.

The chandelier was swaying. In fact, the whole structure of the CN Tower was shaking. An 1,800-foot needle, trembling. Rudy grunted. He sat up out of his trance and in his old-man voice asked, "What the rass a-go on?"

No one answered him. The bottles of alcohol on the bar started to clink together. The chairs shuffled around under the dinner tables. The lights flickered, and there was a low, tooth-rattling hum. Ti-Jeanne's head felt stuffed full. She could hear the rhythm of the blood vessels in her brain, pounding like drums. Rudy was standing. He tottered on his ancient legs, grabbed for the edge of a table to steady himself. "Must be an earthquake," Barry said nervously. He took a small step and looked around as though he could see the source of the disturbance.

Ti-Jeanne was facing one of the windows that ringed the observation deck, so it was she who saw the flash of white light flower in the night sky, zigzag down, and strike the glass. The building flashed into the negative against her abused retinas. Black flared to blinding white, colour to dead black. The structure of the tower creaked. Outside in the miles-high air, Shango Lord Thunder drummed his rhythm while Oya of the storm flashed and shattered the air like knives. Ti-Jeanne had an impression of an ecstatic woman's features, silver dreadlocks tossing wildly as she danced around a hugely muscled, graceful man who clasped a tall drum between his knees. The lightning flashes crawled, whipping around the length of the tower. The first of the Oldest Ones had arrived.

Rain pelted down like boulders. The lightning cracked fissures into the tower's structure, and water began to leak in, buckets of it. The water traced forms along the wall, and two majestic Black women stepped out from its current: graceful Oshun and beautiful Emanjah, water goddesses both, anger terrible on their unearthly faces.

Crack groaned. His body twisted. His skin erupted in suppurating sores. Ti-Jeanne could see the halo of the spirit inhabiting his head, overpowering his own spirit. Shakpana, lord of disease. Crack reached a palsied hand to Barry for help. At Shakpana/Crack's touch, pus-filled buboes blossomed on the other man's body. Barry trembled, clutched at his own throat, and fell dead to the ground. His corpse began to swell immediately with putrefaction. Oshun wrinkled her nose in distaste and fanned her face with the intricate cutwork fan she was holding. It appeared to be made of beaten gold. She delicately picked up the hem of her white-trimmed yellow robe and stepped out of the way. Her sister Emanjah simply quirked an eyebrow in amusement. The tribal scars shifted on her cheeks when she smiled.

Then Ti-Jeanne felt the beneficence of Osain, the healer, leaching the poison from her body. Her burns and cuts healed. She could move again. She was holding Osain in her head, but it was as though he were cradling her consciousness in his hands, allowing her to remain aware simultaneously with him. Ti-Jeanne sat up and thrust off the black bag. She felt both light and heavy, part spirit, part flesh. Her eyes searched and found the knife with which Rudy had tried to bind her. It had kept its weight of gunpowder. With her spirit strength, she melted the knife where it lay. It shrank into itself in a glowing lump of slag, leaving the last mound of gunpowder unfired. "No," she said simply to her grandfather.

Ogun-who-wields-the-knife nodded his satisfaction at her. He picked up the red-hot lump of metal and popped it into his mouth like a toolum candy. He smiled, pleasure in every deep line of his broad, brown face. He licked the last sweetness of the iron off his fingers, then with his square, strong blacksmith's hands, he bent to the floor, brushed the gunpowder away, and was gone.

Lightning cracked once more, then the storm vanished as suddenly as it had arrived.

"One more of we left to appear, cousin," said Osain with her lips. Rudy fled to the elevator and started frantically pushing at the button.

The pressure in Ti-Jeanne's head was almost gone, now that the Oldest Ones had manifested. Except for Legbara. Where was her Eshu?

She understood then. She knew why the Jab-Jab was always grinning. She laughed, starting deep in her belly. She laughed at all her fears, all her sulks. She laughed for the pleasure of knowing that Mi-Jeanne's and Gros-Jeanne's spirits had reached home safe to Guinea Land. She laughed at the sorry man who had thought he could hold death forever in a calabash. She laughed, because now she knew who the Jab-Jab was.

The elevator dinged. The door opened, and there he was, tophatted, skull-faced, impossibly tall. He held a pretty sprig of nightshade coyly in front of his mouth and giggled along with her. Papa Legbara, Prince of Cemetery. Her Eshu. The Jab-Jab.

He was supporting a child in his other arm. Her arms were wrapped trustingly around his neck. She turned her head to look at Rudy, and the lips of the deep slash in her neck rubbed against each other. Rudy's toothless mouth dropped open. He mewled and backed away. "Yes," said Legbara in his death-rattle voice, "is you send this one to me, Master Sheldon. In fact, all of these my children." He stepped out of the elevator, followed by ghoul after ghoul, many of them children, all bearing the marks of Rudy's knife on their bodies. A man dragged himself along the floor on the stumps that had once terminated in hands and feet. Melba held her own skin draped over one arm. Her stride was determined. And . . .

"Mami," Ti-Jeanne said. Her grandmother smiled proudly at her. Her chest gaped open where her heart had been removed. "You do good, sweetness," Mami told her.

"No!" It was Rudy. "Oonuh can't touch me! I move beyond where the powers could reach!"

Mami turned to him, hands on her hips. "Rudolph Sheldon. What a man I take for my husband, oui? You have to understand, Rudy. The powers deaf to you, is true. Them won't come if you call. But is not you call them this time."

Rudy tried to flee, hobbling on his aged legs. His face was a mask of terror, lips gaping. He tripped over Barry's corpse and fell hard. The distended cadaver split open under his weight. The stench was appalling. Whining, Rudy tried to wipe the gore off his body and crawl away from the corpse at the same time. The ghouls silently blocked his way.

"No, master," said Legbara. "You ain't going nowhere. You try to give me all these deaths in exchange for you own, but I refuse the deal. I give them all back to you."

Rudy screamed as the weight of every murder he had done fell on him. Ti-Jeanne had to look away then. The sounds coming from him were bad enough: a desperate plea for mercy; a choked-off gargle; a cracking; then a wet, ripping noise. When she looked back, the chunks of flesh lying there looked like something that should have been on a butcher's block. It was fair, but it sickened her.

"Papa," she said to Legbara, "take him away, please. Rudy, I mean."

"Your grandfather," Osain reminded her.

"Yes." Though it had come to this, he'd been her grandfather, her blood.

A deep, warm voice interrupted. "Nah give the child any more to fret about, Osain. Me know say she not going forget is who blood she come from." It was Emanjah. Her blue-and-white robes clung to her ample body like water droplets on skin. She was very beautiful. "Sister," she said to Oshun, "help me wash away this garbage, please."

The water leaking into the room was already ankle deep.

226

Now it rose, swirling, as high as Ti-Jeanne's knees. She shivered in its cold. She could see fish dancing in it, could hear the cry of gulls. For a second she thought she could smell the sea. Then the flood subsided. Barry's body and Rudy's remains were gone. Oshun and Emanjah had taken them away. Ti-Jeanne felt a longing pull at her. Emanjah's voice had had something of her mother's in it.

The elevator door opened again, and the ghouls all trooped into it. Mami blew a kiss at Ti-Jeanne. Legbara set the little girl he was carrying on her feet. "Go on, sweetheart," he said to her. "I go follow soon." But she clung to his hand, looking at Ti-Jeanne. Then in a soft voice (for much of the air was whistling out through the slash in her throat), she said to Ti-Jeanne, "I'm Emily. Tell Mumtaz. She'll remember."

Then she turned and ran into the elevator to join the others. The door closed to take the passengers back down into the earth.

"Crick-Crack," said Crack Monkey. Ti-Jeanne gasped and whirled around to face him. Shakpana was still riding his body: Ti-Jeanne could see the halo surrounding his head. The lord of disease laughed at her, a sound halfway between a wheeze and a cough. "Like you still can't take a joke, doux-doux!"

"That ain't funny!"

"No, I guess you right." Crack's voice was fading fast. His eyes were sunken in his head, his lips cracked and dry. He was probably burning up with fever. His sores oozed. His spirit light was fading. Shakpana was riding him to death. But

Crack's eyes blazed out at her from the dying body, hatred flashing from them. Ti-Jeanne feared his gaze alone could strike her. She stood well out of his way. She looked around for something heavy to beat him off with, if she had to. But Crack dropped to his knees, huffing for breath. "Just a little more," panted Shakpana with his lips.

Crack slumped to the ground. The Shakpana glow left his head. His spirit casing dulled and frayed away to nothing. He was dead.

"Good," said Osain. "That bud pinch off the vine."

"Well, brother," came a voice like the wind creaking in tree boughs, "what you still doing there in my daughter head?" The Jab-Jab was walking on its hands around the room. Its legs waved awkwardly in the air. It crooked its head up at Ti-Jeanne inquiringly. She couldn't help it. She laughed.

"Legbara, your daughter still need plenty healing yet," said Osain with her mouth. "Body get better, but spirit still bust-up, I think."

"Is okay, Papa Osain, thank you," Ti-Jeanne told him, a little surprised at her own audacity. "I think you start the healing good already. I could do the rest myself."

"All right, cousin. Till later, then."

"Later." *Later?*

"Walk good." And her head was her own again. She could see the sun coming up on the horizon. The day was new.

With a clattering noise, the Jab-Jab righted itself. It cackled at her, patting its two-by-four belly in self-congratulation.

"Heh-heh! Daughter, ain't I tell you you go be Duppy Conqueror this day?"

"Is allyou do all this, Papa, not me."

"Well, is you call all my duppy to come do your bidding. And child, you do a thing I never see nobody do before. For a few minutes there, you hold eight of the Oldest Ones in your head one time." His face got serious for a minute. "Don't try it again, eh? It could burn your brain out."

"No, Papa."

She was speaking to thin air. She hadn't slept for two nights. It was time to go home. She took the elevator down to the ground.

CHAPTER THIRTEEN

Beat big drum, wave fine flag-o,
Quashee come to town.
No more fear Jack's obeah bag-o,
Quashee knock him down.

—Traditional song

Daylight made Ti-Jeanne squint. Light glinted off the windowpanes of those mega-high-rises that still had them. She walked east along Front Street. She grinned idiotically at the familiar tall, narrow wedge shape of the Gooderham Building jammed into the tip of Berczy Park. Mami called it the flatiron building. *Had* called it. Sadly, she remembered her last glimpse of her grandmother's face, blowing a kiss. As she got closer to Saint Lawrence Market, she began to see stalls piled high with goods for sale. It was market day. She had forgotten. The sunny day had spilled the marketplace at Front and Jarvis out onto both sides of the street. The clamour of people was deafening. Despite her fatigue, though, Ti-Jeanne edged her way happily through the crowd. She had a yearning to lose herself in this noisy throng of people going about the business of staying alive.

Bob Kelly's cabbages were round and fat this year. She must come back and get some; Pavel had been promising to show her and Mami how to make cabbage rolls. Now it would just be her.

Bob nodded at her, too busy dickering with a customer to stop and chat. She nodded and smiled back. The smile felt so good on her face that she kept it there for a little while after she'd passed Bob's stall.

The next stall was the shoe repair. Sweat trailing down her plump neck into the deep cleavage of her bustline, Emma Joyce was busy tracing the shape of a young woman's patched running shoes onto a scrap of the tire rubber she used to make new soles. For Emma, this was a hot day. She looked up, put her hand to her forehead to wipe it, and saw Ti-Jeanne. Her face did something complicated, then she called out, "Girl, I'm so sorry to hear about your grandma. Jenny told us." Her customer stared curiously at Ti-Jeanne, relinquishing her other shoe out of her hand only when Emma pulled on it.

"I know," Ti-Jeanne said. "I go miss she." She missed her grandmother already. Mi-Jeanne too. It was hard to find her mother and lose her again in the same day. Ti-Jeanne wondered what Emma had heard, exactly, about the whole thing. She didn't feel like trying to explain about Rudy.

"Are you going to carry on now that she's gone?"

"Yes, are you?" Mary Hayward had joined them, wiping her hands on her apron. "Here, take this." She handed Ti-Jeanne a pot of her honey. "Oh, and Jenny's up at your farm. She said she was looking after the baby there until you got home."

A little knot of worry eased. Josée had kept her promise. "Thank you. I ain't know what I go do. I have to think about it."

By the time she was out of the market, she was juggling a half pound of rabbit pemmican—working one rich, meaty strip in her mouth—a bottle of cranberry jelly, a carved gourd rattle ("for the baby"), and Mary's honey. Grief still darkened her thoughts, but the attentions of the market people had soothed her a little.

The sun was at noon. Her breasts were leaking through her shirt. Fortunately her jacket concealed that. Since Baby's birth, she had learned that the first few months of motherhood were about fatigue and leakiness. She hoped Baby was tolerating the cow's or goat's milk that Jenny was probably feeding him. He'd been a colicky baby.

She barked with laughter as she was walking past the Moss Park Armoury Building. Someone had used cement to convert the cannon that stood out front into a massive penis. Plastic shutter rods made a spray of semen. The men lounging on the steps of the armoury snickered at her reaction. The heaviness of loss in her heart hadn't eased, but there was room there for humour, too.

A few minutes later, she was finally home. She stood outside her front door, reminding herself that Mami would not be inside to greet her. Then she remembered Mi-Jeanne's body. She hadn't been able to take the time to bury it when the duppy had been herding her and Tony out of the house. "Oi, Papa," she muttered, "I wonder is what Jenny think when she see *that*?" Well, Jenny was a tough old woman, had seen a lot of harsh things in her time. Ti-Jeanne opened the door and stepped inside. She called out, "Jenny?"

"Ti-Jeanne? Hush. You'll wake them up, dear. Come on upstairs."

Lord, who could "them" be now? She hoped that Tony hadn't made his way back to the farm. She wasn't quite ready to deal with him yet.

Jenny greeted her at the bedroom door with a sad smile and a big hug. *"Yoy,* my darling. I'm so, so sorry about your grandmother. *Yoy, Devla, che choromos.* What a hard thing! May she sleep well, my dear."

Ti-Jeanne held on, long and hard. Finally Jenny led her into the room, one hand still around her waist. Her mother's body was lying in the bed.

She didn't know how she found herself kneeling by the bed. Mi-Jeanne looked weak, but her breathing was deep and regular. She was alive! Ti-Jeanne sat down hard on the bed. Mi-Jeanne stirred a little but didn't wake.

"I found her lying in Gros-Jeanne's room," Jenny said, bending down to put Baby in Ti-Jeanne's arms. "Good thing it was me that found her. She had lost some blood, but I fixed her up."

"Is my mother," Ti-Jeanne whispered.

"I know, dear. She told me when she came to. She was just groaning and twitching at first, and I thought the bullet might have damaged some nerves, but I think she'll be all right with rest."

"The bullet ain't kill she."

"No, it didn't. He was a bad shot, whoever he was. *Te xal o rako lengo gortiano!* May a cancer eat his throat."

No wonder Mi-Jeanne hadn't been able to attack Rudy. She remembered now that she hadn't seen Mi-Jeanne among the ghouls who had finally confronted Rudy. "The duppy must be come back to she body when I free it."

"I don't understand, dear."

"Nothing."

Baby stirred awake, yawned, opened his eyes, and gave her a big, gummy smile. Ti-Jeanne noticed how his whole body seemed to smile at the sight of her. She smiled back, nuzzled his cheek. He was already rooting hungrily at her breast. Ti-Jeanne unbuttoned her jacket, yanked up her shirt, and gave him the nipple.

Jenny patted his head. "He's beautiful, your baby."

"Help me up, Jenny?" A mother found, lost, then found again. This final shock was too much. Ti-Jeanne went into her grandmother's room. Jenny settled her on her side in the bed, so she could feed Baby as she slept.

"You look half-dead, dear. I'll watch over you and the little one."

Dreams took her immediately. They were meaningless pictures only, floating through her head. No visions.

● ● ● ●

Dr. Wright was keying in the hospital code almost before her half-awake mind registered the beeping earbug. Emergency.

"Ottawa General, Cardiac," the operator's voice said. His words deactivated the urgent piping that only Margaret could hear.

"Dr. Wright. You paged me?"

"Ah, yes. Sorry to wake you, Doctor, but you have to get to the hospital right away. It's the Premier. Looks like she's rejecting the transplant."

"Fuck!" Beside her in the bed, Mira groaned and sat up, woken by the sound of Margaret's voice. She was used to these late night calls. She waited.

"Ambulance is on its way to get you, Doctor." In fact, Margaret could already hear the siren screaming through the Ottawa streets.

"Yeah, here it is now." Margaret clicked off, got up, and began dressing.

"You gotta go?" Mira asked.

"Yes, love. Sorry." She leaned over and gave her partner a quick kiss.

The ambulance arrived with a screeching of wheels. Someone was already leaning on the doorbell. Margaret headed for the stairs. She yelled back over her shoulder, "Looks like the Premier's fucking cacking out on me!"

She grabbed her coat, was out the door while she was still putting it on, mumbling a greeting to the ambulance attendant. She clambered into the back of the van. As the ambulance pulled away, Margaret looked up to the bedroom window of the house she and Mira owned. Mira was standing there, waving.

Margaret buckled in, keyed on a monitor, and called Don Fang. The screen showed him in Uttley's room, face still crumpled with sleep.

"What's doing, Don? She in rejection?"

"Well, the heart's rejecting her, actually. Take a look at this." He pressed some keys. Margaret's screen split into two. Half of it was Don's face, the other half a constantly refreshed readout from the CareVue that was monitoring Uttley's progress. Lungs failing. Kidneys failing. Severe skin lesions. "Yeah," said Uttley, "that's GVHD all right." Graft Versus Host Disease. Cells from the donor organs were attacking Uttley's immune system. "Damn!"

"Thought so. Worst case of it I've ever seen," Fang said worriedly.

"Get her on an immunosuppressant drip, fast. OKT5 should do it." That was like detonating a bomb to kill a fly, but it looked as though they had no choice.

Fang gave the order, then said, "The reaction's so extreme. It's like that heart can't wait to get out of there."

When Uttley awoke two weeks later, she would have only vague recollections of an extended nightmare. While Margaret Wright and Don Fang were fighting to establish a symbiosis between their patient's body and its new heart, Catherine Uttley's unconscious mind had been conducting a battle of its own. At some level in her dreams, she'd been aware that the lifesaving organ had been placed in her body, had felt relief and a sense of welcome toward the donated heart.

But then the dream had changed. She had realised that she was being invaded in some way, taken over. The heart's rhythm felt wrong, not her own. It had leapt and battered against her chest as though it were determined to break out. Uttley had been stern at first. "Stop that. You're here to help me. Just settle down and do your job." The heart's frenzied buffeting had slowed to a more regular pace, but then Uttley began to feel a numbness spreading out from her chest with each beat of the heart: down her arms, through her trunk and legs. Bit by bit, she was losing the ability to control her own body. The heart was taking it over. Uttley became alarmed, had tried talking to the alien organ. "Please," she said. "This is my body. You can't take it away from me." But the creeping numbness spread up her neck. She was now completely paralyzed. All she could do was wait for it to reach her brain. She had known that when that happened, she would no longer be herself. Unable to move, unable to save herself, she had felt her brain cells being given up one by one. Then blackness. Nothing.

And then she was aware again. Her dream body and brain were hers once more, but with a difference. The heart—her heart—was dancing joyfully between her ribs. When she looked down at herself, she could see the blood moving through her body to its beat. In every artery, every vein, every capillary: two distinct streams, intertwined. She had worried for nothing. She was healed, a new woman now. "Stupidness," she said, chiding herself for her unnecessary fears.

By the time they let her have visitors, most of tubes were out of her body and she could sit up in bed for long stretches of time without getting fatigued. She felt *wonderful.* She was champing at the bit, impatient to get back to work on her election campaign. She spent most of her waking moments tapping notes into her palmbook.

"Good news, Premier," said her policy advisor, breezing

into her room and immediately yanking his palmbook out of his briefcase. "You just tipped the polls at fifty-two percent support. Without any campaigning yet, even."

"Yeah," Uttley replied distractedly. "Listen, Constantine, I'm going to change my tactics a little."

"What? But I've got the press statements already written, the news spot lined up—"

"Shouldn't be a problem. It's just occurred to me; this volunteer organ donation thing will never work. Human beings will never be eager to deed away bits of themselves, even after they're dead."

"But . . ." Constantine spluttered.

He was usually the one providing the social analysis. Uttley knew that it hadn't been her strong point, trying to figure out why people acted the way they did. But lying on her ass in that bed for so long had given her time to think.

"No, it's easy. We still come down hard on the pig farming thing. That'll keep the animal rights people on our side. But we've got to provide people with an alternative that's just as successful. Can't have the organ shortages of the eighties and nineties."

"What's your plan, Premier?" Constantine was looking at her warily. Probably already figuring out how he was going to convince her back to her original position. Oh, but she admired the man's craftiness!

"We'll do what they used to do in Switzerland. I'm going to propose a new bill, one to create a presumed consent statute for all Ontario residents. It'll state that anyone who dies is a potential organ donor, unless they've signed an opt-out card.

See," she said, sitting up eagerly to explain it, "no one will be forced to be a potential donor. Anyone can sign the opt-out card, and their bodies will never be touched. But most people won't bother. Constantine, one donor cadaver can benefit fifty people! In the old days, twenty or thirty people would die each year in Ontario while they waited for transplants."

Constantine frowned at her. "Excuse my bluntness, Premier, but when did you develop a social conscience?"

That took her aback for a second. Had she become so different since her operation? Was she losing her edge? No, couldn't be. "Don't get your panties in a twist, man. Stupidness."

"Huh?"

"It's called 'enlightened self-interest,' right? Solves the Virus Epsilon problem, and makes me look good, too."

"Yeah, makes sense." Constantine was already tapping figures into his palmbook, figuring the odds, plotting their course.

Uttley laughed. "You're not a policy advisor; you're a goddamned bookie."

He looked up with a predatory grin. "And your bookie says the odds look good. We can do it, Premier."

"I know we can." She settled contentedly back into the pillows. "There's another thing, too. We're going to rejuvenate Toronto."

"Premier, you know that project has always been death to politicians. No one's been able to do it yet."

"Yeah, 'cause they've tried it by providing incentives for big business to move back in and take over. We're going to offer interest-free loans to small enterprises that are already there, give them perks if they fix up the real estate they're squatting on."

"What small enterprises? The place is a rat hole, complete with rats."

"Oh, I don't know. Something tells me we'll discover that there are quite a few resourceful people left in Muddy York."

CHAPTER FOURTEEN

There is a brown girl in the ring, tra-la-la-la-la,
A brown girl in the ring, tra-la-la-la-la,
A brown girl in the ring, tra-la-la-la-la,
And she look like a little sugar plum (plum, plum).

—Traditional song

You put small-leaf thyme in the peas and rice?"
"Yes, Mi—yes, Mummy."

Sitting at the kitchen table, blind Mi-Jeanne dandled Baby as she spoke to Ti-Jeanne, who was working over three huge pots at the hot stove. Baby kicked and chortled happily. For some reason he seemed a much more contented child now.

"And you sure it have enough rabbit stew and curry goat?"

"Yes, man!"

Ti-Jeanne was finding it awkward, having her mother back. There was a lot between them that Ti-Jeanne would have preferred be left unspoken, but after twelve years of silence, Mi-Jeanne was eager to unburden herself. In the nine days since the spirits had helped her to breach the CN Tower, Ti-Jeanne had learned more about her mother, grandmother, and even Rudy than she had ever known. The knowledge was uncomfortable. She would rather not have known about the passionate, violent love her grandmother had had for an insecure bully who had finally hit her once too often. And why did she need to hear about soft-spoken, dignified Dunston, the man who had been one of Mami's flock and had become her lover?

But the most difficult to listen to was Mi-Jeanne's tearful admission of how much she had resented the daughter she had brought into the world. "When Daddy find out I was making baby," Mi-Jeanne had told her, "is like he cut me dead. I used to be he doux-doux darling, he little girl, but not after that. And after you born, you eat up my whole life. It was 'baby need this, baby need that.' I couldn't take it. I sorry to admit it to you, Ti-Jeanne, but I couldn't take it."

Shame made Ti-Jeanne's face hot. It bit too close to the bone. She knew what her mother had been feeling.

Ti-Jeanne felt as though she and Mi-Jeanne were doing a cautious dance around each other, negotiating terms. Between that and preparing for Mami's nine-night, she had barely had time to acknowledge the grief she felt at Mami's loss.

It was Jenny who had insisted on the nine-night, a wake for the recently dead that would calm the dead spirit and point out its way to Guinea Land, sent off with the love of the living it must leave behind. "This is how your granny would have wanted it," Jenny told them. "A shasto, a party, to send her soul off with joy. This is her way."

Thank God for Mami's flock, eager to teach Ti-Jeanne their rituals. They would hold the ceremony in the palais and, afterward, a feast for anyone who cared to come. Ti-Jeanne had made sure to send word to Josée. The street rats that had helped Ti-Jeanne nine nights ago would eat well. Though it couldn't ever make up for Chu.

Roopsingh had donated some of his precious store of curry and the use of three institutional-size cooking pots to the undertaking. "Me and Gros-Jeanne ain't always walk good, you hear? But is she save my leg when I get blood poisoning that time."

In fact, the gifts that were pouring in from Mami's past patients meant that Ti-Jeanne had not had to use too much of her winter stores. There had been rabbits from Paula and Pavel; wild rice from Frank Greyeyes; and, priceless beyond words, a jug of deep red sorrel drink from old man Butler, he who depended on Mami's foot-itch paste every winter. Caribbean sorrel bush wouldn't grow in Canada's climate. Old man Butler had made the drink from some of his pre-Riot hoard of the dried fruit. As he presented Ti-Jeanne with the jug, he'd said, "Me only had 'nuff for you and your family, seen? Nobody else to get. You, and Mi-Jeanne, and the baby. But mix the baby own with little water, you hear me? It too acid for he belly."

Someone pounded at the door. "I going to see who it is," Ti-Jeanne told her mother. It was Bob Kelly, with three of his cabbages. And a bad cold. Ti-Jeanne showed him into the examination room and gave him some of Mami's horehound cough syrup. She'd have to make more soon. Hard on his heels came a woman with a dislocated shoulder.

"Let me see to she," said Mi-Jeanne. Her sensitive hands clicked the joint back into place almost painlessly. Then came a man bearing his little son, screaming from the pain of an earache. And a young man with food poisoning from eating something he'd scavenged from the dump outside the market. The day went by quickly as Ti-Jeanne and her mother dispensed medicine and tried to keep an eye on the cooking and on Baby. Ti-Jeanne heard herself mutter a "Thank you" to her dead grandmother for insisting that she learn how to treat the sick.

At one point, pot spoon in one hand and medicine dropper in another, Ti-Jeanne walked wearily out to the front porch and sat on the railing. The cold air cleared her thoughts. In the surrounding park, the large, bare trees blew in a slight breeze. Ti-Jeanne relished the few minutes of peace. Harold the goat was tugging at the last few clumps of grass of the season. His grazing brought him close to the porch. Suddenly he looked up at Ti-Jeanne and sneezed, "Eshu!" Briefly Ti-Jeanne could see his bones through his flesh. Another vision, a joke from her spirit father. She laughed. "Legbara, is you sending me all these sick people to treat, ain't?"

No answer.

"Well, Papa, look my answer here. I go do this for a little while, but I ain't Mami. I ain't know what I want to do with myself yet, but I can't be she."

The goat gnawed at an itch on one hind hoof and walked on.

No one else came to the door until dusk, when it was time for the ceremony. Maybe Legbara was satisfied with her answer.

Now the flock had taken over the palais, and the drumming had started, Mami's send-off party. The bulk of Paula and Pavel was taking up fully half of one of the short pews. Paula cradled a sweet, round-faced newborn girl to her breast. Delivering that baby without Mami's guidance had almost been more terrifying for Ti-Jeanne than facing her grandfather in the tower.

Bruk-Foot Sam was leading the chanting, a call-and-response that the flock seemed to know well. Mi-Jeanne sat tall and proud in one of the pews, hands folded in her lap, tears running down her cheeks. *It look like she tear ducts get leave behind when she jook out she eyes,* Ti-Jeanne thought. She shuddered at the image of her mother desperately mutilating herself.

Eshu's stone head glistened with white rum. Frank Greyeyes stood up and presented his pipe to the four directions, redolent with burning tobacco. Eshu would like that. Holding Baby, Ti-Jeanne crept out through the open doorway. She still didn't feel a part of these ways that had been so much a part of her grandmother's life.

Jenny was coming up the path, leading Tony by the hand. His arm had been bandaged against his body, leaving one sleeve of his jacket empty. He looked sorrowful, apprehensive. Silently Ti-Jeanne went to meet them. Tony said her name softly, then stopped. It was Jenny who spoke up for him. "He's sorry, darling. He wants to do penance." Ti-Jeanne scowled. "It won't bring your granny back," Jenny said, "but her soul's at peace now. It's his that needs the healing." Then she went into the palais, leaving the two of them to stare at each other.

Jenny was the only one outside the family who knew the truth of what had happened. How could she talk so casually of Tony needing healing? What about the rest of them? He had *killed* Mami!

"Ti-Jeanne," Tony said, "I can't ask you to forgive me. Nobody could."

She just stared at him stonily.

"If you saw what I saw, what Rudy could do . . ."

"I did."

He sighed, almost a sob, and looked at the ground. "Yes, you did. And you faced up to it, despite the odds, despite being frightened." He looked at her again. "I don't think I could have done that. I don't know how a person learns to be so strong."

In the palais, the drumming reached a new intensity. Ti-Jeanne turned to look. Bruk-Foot Sam was dancing Damballah, his twisted leg carrying him as ably as the well one.

"Since I felt that drug in my body, the full bufo drug, I mean, I can't slash any more. I can't put that stuff in my veins. Ti-Jeanne, I'm so sorry that I did this to you and your family."

His face was a mask of grief. Ti-Jeanne looked into his eyes, feeling none of the desperate obsession she used to have for Tony, none of the longing for him to make her life right, either. And, to her surprise, no hatred, not really. Just pity. Her heart was free. She couldn't forgive him yet, but maybe one day . . .

She took a deep breath. "Go on inside and say good-bye to she."

A little of the pain lifted from his features. He reached out and patted Baby on the head. Baby blinked but only seemed a little startled. Ti-Jeanne waited for her child to object to his father's touch, but it didn't happen. Tony looked at her, sadly, once, and hesitantly entered the palais.

Ti-Jeanne still wasn't ready to rejoin the service. She sat on the stone steps of the crematorium and began playing peek-a-boo with Baby. He chortled at her, his fat cheeks bulging. The sight filled her with glee. She grinned back, then gently pulled his tam down to protect his ears from the cold. She smiled at him. "So, bolom baby," she said, "what we going to name you?"

Wire bend, story end!

ACKNOWLEDGMENTS

I still don't quite believe that I've done this. Writing a novel feels like wrestling a mattress, and it was accomplished with the help of so many people. Effervescent thanks to:

My mother, Freda; my brother, Keita; and my family, for endless support, encouragement, and belief.

The SpecHeads; Bob, Brent, and Laurie, for lively, intelligent dissection of my manuscript. Hope allyou like how I put it back together. And to David for loving, honest critique. And Peter (Driver Man) for science expertise—if I got any of it wrong, it's my fault, not yours—and general sound advice.

The cast and crew of the 1995 Clarion Science Fiction and Fantasy Writers' Workshop (it was sticky and there weren't any ducks), and to Bob and Laurel, who lent me the cash to get there, and the Cultural Human Resources Council, which ultimately helped me pay the whole tab.

Derek Walcott for writing the play *Ti-Jean and His Brothers*, one of the first examples of Caribbean magic realism I ever read.

The arts councils that have supported my writing: Canada Council, Ontario Arts Council, and the Multiculturalism Programs of the Department of Canadian Heritage.

The African Heritage collections of the Toronto and North York Public Libraries, which are resources beyond price. I didn't know a lot of this stuff; I looked it up.

Every friend who's ever listened to me moan that I can't do this, it's too hard, no, I can't come out and play 'cause I gotta write another thousand words. Especially you, Sudharshan. And Winsom, for support and jubilations.

I'd like to thank the Academy . . . oh, all right, I'll stop now.

• • • •

And hekua to all my ancestors for walking the path before me and lighting my way.

As the only one in the family without magic, Makeda has decided to move out on her own and make a life for herself among the claypicken humans. But when her father goes missing, Makeda will have to find her own power—and reconcile with her twin sister, Abby—if she's to have a hope of saving him...

Please turn the page for a preview of

Sister Mine

Available in March 2013

I have no coin;
To take were to purloin:
I have no copper in my purse,
I have no silver either.

Score!" I said to the scruffy grey cat sitting on the building's loading dock. "She'd never even think to look for
me here!"

The cat replied with a near-silent mew and set about cleaning its face. One ear was ragged from a long-healed injury.

I double-checked the scrap of paper I'd torn out of the
Classifieds section of the *Toronto Star*. Yup, this was the place
that was looking for tenants. It didn't look like so much, sitting
there on a downtown corner. It was a blocky, crumbling cube
of a warehouse. Looked like it had a basement below ground,
two storeys above. It was wedged between upscale high-rise
condos and low-rise co-op townhouses.

There were buildings in this city that went to hundreds of
floors. Your ears'd pop from the altitude change just going up
in the elevator. But those sparkly new structures, they needed
the reflected gleam of sunlight off their chromed and mirrored

surfaces in order to shine. This building, it sucked in light, and the glow it gave back couldn't be seen in daylight or in Toronto's overlit night. Not by purely claypicken eyes, that is. I could see it, though. One of the few perqs of being a crippled deity half-breed. Although I had no mojo of my own, I could sometimes get a glimpse of the glow-on that some things and people had. Not as strongly as Abby could. Still, if I squinted exactly the right way, for just a split second, I'd see a flash bounce off Shiny people and things. Like the green flash on the horizon just as the sun sinks into Lake Ontario. That warehouse had some Shine to it. Inanimate objects can get that way when they've rubbed up against the ineffable for a long time. The building's faint burr of Shininess was my first clue that I might like living there.

The exterior paint job was something else, in a wacky way that I liked. Probably years before, someone had slopped teal green paint onto the raw brick. They'd used a dark, muddy purple for the exterior window rims and sills and the edging around the roof. Then for good measure, they'd lined the inner surfaces of the windows' rims with dark yellow, kind of a mango colour. Made the windows look like the insides of baby birds' beaks when they gaped them wide and demanded food from their exhausted parents.

When he'd realised he was slipping, our dad had signed our childhood home over to me and my sister. Since Abby and I had to live in the world, it was best if we had claypicken legal documents to prove that the place was ours. But I'd had it with living under Abby's wing. She could have my share in the house. I was going to go it alone from now on. My pulse leapt at the thought.

• • • •

"I think a tree talked to me today," I told Abby, hating myself for doing this again, for coveting mojo so badly that I kept trying to talk myself into believing I had it. I'd never been able to read trees before, so why would I suddenly now have developed a knack for it? I waited, toying with the food on my plate, sitting at Abby's expensive mahogany table, eating off her handmade plates from some artists' studio over in the Distillery District, staring at the graceful young oak tree in Abby's front yard through the leaded glass of Abby's antique stained-glass living room window. In my own house, I cotched like a boarder.

• • • •

Teal with purple edging and yellow accents; Abby would hate the place. She would especially hate that it was crass enough to have a name. Hand-painted in toppling white letters over the entrance were the words CHEERFUL REST. Abby's lips would curl at the inept lettering, the building that looked like a squat for homeless people. Me, I thought it was neat. Plus it would intimidate her. Even low and funny-looking as it was, even in broad daylight, Cheerful Rest managed to loom. Abby would be able to see that, probably more clearly than I could.

The old cat had finished its ablutions. It sphinx-sat on the loading dock in the springtime sun, watching me through half-closed eyes. I could hear it purring though I was a good few feet away. Its body swayed a little to the rhythm of the vibrations.

• • • •

Abby didn't reply right away. I looked across the table at her. She was staring out the window, slowly and carefully chewing. I'd made us an excellent dinner, stewed guinea hen and manioc with batata dumplings and an arugula salad with crumbled blue cheese. No wonder Burger Delite wouldn't let me do anything but bus tables and wash dishes; I was too good for them.

• • • •

The building's Shine wasn't a flash, but kind of an aura. But it felt like mojo, or tasted like it, or something. How had it come by that Shine? Would it somehow spell trouble for me if I moved in there? I had a bad track record of not getting along well with the Shiny; the Family on my dad's side, my haint. Abby.

• • • •

"Abby, I'd swear it really did talk. A crabapple tree in that park at Queen and Sherbourne. I think it asked me where Dad was. Said it hadn't seen him in a long time."

Abby whipped her head around from the window to glare at me. "Stop it. Just stop it. Why are you always saying things like this? You're embarrassing yourself. And me."

"But—" Why did I say things like that? Because I couldn't help myself. Because I craved more than anything else to have a little mojo of my own.

"Makeda, I don't care whether it's desperate wishful thinking or a stupid little trick you play to impress, but it's really cruel of you to play it with Dad lying helpless in palliative care."

*Oh, gods, why couldn't I ever stop doing this? Abby was right.
I was only shaming myself.*

• • • •

A lean black guy came round the corner. He was wearing
faded black jeans rubbed thin at the knees and a black Revolting
Cocks T-shirt, so worn that it was almost grey. The left shoulder
seam had split open. He had a big, wild 'fro. His left foot was
shod in an orange high-topped canvas sneaker, his right foot in
a purple one. He smiled at me before unlocking and yanking
open the heavy back door that led inside the building, letting
out a grungy roar of miked rock drumming. Sounded live, too,
like a practice. The guy made an apologetic shrug. He spied
the piece of torn Classifieds in my hand. He smiled. Over the
racket, he shouted, "It's only this noisy on the weekend!"

So if I moved in here, there would be music, and musicians.
Plus there was a brother, apparently living here, who liked
punk. So it wouldn't be like I was trying to single-handedly
desegregate the place, either. Nice. I smiled back at him and
relaxed a bit. Music was the most fun part of living with Abby.

He said, "Hey, Yoplait!"

Yoplait?

The cat twitched one ear in his direction.

The guy jerked his chin towards the open door. "Come on!"

The cat looked over its shoulder at him. Stood. Went over
to him. The door was hydraulic, and took a few seconds to shut
behind the guy and his cat; long enough for me to hear the drumming clang to a halt, someone saying something muffled into the

mike, a laugh, the drumming starting up again. Looked like the guy had gone up a short flight of stairs. I'd gotten a brief whiff of stale beer from the open door. There were two-fours of empties stacked outside. Some kind of club space in the building?

The door closed completely, and I was left with only the endless Toronto traffic sounds.

Longing tapped me on the shoulder and enclosed me in its arms. I wanted to live here, be fully independent of Abby and Uncle, start learning how to exist as the mortal I was. I bet Cheerful Rest was some kind of claypicken artists' space, where people used scavenged milk crates and bricks and wooden flats to customize their units. There'd be flyers stapled to the walls, advertising bands and readings and gallery openings and dance performances. Would they even let me into a place like that? I wasn't really an artist. I was just an artist's hanger-on who liked to tinker. I'd always wanted to live in a warehouse. A real warehouse, with high ceilings and exposed brick and pipes. And best of all, Abby wouldn't know where I was if I didn't tell her. We'd quarrelled last night, and again this morning. I'd told her I was moving when I stormed out a few hours ago, but I always said that when we fought. Today, though, I meant it. Standing outside Cheerful Rest that warm spring afternoon, sensing its warm-blooded Shine and waiting for the guy who ran it to show up, I meant it. I was finally going to break free of the hold my sister Abby had on me. She could get kinda clingy. We'd always lived together. She lost her shit if I didn't attend a performance of hers. And to tell the truth, I missed her if I didn't see her for a few days. But she really got on my freaking nerves all the time! Today, I was cutting the tie that bound us, locked together like the conjoined twins we used to be. I'd get my own place, tell Abby in a few months where I was living, and by then, she and I would have gotten used to being a little less intertwined in each others' affairs. I could begin to figure out how to live my own life.

It was partly my own fault. Abby'd been so dependent on me in the first years of our life, and I'd gotten used to it. They'd separated us physically, but emotionally, Abs and I couldn't seem to let each other go.

• • • •

"Abs, can't you even give me the benefit of the doubt? Why in hell can't you accept that maybe you're not the only special one?"

Abby slid her cane off the back of her chair and pulled herself to her feet. "Because you don't hear trees talk. You never did. You started pretending you could after you overheard Cousin Flash calling you that silly name."

"The donkey. Yeah. But that's not when I started doing it."

"When you started to make believe you could do it."

"I started it after you called me the same name to my face." *Too late, I realized I'd just practically admitted I was talking shit about speaking to trees. My cheeks flaring with embarrassment, I pressed on, "The sister I shared all my secrets with. The sister I looked after until she could do it herself."*

She swallowed. Took a breath. "Children can be cruel. They say mean things to each other, play nasty tricks. How about that time you shortened one of my crutches?"

"That's not fair!"

"Just a half inch. And me so used to being uncomfortable in my skin that I didn't notice it for awhile. My shoulder ached that whole day and the next, and I couldn't figure out why."

"It was just a prank. A stupid kid prank."

"And me calling you Donkey was just a stupid kid thing. Get over it, Makeda."

I folded my arms, looked out the window. "That tree could have been talking to me," I muttered. I sounded about five years old. I detested myself for it. I hated my compulsion to go on about this stuff. The wind in that tree, it had kind of sounded like words in a different language. I just figured maybe that's what Dad heard when plants talked to him. Maybe it was just like a different language, and I could learn it. Or maybe I was just being an ass. I knew how to do that.

• • • •

A grey-beige hatchback, new, pulled into the building's three-car gravel parking lot. I moved out of the way. The door whispered open. The man who rolled out of the car was a big guy, white-looking, with straight, light brown hair that stopped just short of his jawline. He was wearing a two-piece suit the same colour as his hair, white shirt underneath. Brown dress shoes, their leather creased across the toe box. He was sweating even though it was a cool spring day. He gave me a distracted glance. "You Mak...Makky...?"

"Makeda," I said, moving forward and extending my hand to shake his. "And you must be Milo?" He was about as Shiny as day-old bread. So he wasn't the source of the building's glow, then.

"Yeah." His hand was cool and meaty. "Come inside," he said.

As I turned to follow him into the building, I fretted. Didn't have any references to give him except Abby, and I didn't want to bring her into this. I'd been fired from or left the last four jobs I'd had. They hadn't felt real to me at the time. Even Burger Delite was just something I did to prove to myself that I could, until today. Abby made money, I knew that. I'd never been too clear on the details. Me, Dad, and Abby, we'd never been wealthy, but if things were getting too lean, Uncle would glean some valuables from the dead for us. Never anything that next-of-kin might be needing. Lots of people died in ways that made the cash in their pockets or purses inaccessible by claypickens. Today, though, my ignorance could bite me in the ass. When Milo did his credit check on me, it'd reveal a tendency towards bouncing cheques—not all the time, just a lot of the time—low earnings, and a spotty work history. It'd never been a problem before. I did some quick math in my head. Paying my own way was going to be tight. The rent on a rundown place like this would be cheap, wouldn't it? Fact was, I hadn't really thought my grand storm-out through. Milo walked me around to the front of the building and unlocked that door. From here, the drumming was muffled. He frowned. "You won't have that noise all the time," he said. "If they have a weeknight show, they stop by 11 p.m."

Weeknights too, huh? That could get a little rigorous. "That's fine," I lied. "I'm sure it'll be okay." Maybe it wouldn't be so bad.

"They practise during the days a lot, but most people are out at work then."

"I usually work the evening shift. But I'm used to sleeping through the sounds of music practice."

"Yeah? You know some folks in the biz, then?"

"A few." Milo led me into a tiny, stuffy office on the main floor. One scuffed desk, dark brown Formica fake wood grain. No chairs; Milo perched on the edge of the desk while I bent over it to fill out the application form with the chewed ballpoint pen he lent me. "It's a good place," he said absently. "I gotta get another super, but that won't take long."

"A super what?" I was only half-listening. *Three* references?

He laughed. "Superintendent. I'm not here every day, so if you need anything, just ask Brian or one of the other tenants. They'll help you. Only not the chick in 213. She's a little crazy. Nothing to worry about! She gets nervous around strangers, is all. If she stays on her medication, she's just fine. I'm giving her a break on her rent till she's back on her feet. In any case, Welfare sends her rent cheque right to me, so no worries there. Anybody else can give you a hand if you need anything, and you have my number."

Yeah, sure he was doing it out of the goodness of his heart. Sweet deal for him, guaranteed rent.

Whatever. He was talking as though I already had the place. That was a good sign. Nervously, I handed him the completed application form. He glanced at the badly photocopied sheet of paper. "No references?"

I'd skipped that part. "I'm not sure what those are, exactly," I replied.

He narrowed his eyes at me. "People who can vouch for you."

"Oh!" I could use Aunt Suze as a reference. I took the form back from him and scribbled down her name and contact information. Thought about it some more, then added the name and phone number of my boss at Burger Delite, even though I'd already written that in the "employment" section. I couldn't put my uncle's name down; Death didn't exactly have a physical home address or phone number. Or a reliably corporeal body, for that matter.

Maybe Milo would be satisfied with two references. I slid the form back across the table to him. He started reading it again. He said, "You have any pets? No pets allowed in here."

So did he just not know about the grey cat I'd just seen? "No pets."

"You don't throw loud parties, do you? Or have loud hobbies, like woodworking? Had a guy in here once with a table saw. Disturbed the other tenants."

I laughed. "No, nothing like that." He was worried about one person having a party, but he had a rock band practising on the main floor? "I make little wind-up toys. You know, from discarded nuts and bolts. Just something I do to pass the time. Give them to people as gifts. It's not noisy. Mostly I use glue and a screwdriver."

"No soldering? Can't do anything in here that's a fire hazard. You won't even have a stove in your unit."

"What? How do people cook, then?"

He frowned irritably, as though I'd asked him something bothersome and insignificant. "I think there's a microwave in that vacant unit. And there's a kitchen down the hall, with a shared fridge and stove. It can get a little skanky in there, but it's okay."

I bit my lower lip. Store my meds in a communal fridge, where anyone could walk in and help themselves to them? I didn't think so.

"And by the way," said Milo, "the unit doesn't have bathroom facilities, either. You'd have to use the shared shower and toilet down the hall." He saw my face. "Most of the units don't have bathrooms. Only the supers' units do. This is warehouse living, remember? It's pretty bare bones. But you can fix your unit up any way you like. Paint it, whatever. Brian, he built an honest-to-god loft in his. It's like he has a two-storey apartment. Has these heavy stage curtains running along rods he put in the ceiling. Uses them as movable room dividers. It's the darnedest thing. Girl downstairs is a dancer. She built a sprung wood floor in hers, so she can practise."

"Okay," I said doubtfully. This was the experience I'd wanted, but now it wasn't sounding so hot.

In my pocket, my cell phone buzzed. Probably Abby, calling for the umpteenth time today. I ignored it. Let her fret. "And how much is the rent?" I asked Milo.

He named a figure. I swallowed. It was decidedly more than I'd been contributing to the joint household fund that Abs and I split between us. "That's fine," I said, lying through my teeth. I'd have to see about picking up another shift at the restaurant. And about trying to subsist on the free food I got there when I was working. In a pinch, there was always Uncle. Milo was still peering at the sheet. "What do you do at Burger Delite?"

"Dishwasher." I looked down at my feet. I'd been so proud about holding down a claypicken job, but today, in the face of how inadequate my salary was going to be for just the basics, it felt as though I were confessing to some sort of character failing. I made myself meet Milo's eyes. "But they say they're going to move me up to waiting tables soon. I'll get tips then." Gods, that was even worse. Like I was begging him for shelter.

He pursed his lips, studied the sheet once more. "You've been living at your last place of residence since you were...what? Sixteen?"

"Yes, but—" All my life, actually, but I'd fudged that part of the form.

"And the owner has the same surname as you? Who is that, your mother? You still living at home?"

"No! Not exactly. Abby's my sister. We're co-owners."

He raised an eloquent eyebrow. "So why are you leaving your own home? If you don't mind me asking."

"She and I, well, we aren't getting along. I'd rather she didn't know where I was living." Damn. I hadn't wanted to get into this. I'd hoped he'd think that I'd been renting my previous place and just happened to have the same surname as the owner. Guess that was dumb of me.

"But it's your house, too? I don't get that. You walking away from your own property?"

"She can have it." His prying was starting to make me a little cranky. Was this how it would be, living whole hog in the claypicken world?

265

"You don't owe her money or anything, do you? I don't want to take on an unreliable tenant."

I laughed, trying hard to sound like someone who would never, ever "forget" for two months in a row to pay into a household fund. "God, no. That's not why I'm leaving. She's just always up in my business. Nosy."

He frowned. "Can't have any drugs in here, you know."

Oh, no, he did not just say that. I growled, "I'm black, so I must be a dealer? That it?"

He laughed an easy, non-defensive laugh. It threw me. "Hell, no. I was one at your age, though. And when my first wife started to get too curious, I told her to stop being so nosy. She didn't like that one bit, I can tell you. We were divorced within a year. So the word *nosy* kinda sets me off sometimes."

Nonplussed, I said, "Don't worry. Dope's not my thing. Bottle of Guinness with dinner is more my speed. And early to bed when I can. Those shifts at the restaurant are brutal."

He perked up even more. "You drink Guinness? That's the good stuff. Not like the dishwater the rest of the guys in here swill. You drink it cold?"

I shook my head. "No. You hide the flavour that way."

"Good girl."

The word *girl* made me feel bristly all over again, but I wanted this place. If he wanted to make patronizing small talk, I could play along a little. Milo looked me over, considering. "Mak...Makeda? Listen. Ordinarily, I wouldn't rent a place to someone..." He put the paper down on the table, pushed it away from himself. "I mean, no references, minimum-wage job. I notice you didn't put down any previous employment, either."

"I've had other jobs! I just—"

"Here's the deal." He sighed, set his shoulders as though he'd just come to a decision. "You seem like a nice girl. I'd like to make you an offer."

Now it was my turn to raise an eyebrow. "You would, would you?"

He smiled. "Oh, no, my dear. Nothing like that. Nothing at all like that. I need a new assistant superintendent to help Brian out, fill in when he's not around. Sounds like you're pretty handy? Know one end of a hammer from the other? It's easy work, doesn't need more than an hour or two a week, sometimes not even that."

"So, how would this arrangement go?" This could work out, after all. If Milo let me have the unit in return for replacing the occasional washer, I could maybe drop down to one shift at Burger Delite instead of two, still be making enough to get by. Not take handouts from Abby and Uncle for every little thing. Make a real go at having a claypicken life, since I was never going to have the other kind.

"I'd reduce your rent by a couple hundred," Milo said.

My happy bubble fantasy popped, leaving a sting like liquid soap. "Two hundred? That's it?" That wasn't even a quarter of the rent he was asking for the unit. Which, it suddenly occurred to me, he hadn't shown me yet. Milo nodded. "One fifty, two hundred, something like that. You'd have your own bathroom."

Did the fool think I hadn't noticed how the "couple hundred" reduction in the rent was turning into one fifty? "Can I see the unit?" I asked coldly. Might as well, since I was there. But no way was I falling for this guy's penny-pinching con job. There had to be plenty of apartments in this city, if you weren't too fussy.

He led me up the flight of stairs to the second floor. Iron railings, painted in peeling black enamel. The stairs were steel-reinforced slabs of concrete, worn down by years of foot traffic, each step canted at a slightly different angle than its neighbour. I liked that. I liked things that had been solidly made and that wore the evidence of hard use, of survival.

The second-floor hallway was cool and dark. The walls were the same colour as the outside of the building. There was a musty, old-building smell. Only to be expected. Not like I was going to be living in the hall, anyway, right? There were doors lining the hallway on one side, an open doorway halfway down on the other side, leading to what looked like some kind of common room. There was a battered couch in there, an old Formica table, a couple of rickety chairs. And sure enough, posters tacked to the walls; some band playing at the Vault last week, old cartoon film fest at the library this weekend. That room was painted a deep pinkish red. The paint on one wall wasn't just flaking, it was bubbling. Moisture beneath it. Milo noticed me looking at it. "Had a bit of a leak in there last week. Spring rains, you know? I'm having it fixed."

I'd heard about his kind. He was just your average slum landlord. I kissed my teeth in disdain. Milo blinked at the sound, but clearly didn't know what it meant. Any one of my relatives would have, on either side of the family. Hell, any black person pretty much the world over would have known it. Milo unlocked one of the units on the other side of the hallway. "Just had it painted," he said proudly. "This is where the previous assistant superintendent lived."

He pushed the door open and went in ahead of me. "Oh," he said, "I guess Brian hasn't gotten around to painting it yet. Looks kinda cool though, right? Artsy."

A faint scent wafted out of the room. Spices? Was that nutmeg? And some kind of fruit? My mouth watered. I stepped inside. I asked, "Did the previous tenant like to burn incense? I can smell—"

"No incense burning allowed in the units. No burning of anything." He clearly wasn't the least bit interested in what the previous tenant used to do in here.

The space was big. The walls were a creamy white, reaching up and up to the high ceiling. A previous tenant had painted curling vines climbing up the corners. Probably the same someone had painted the Styrofoam ceiling tiles in a skyscape of blue sky and massing white clouds. "That colour," I said to Milo, delighted. I pointed at the ceiling. "It's haint blue."

He squinted up at the ceiling. "Is it? I scored a lot of tins of it in a closeout sale a while ago. Don't think Brian's used it all up yet."

I smiled. "No, it's okay. I kinda like it." More than that; I felt oddly at home. The blue of the ceiling was the same colour as the porch ceiling of our—of Abby's house. Dad had done that for me, ages ago. Ghosts can't cross water without help. Plus they're stupid. Get the right shade of blue, paint your floor or ceiling with it—doesn't matter which, cause ghosts don't have a right way up—and they'll mistake it for the glint of light on water and be unable to pass. Paint your porch ceiling that colour, and your door and window frames, and you have a haint-proof house.

There was more. The nubbly concrete floor had been coated with a semi-gloss St. Julian mango yellow, layered on so thick it was like enamel. The building had looked a bit creepy from the outside, but looks could be deceiving. Now that I'd seen this part of its insides, I loved the place. "It's cute," I said, trying for nonchalance. The window in the opposite wall was open a crack, letting in birdsong on a ribbon of cool, sweet air that leavened the unit's damp, musty smell. The street noises were a distant background rumble. With the vines, it was like a picnic in the park in here. My bed would fit nicely right over by the window, give me a bit of a view of the outside. Abby'd just bought a new microwave. I could take the old one off her hands when I went to pick up my chest of drawers. Hooks on the walls for any clothes that needed hanging, my workbench and chair. Maybe a card table and a couple more chairs once I could afford them. For when guests came over. I could have guests! That was the kind of thing that claypickens did, wasn't it? But the rent, ouch. Boldly, I asked, "You said three hundred off the rent?"

He frowned. "Two hundred."

Gotcha. I'd tricked him back up to the full discount he'd promised at first and then tried to welch on. It was still more than I could afford, but I was enjoying playing with the bastard now. Lead him on, make him think I was going to take the place, then shake my head and walk out of there. "Two hundred. Could I get that in writing?"

"Sure. And there's a bar fridge around here somewhere you could have. I'd get Brian to put it in here for you."

That'd solve the problem of where to keep my meds, at least. If I was going to take the place. Which I wasn't.

"So. You like it? The bar fridge could go over there." He pointed to a wall with an electrical socket.

"I don't know about this..."

The hint of fruits stewed in honey and nutmeg intensified. Cinnamon, too? And maybe a bit of orange zest? It like the scent was seeping from the walls. The Shiny building was flirting with me! Sometimes Shiny objects developed self-awareness, and something a bit like personalities. I smiled regretfully, shook my head. Milo looked at his watch. "Miss, I have to go. No rest for the wicked, and all that. Would you like the place or not? You're not going to find a deal this good anywhere else."

Couldn't I? I opened my mouth to tell him no.

"Like hell you're moving out. You know you're going to stay right here, where the living is easy."

Abby thought she knew me so well. I said, "I'll take it."

READING GROUP GUIDE

Discussion Questions

1. In *Brown Girl in the Ring*, Nalo Hopkinson envisions a post-apocalyptic Toronto in which violent riots have led to the collapse of the city's economy and political system. Many have fled the central city, and those who remain rely on a barter economy and herbal medicine. Meanwhile, there are exclusive "elite" megamalls, and hospitals are so expensive that only the rich can afford them. Do you think this is a realistic vision of the future? Why or why not?

2. When Ti-Jeanne stands up to Mami about helping Tony, there's a moment when Mami acknowledges that Ti-Jeanne has become an adult. Their relationship shifts: They're now two women instead of an adult and a child. What do you think makes someone an adult? Is Ti-Jeanne really an adult? Is Tony? What about Josée, the leader of the street children?

3. Do you think Ti-Jeanne did the right thing in leaving Tony before having the baby? What would you have done in Ti-Jeanne's place? And why is she unwilling to tell Tony that the child is his?

4. Ti-Jeanne has the power to see the manner in which people will die, but she cannot see her own. Would you want to know about your own death?

5. Look up descriptions of the major Orisha spirits. Why do you think Ti-Jeanne is chosen by Legbara?

6. At the end of the story, Premier Uttley puts forth a proposal for a "presumed consent" organ donation, in which anyone who dies is a potential organ donor, unless they've signed an opt-out card. Do you think this system is ethical? Is it ethical to raise pigs to harvest their organs? In your opinion, what's the best way to handle organ donations?